WAGER TOUGH

ALSO BY TOM FARRELL

THE WAGER SERIES

WagerEasy

WAGER TOUGH

To Steve,
Thanks! See you at
the next MeDecker!

Tom Farrell 8-27-21

TOM FARRELL

Wager Tough©2021 Tom Farrell
ISBN: 978-1-7365932-1-9

Copyright notice: All rights reserved under the International and Pan-American Copyright Conventions. No part of this book may be reproduced or transmitted in any form or by any means, electronic or mechanical, including photocopying, recording, or by any information storage and retrieval system, without permission in writing from the publisher.

This is a work of fiction. Names, characters, organizations, entities, places, events and incidents are either products of the author's imagination or are used fictitiously. Any resemblance to actual persons, living or dead, or actual events is purely coincidental.

Editing by Steve Parolini
Copy Editing by Susan Brooks
Cover Design by NovakIllustration.com
Typesetting by NovelNinjutsu.com

www.tomfarrellbooks.com

1

WEDNESDAY
August 2014

I stood on the top concourse of Coors Field beside the clock tower and looked down. I imagined the headfirst fall Zany took over the rail in the middle of last night. His mangled body four stories below now marked by nothing more than a rust-red stain on the concrete.

"Remember, Eddie," Zany had told me one summer years ago "lots of handicappers want to boil everything down to a system. They want to use numbers for speed and pace. But you can't simply reduce a race to a number and hope to win on a regular basis. You have to think of the things nobody can measure with a stopwatch. You got to think about 'heart.'"

That advice had paid off over the years. But Zany showed more heart that summer than I'd ever seen in my young life. He'd taken a spill off Uncle Mike's horse, Splendid Runner, and had suffered serious injuries as a result. At first, he came to the track in a wheelchair, then a walker, and then crutches. The pain etched in his face. I'd helped him back and forth to his car, placed bets, and fetched drinks. It surprised me that he had to count on betting the horses for income. Back then, I thought all jockeys were rich.

Traffic lined the streets around the Denver ballpark. The rooftop bars and blaring hip-hop music shook up the weeknight doldrums. Behind the squat buildings of LoDo loomed the city center, skyscrapers that provided nesting ground for high-salaried types.

Zany had left Chicago after that summer of rehab and rode at small tracks and fairs out west. Each year the number of mounts decreased until the stats stopped ten years ago. I was surprised he could ride at all considering his back problems. But what else could he do—riding and the horses was all he knew. Then I answered my own question. He also knew gambling. So, he had become a bookie.

I turned and concentrated upon the crowd. A group of young people, beers in hand, pushed each other, laughed and screamed, then stumbled off the escalator. I watched for my witness, the one the police did not yet know about.

Across the vacant picnic area near the concourse railing, smokers congregated in a designated area. Rare to find a quiet spot to smoke with a view. What a lousy time I'd picked to quit.

Even as the third inning ended, fans continued to stream to the grandstands. I saw a woman break away toward me through the picnic area. She wore work clothes—an ultra-short, black cocktail dress and high heels, and talked on her pink, rhinestone-encased cell phone. She had the kind of body that forced me to do a double-take.

I walked up to her.

"Are you Eddie O'Connell?" She put the cell phone away, brushed back her long, black hair, and looked up at me.

"That's right," I said. "Are you Amity?"

"Do you have my money?"

I always enjoy a warm, economical greeting but I was glad she'd arrived. "Over here."

I directed her a few steps over to the clock tower, away from the flow of the crowd. No need to make things too obvious.

She snatched the five twenty-dollar bills. "What's this? My feet are killing me. It must be important for Mags to set this up. I should get double."

Mags, the head of the local crime chapter in Denver, took orders from Burrascano back in Chicago, the man who'd hired me and Uncle Mike to find Zany's killer. Zany was connected and everyone knew it or should've known it.

I considered Amity's play for more money from her angle. I noted her chipped front tooth. I wondered what the tooth might cost to fix and who slapped her around and what she'd look like with a perfect smile. I reached for more cash.

She sighed but flipped the cash expertly between her fingers and into the black sequined evening bag strapped over her shoulder.

"Now what?" she said.

"Tell me what happened with you and Zany that night."

"What about it?"

"Look, Mags wants answers. Make it easy on yourself."

She pulled out a stick of gum and chewed. "Fine."

"Where did you meet?"

"On the first floor. Zany bought me cotton candy and we came up here. This is such bullshit. I don't know anything."

I needed to get to the place where Zany was tortured. I took a step back from the railing. "Show me where."

She headed off into the flaming orange sunset over the Rockies to the west and the smoky haze from the grills. Besides the aroma of burgers and brats, I smelled something else. It was a pungent campfire smell. I'd heard about the fires burning out west in the record drought and heat, but didn't figure the smoke could drift this far.

Amity twisted a path through the string of concession stands to a boarded-up stand farthest from the flow of traffic. It was an eight- by ten-foot free-standing structure.

Why Zany would have a tryst inside this closed-up stand would never be answered. The structure remained unguarded, not even a strand of yellow police ribbon.

"How often did you come here?" I asked.

Her phone rang. "A few times."

"Turn the phone off. Did you come up here with others?"

"No. Absolutely not." She took out the phone, peered at the number, and turned it off. "Zany was the one with the key."

Her eyes had become childlike upon demand like an actor's eyes. She'd drawn her arms tight around her chest as if chilled, despite the day's record heat that still languished through the dusk. No doubt she'd heard all the rumors of what happened here. If she knew the details from the police report about the cigarette burns, the bruises, the broken fingers and gouged eye, the lacerations around the testicles, maybe she'd find a new line of work. Or maybe not knowing was worse.

I took a look around. "Stand there."

Using Amity as a shield, I pulled the pick from my pocket and went to work on the padlock. I practiced on this type of lock in the dark so I jimmied it open in seconds.

I swung the door open. The few photos in the police report showed the blood stains and ripped-open boxes.

"C'mon." At six-foot-three, I had to duck to enter the shadowy enclosure. "Let's take a look."

She stood in the doorway and then followed me in. "It looks different. There were stacks of cardboard boxes all over and beer kegs there under the counter."

I liked that she volunteered information. "Tell me what you did."

"What are you, some kind of pervert?"

"Think through what happened. Where did you stand?"

She glanced around the dark chamber as if disoriented. "About here." She moved a few steps. "Against a stack of boxes."

"Then what?"

"I took off my dress."

"And."

Her lips turned into a pout as she hesitated. "We started to kiss."

"On the lips?"

"No. On his cheek. I unbuckled his pants."

"Then what?"

She looked away and blushed. This modesty seemed to surprise her. Then the crowd roared, shaking the rafters of the shed like the hand of God rattling dice, and she cried out. "He didn't want to do it."

"What?"

"He wanted to go. He paid me but then told me to leave."

"He paid for nothing?"

"Yes."

"Why would he do that?"

"You don't understand. Zany was a gentleman."

"Did someone knock on the door or cause him—"

"No."

"Did you see someone?"

"No, no one."

"Maybe one of your wacko boyfriends," I said.

"No."

"Did you bind Zany's hands?"

"No, Zany never . . ."

The Formica shell started to break apart. "What happened?"

"Nothing. Who would do this?" She covered her face with her hands and sobbed. "Why?"

The same question ran through my head. At least I could eliminate her as a suspect. The killer or killers must've followed her up here, waited, and then bound Zany after she'd left. The fun started after the crowd went home and the stadium turned dark.

"You took the money and left?"

"Yes. I asked Zany to take me back, but he wouldn't."

"Why not?"

"Zany had to go somewhere."

"Where?"

"I don't know. Wait. The Kelso Club."

"Did he say why?"

"No. I think he had to meet someone. That's all. Said he had to work to set things straight."

"That's it?"

"I don't know what he meant."

"This Kelso Club, is it your strip club?"

"God, no. It's a fancy place. I've never been there before."

"Did he say who he planned to meet?"

"No."

Her legs began to wobble. She reached out and leaned against the wall "Let me out of here. Please."

I took a step to the side and helped her out. "You got anything else you can tell me?"

She took a big gulp of air. "No, that's all. I swear."

"Call me if you think of anything more or if anyone contacts you." I handed her a slip of paper with a number.

"I will."

She took several unsteady steps, then gained traction and ran down the concourse to the stairs.

It was probably the same direction she went that night. I looked into the lines of people at the concessions and tried to read faces. The killer had stood in a crowd like this one, waiting for Amity to leave.

I inspected the concession stand once more before I closed and locked the door. The walls had done their job and broke down my one witness. It wasn't much but it was something.

How long had the torture gone on before Zany was dragged over to the clock tower? The walls got to me too.

I gazed out over the city. What sort of monster was I looking for?

2

THURSDAY

The next morning, I went to Zany's store. I stood in front of the address I'd been given, a two-story, red-brick building with no sign out front. It was hidden away on a side street adjacent to an Irish pub across the alley to the east and a small parking lot to the west, only a few blocks from the baseball stadium. It blended into many of the old warehouses in the area. If I drove past and blinked, I'd miss it.

Every gambler thinks he can run a book better than the bookie and I was no exception. The only problem was that it wasn't my operation, it was Zany's and now Burrascano's. If I ran it into the ground, I might find myself six feet below it. They don't teach that kind of pay for performance in business school.

Inside the small lobby, a single potted plant wilted from the sun streaming through the south-facing windows. I checked the names of the businesses on the directory and found Team Player Collection Agency located on the basement level.

Team Player was a company owned by Joey L, Burrascano's right-hand man. If the IRS asked questions about Zany's tax returns, the company provided cover.

Downstairs, the door was locked. I'd arranged to meet with one of Zany's employees.

What did I know about running a store? The surviving employees would see right through me. I was the guy who called in bets and lost his ass, not the guy who made precise last-minute adjustments to the line as action poured in. Maybe I could fake my way through it. At least until college football kicked off a week from now.

From placing my own bets, I was familiar with the software Zany used and Uncle Mike told me to contact our local Chicago bookie, Oscar Colasso if I had questions about running the store. Oscar was the guy who'd turned over my gambling debt to the mob for collection. This job would make my gambling debt go away with the understanding I wouldn't gamble again.

I wanted to find Zany's killer and clear my gambling debt, but the job assignment wasn't a slam dunk for Burrascano. Since Uncle Mike was sidelined this time around due to an injury on our last job in New Orleans, I would be on my own. Certain people had voiced objections to a solo assignment. Uncle Mike was a former Chicago homicide detective, what did his nephew know about solving murders?

I knocked. There was no answer. I checked my watch and knocked harder.

The door opened. "Are you Eddie?"

The woman who seemed too young and out of place answered. I thought she might be lost and that would make two of us. She had a pretty face without makeup, auburn hair, and a trim figure. Her reddened eyes said she'd been crying. She extended a hand.

It was a confident handshake. "That's right. You're Rudi?"

"Yes, Paula Rudinger but everyone calls me Rudi."

Inside, rows of workstations extended the length of the building to the concrete wall at the opposite end.

"Where is everybody?" I hoped everyone hadn't quit.

She shot me a look. "Too early. East coast games won't start for another hour. You said you wanted me to show you around?"

She gave me a tour past the workstations to a break room and then to the offices along one wall. Posters of local teams and sports heroes bordered the space.

She explained how each station was equipped with the latest technology and discussed the number of clerks employed during peak periods. Some stations were laden with family pictures and personal items. Sweaters hung over the back of some chairs. It was reassuring to discover people were invested in this business I had to run.

It was a chance Uncle Mike and I had to take. If Burrascano called in a gang of known mobsters to run the store, the killer would never surface. But if someone like me was running the place, the killer might think he could take advantage of the situation. Of course, it also meant I'd have to keep the business afloat and I wasn't sure exactly what that would entail.

She pointed. "This is my office and the one in the corner was Zany's. We got a sweet deal on all this from the prior owner who went out of business."

"Gambling problem?"

"How did you guess?"

We stopped outside Rudi's office. A cardboard box sat on the desk.

"Organizing some stuff?" I had asked her over the phone if she could provide me with some information.

"Cleaning out my desk," she said.

A cold wave of fear swept down my back. I didn't know what Rudi's duties included, but based on the simple fact she had her own office, I assumed she played an important role. I needed Rudi to maintain the status quo.

She was the contact provided by Joey L. A well-respected mob veteran in his seventies, Joey L was Burrascano's emissary and gave us certain mob insight that helped us to solve more than one case. It was Joey L who had convinced Burrascano to let me handle the Zany investigation on my own over the objections of others. It was important to get justice for my old friend, Zany, and just as important to prove Joey L right. I had to keep the store running like Walmart.

I kept my voice matter-of-fact. "You're cleaning out your desk? Why?"

She shrugged. "Want to see Zany's office?"

She took out a key and unlocked the door and then went inside.

It was almost three times the size of her office. A massive antique desk stood below a small sidewalk-level window.

Opposite the window was a large trophy case. A leather couch sat against one wall, surrounded by a bevy of hanging plants. A shiny pair of jockey boots sat poised on an end table beside a lamp. In the corner stood a leather-handled derby walking cane.

"It's all yours," she said.

I was willing to swap it for her office. Anything to get her to stay. "I wish it wasn't this way."

"Why? What do you care? I'm sure it's what you wanted."

"It's not." Could I trust her? If not, she could spread gossip through the ranks.

"Isn't it all you dreamed about?" she said. "Where did you say you were from?"

"Chicago." I'd flown out yesterday, the day after Zany's murder. My first time ever in Denver.

"You must've compiled quite the impressive resume to be awarded this prize. I thought they'd send some goon. You're younger than I expected."

I bristled. "What did you do for Zany? You were one of his bookkeepers?"

"The manager."

The way she looked down at the desk and then walked over and placed her hand on the headrest of Zany's big leather chair told me she had something more than a business connection to Zany.

"I bet you're important to the operation," I said.

"The place won't run without Zany or me."

It certainly wouldn't run with me in charge. I talked fast. "You think that's what Zany would want, for this place to close? Because, believe me, it will close if you leave. I'm not some hotshot bookmaker from Chicago."

She looked down at the desk then up at me. Tears welled up in her green eyes. Zany must've been a decent guy to earn those. "Are you some mob guy?"

I came around the desk beside her. A framed picture on the desk of her and Zany with wide smiles. An older Zany than the one I knew, with one arm around Rudi's shoulders. What would she do if she knew Zany had planned to meet Amity the night he was killed?

"No, I'm not," I said. "Do you want whoever did this to go unpunished?"

"I don't know. Of course not."

"I need you to stay. We want the same thing."

"What's that?"

"I want to find Zany's killer," I said.

"Why?"

I saw the pictures plastered all over the wall of Zany, the jockey, in the winner's circle. Too bad none of them were of Splendid Runner. "I once stood in one of those pictures with Zany." I pointed.

"Bullshit. Zany hadn't ridden in ten or fifteen years."

"My uncle owned the horse."

"What was its name?"

"The horse? You probably never heard of it."

She had her hands on her hips. "Try me."

"Splendid Runner."

She looked at me as if I'd handed her a winning sweepstakes ticket. "Your uncle owned Splendid Runner?"

"Right. The horse had potential. Zany thought so too."

"Did you see the race?"

She asked the question with trembling lips as if we might share something. The way somebody asks where you were when 9/11 happened.

"It was awful. When Zany went down, we thought he was dead."

"He talked about it. But he didn't remember much. Just how he woke up in the hospital."

It made me proud to share a little piece of Zany's history. "Zany came back but he was never the same."

She nodded and tried to catch her breath, fighting back more tears. She looked up at me. "We were seeing each other. My husband and I filed for divorce. Zany didn't talk much about his racetrack days, but he talked about that horse."

"He did?"

"Zany could be irritable. Especially late at night. He got headaches, terrible ones. Sometimes his back hurt him so bad he had to use a cane. He cursed that horse. Called it Devil's Runner."

He used to tell me how he thought Splendid Runner might be his one chance to hit the big-time, get into the Triple Crown. He must've been in real pain to call the horse "Devil's Runner." Maybe laying blame had eased the pain. "Zany took a rough spill."

"You're here to find out who did this?" she asked.

Doubt flashed in her eyes. But hope was also lodged there.

"Right," I said. "I drew the short straw."

"Funny."

"Don't tell anyone. No, really. It's important. As far as anyone knows, I'm here to run the store. Collect the gambling debts and keep things running. A bartender from Chicago."

"So, you need me."

"Yes."

Maybe I should tell her about the past jobs Uncle Mike and I had done. That my uncle insisted a killer be turned over to the police. A strange bargain, but knowledge meant more to Burrascano than spending money on a "hit."

"Okay, Eddie O'Connell. There's more to you than meets the eye. You knew Zany, and your uncle was the owner of Splendid Runner."

"So, you're in?" I wanted a declaration of allegiance to the cause.

She looked at me and then back at the pictures on the desk. The cautious, measured way she seemed to think things through told me she had a calculating mind. She'd need it to run a store like this.

"Fine. I'll get that list of delinquent customers."

I knew what she meant: *"I'll give you a chance and see what you've got."* I'd bought some time.

Was it fate? Did Splendid Runner bring us all together in some deal with the devil? Absolutely. The horse was my first winner, my lucky charm. Zany would've loved the fact that Splendid Runner brought Rudi and me together. It was as close to a sure thing as I'd ever get. Rudi might not swear allegiance, but I did. To her.

3

Rudi walked back into Zany's office. "Here's the list of people who owe Zany's store."

"Which one should we see first?

Rudi didn't hesitate. "Michael Mulholland."

I looked down the list. The guy owed eighteen grand. "Why him?"

"He's my divorce attorney and he's not calling me back."

"Great." My first collection call and not only did I need to make an impression on Zany's customer base, I'd need to show Rudi what I was worth.

I had to get to know all I could about Zany. His habits, his routines. The kind of people he knew. Bookies were secretive. Money changed hands in the shadows like drug deals. Records were kept hidden in case of a raid. The simple act of pulling a list of debtors would be a monumental task if not for Rudi. The old days of rice paper were over but today's computer software encrypted customer information.

Rudi agreed to drive and I followed her through the back door down the alley to a parking garage. I planned to lure Mulholland out of his office. I needed a show of force but I couldn't start busting knee caps and breaking fingers.

We found her SUV on the first floor of the garage. I looked over the Yukon. "Nice wheels."

"Last year's model but I got a great price. Don't you have a car? I thought you were a big-time investigator."

I appreciated the good-natured ribbing and the smile that came with it. It lifted the dark cloud that hung over Zany's death.

"My hotel is down the street. Took a cab from the airport." I didn't want to tell her about my rental. The Crown Vic would be kept under wraps except for special projects. I wanted Rudi to drive me around and show me the city. I needed to learn Denver's streets and neighborhoods. I also wanted her take on these deadbeats.

I didn't like the word "deadbeat." I'd been one until this job where my portion of the fee, plus a liberal discount from Burrascano, bought me a ticket back to respectability. But deadbeat was still better than the alternative: "welcher."

"How did you end up with Mulholland as your divorce attorney?" I asked.

Rudi pulled out and we zipped up Seventeenth, one-way east, through the business district.

"I got his name from a friend."

"Has a good practice?"

"With the retainer, he charged and the hourly rate, he must do very well."

A possible love triangle between Rudi and Zany and the husband sparked the genius detective inside me. "Your divorce isn't final?"

"Nope. Just filed the damn thing a few weeks ago. I should've filed long ago." She gunned the SUV. I reached for the grab handle above. Maybe I should have changed the subject to traffic safety. Instead, I kept it up. "What did your husband do?"

"We came out to Denver for this hot sales job." Her special emphasis on the word "hot" came with anger and sarcasm. "Warren lasted all of six months. He's been in and out of work since."

"Where did you move from?"

"A little town outside of Omaha. Everyone moves away to find work unless you live on the family farm."

"Is Warren working now?"

She cut off a car and swerved into another lane, headed south on Broadway.

"Are you kidding? His full-time job is to make my life a living hell. He's out there right now charging up our credit cards. You know what he did?"

"What?"

"Warren sent a letter to my parents telling them I worked for a bookie and that's why *he* had to leave me. After I kicked *him* out."

"Sounds like a piece of work." Broadway sliced through a wide, forested park. I spotted the golden dome of the State Capitol on a rise to the left.

"First letter he's ever written. Never talked to my parents on their birthday or anything. Bastard."

I liked the look of the city and the lack of traffic compared to Chicago, but I wanted her to slow down. We passed some state administration buildings in silence, and I decided to risk more. "Any kids?"

"No, thank God. A close call, too. Everyone in my class married our high school sweethearts. We sat in the bleachers every Saturday night and screamed for our team. Stayed up all night to work on some damn float for the Homecoming Parade or the Harvest Parade or whatever. Everyone I know has kids now."

Rudi shifted in her seat then took a left down Sixth and accelerated through a yellow light.

"Watch that car," I said.

She hit the brakes in time then cut over to Speer Boulevard. I lunged against the seat belt and took a deep breath.

"I'm not exactly buying into all the old traditional bullshit anymore. If my folks want me to quit, that's just too bad. It's my decision to work for a bookie."

"Much farther?"

"Mulholland's office is up ahead in Cherry Creek. What about you? Married?" she asked.

"Divorced."

"Lucky you."

We drove a few more miles in silence. I needed to think about how to squeeze eighteen grand out of this attorney, while at the same time get him to pay attention to Rudi's divorce case. We drove through blocks of trendy shops and shiny office buildings.

"I can't believe you were able to get Mulholland to see us," Rudi said.

"I didn't."

"What? I thought you called."

"If I had to set up a meeting with deadbeats, I'd never collect a dime. Surprise is more fun. Call him and say you're on the way over. Say it like you mean it. Find out if he's in the office."

"Really? Because I can be a real bitch if I put my mind to it."

"Don't hold back."

At a red light, Rudi pulled out her cell, identified herself, and asked for her attorney. "Mr. Mulholland is in conference? Look miss, I gave that bloodsucker a retainer so he'd represent me. That means returning my calls. I have a real problem, and if he's going to ignore me, I have a right to know. I'm on my way over. My husband calls every night, laughs, and hangs up. How would you like that? I need Mr. Mulholland to do *something*." She stopped and listened then turned to me. "She hung up. Want me to call back?"

"No. And remind me not to piss you off."

"You better not."

I directed Rudi to drive slowly through the parking garage of the lawyer's office and found a spot near the building's exit. "Stop here."

We didn't have to wait long before a man ran out the door into the garage.

"There he is," Rudi said. "The chicken shit."

Mulholland was a short, thin man. He wore a dark suit and a conservative striped tie that pinched the skin around his neck.

I jumped out of Rudi's SUV and met Mulholland by his white Porsche. I introduced myself and the attorney ignored me and opened his car door. I stepped in front of him and slammed the car door.

"Take it easy, pal. This is Paula Rudinger. Remember her?" I bobbed my head toward Rudi who walked over. "A client. Or did you forget after cashing the retainer?"

"Do I know you?" Mulholland said.

"I'm Zany's replacement, Eddie O'Connell. You owe money. A lot."

Mulholland ran a hand over his forehead and across his bald head. He gritted his teeth. "Zany's dead."

I suspected people might think their debt died with Zany, but I was here to make them see the light. "Think again, counselor." I relished the sick expression on the attorney's face. The job had its perks.

"I don't have time to deal with you now. I have an emergency hearing."

"No briefcase?" I looked at Rudi. She had a big smile.

"My file is in the car."

I opened the car door and looked inside. "That's funny. All I see in there are racing programs. Maybe if you eased up on the horses . . ."

"I'll get a check over to you. Now get out of the way. Be careful with my car—"

"I don't think I want your money after all. I kind of like this car," I said. The attorney hadn't raised a dispute about the amount owed to Zany.

He shot me a quizzical look.

I gave him a wide smile. "I just got out here from Chicago and need a car to get around. I'll take it as collateral until you pay."

Rudi held one hand over her mouth, perhaps concealing a smile.

"You don't have any security interest in my car," Mulholland said. "I'll pay."

"Screw that legal bullshit. How much do you charge an hour?"

The attorney cleared his throat. "That's a confidential matter."

"Rudi, how much?"

"He told me four hundred eighty-five dollars per hour. Unreal," Rudi said.

"You know, Mulholland, I need a lawyer every now and then. I got all kinds of stuff—bond hearings, assault." I inched closer. I didn't like his tie. "They tell me I've got a problem."

"This isn't fair," Mulholland said. "You haven't given me a chance."

"What about Rudi's unanswered phone calls?"

"It won't happen again, I swear," Mulholland said.

"If it does and if I don't get Zany's money today, I'm not going to be so nice." I looked down on Mulholland. "And one more thing."

"What?"

"I want it in cash."

"Okay, okay."

Eighteen grand would help the store's bottom line. "Now go over there and talk to your client. Act like you give a damn about her case."

Mulholland and Rudi huddled up near the entrance. My star manager seemed happy.

There was something in Rudi's complaint about Warren's incessant calls that had caught my attention. Something I didn't like. I heard fear in Rudi's voice.

4

Rudi and I did several more collection calls at a bowling alley on Colorado Boulevard that yielded a substantial down payment and the promise of monthly installments. Like most bookies, Zany operated through every strata of society.

We then returned to the store to meet with the employees whose shift began an hour before the start of the evening's east coast baseball games. They were anxious to check out the new boss and crowded around. Three men and four women. They were a tight-knit group and looked to Rudi for direction. Once more I silently thanked Rudi for staying.

After the introductions, Rudi and I sat down to discuss finances. I learned the store only had enough cash to last a week. Zany kept his cash hidden and nobody, Rudi included, knew where. Burrascano would expect me to find Zany's stash.

The receptionist buzzed Zany's office—now my office— and asked for Rudi. She took the call in a cool and professional manner. Her face turned several shades of red and purple as she tried to get in a few words of explanation to the caller. After several minutes, she hung up and her face turned grim.

"We have to go. You've been summoned," she said.

Rudi explained that her divorce attorney had contacted Preston Williston, the President of the Kelso Club, to complain about my strong-arm collection tactics. Preston demanded my immediate presence to answer questions. Mulholland had accused me of harassment.

What harassment? I didn't slap him around or smash the windshield of his car. And who was Preston Williston?

I took a deep breath and let Rudi explain things. She told me that the Kelso Club was where all the store's high rollers played. Most days Zany took more action at the club than he did in-house. Without its members, we'd be forced to close.

That wouldn't sit well with Mags, the local crime boss, who depended on his cut, or the boys back in Chicago. Rudi led the way to the club. It was four blocks away on another side street in LoDo, so the walk gave me a chance to cool down.

The late afternoon sun aimed a death ray of heat straight into my face. Commuters dashed past toward the light rail and tried to find what shade they could from the historic, red-brick warehouses that lined the block.

I turned to Rudi. "They better not ask me to apologize."

"Look. You need to do whatever they ask. The club is a gold mine and to keep the members we have to keep Preston happy. I blame myself. Maybe I was too upset about my divorce. I should've warned you about that."

"You couldn't predict what Mulholland would do. How did Zany handle the Kelso Club members who owed?"

"They drove him nuts." Rudi circled around a homeless person holding a cardboard sign while planted on the shady half of the sidewalk. "He coddled them. Sat down and talked with them. Gave out ultimatums. Threatened. Nothing worked."

The rich bastards didn't deserve to slide. They acted like Zany had done them a favor by taking their wagers. For the sake of the store, I had to cut these guys off. But I couldn't walk into the club, introduce myself, and lay down new rules. I had to stay in control.

Collecting gambling debts, a debt based on an illegal activity, was a bluff. You didn't want to push the debtor toward the authorities. It was a different story in Chicago where collectors operated under the mob's protective umbrella of rumor and innuendo. Run to the cops and they'd laugh at you and club you with a nightstick to cure you of stupidity. But here in Denver?

After walking a couple of blocks west, we stopped at the red light to head south, away from the baseball stadium. Rudi looked toward the park and nudged me. "They said Zany fell off the stadium. Unreal."

The cops hadn't disclosed everything to the media, but Burrascano's sources had leaked what really happened. That Zany had been tortured and thrown off the top floor late at night.

I asked Rudi what she knew about the night Zany had been killed. She said it'd been a Kelso Club-sponsored "night out at the ballpark," although Zany had supplied the tickets. Buying his customers tickets to a sporting event had always been good for business, she said. People would return the favor by making a wager with their bookie-benefactor. She hadn't attended because of an appointment with Mulholland, but the attorney canceled at the last minute. Another source of aggravation with her divorce attorney.

She didn't know if Zany planned to meet anyone after the game or if he had any dispute with a member. Amity still offered the best clue. I didn't share that with Rudi.

Zany needed to go to the Kelso Club that night to straighten something out. Most likely a dispute. I needed to find out who Zany had planned to meet and why. A good reason for me to make peace with Preston Williston.

"That's it, up ahead," Rudi said.

A rounded, burgundy-colored awning in the middle of the block came into view. It extended out from the building to the street, the gold, cursive lettering embroidered on the side: "The Kelso Club."

I wasn't sure what I'd expected but this wasn't it. The building took up almost half a block. Five stories high, including the penthouse on the top. The upper floors gleamed in the late afternoon sun. Plants from the penthouse patio hung down over the walls.

Although the building maintained the exposed original red brick like most of the converted lofts in the area, the Kelso Club sported additional architectural amenities. Black steel beams reinforced each level and framed the upper windows to provide a solemn grandeur. Shaded black glass wrapped the upper floors, reminding me of a poker player's dark sunglasses.

The front of the building faced east, cloaked in shade. As we got closer, I noticed how the building extended back to the alley, farther than the other buildings on the block. Expensive cars flocked to a valet stand like honeybees to a fragrant rose. A valet gunned the engine of an apple-red Ferrari.

At the entrance, a security guard nodded to Rudi then returned to his debate with the doorman about the merits of the free-agent signing of a defensive lineman by the Broncos. The doorman tipped his hat to Rudi and opened one of the oversized bronze doors. The sign provided a cold welcome: "Private—Members Only. Trespassers will be prosecuted."

Inside, any evidence of a warehouse had been replaced by marble floors and high ceilings. It reminded me of one of the century-old bank and trust buildings that lined Chicago's LaSalle Street.

To the left, a wall of glass enclosed a formidable array of fitness machines. Colorful works of modern art reached from floor to ceiling.

Another security guard manned a bank of video monitors behind a long counter.

Rudi smiled at the white-haired guard and introduced me. I shook Raymond's hand as he offered condolences for Zany's loss. I thanked him and followed Rudi to the elevator.

The place gushed money. I leaned over to Rudi. "I don't see why these members can't pay us." More than sixty percent of the store's debtors were Kelso Club members; they accounted for eighty percent of the total outstanding receivables.

"Hush." She led me a few steps away. "Zany isn't the only outlet in town. Lately, this guy Peter Leister has made a big push."

A dispute over territory could supply a motive for murder. Dressed up as a possible sex crime, rather than a simple assassination, it would throw Zany's mob connections off track.

"Did Zany get along with Leister?"

"I'm not sure," Rudi said. "Some things Zany didn't share with me. He could be a loner. Zany's jockey career hit on hard times after Chicago. He talked about drifting from one track to the next, trying to get live mounts, and fighting to make weight. A drug habit didn't help but he finally kicked it."

We walked back and joined several other members at the elevator. Perhaps the key to Zany's murder could be found in the Kelso Club.

5

I FOLLOWED RUDI OUT OF THE ELEVATOR ONTO THE SECOND floor of the Kelso Club that opened into a comfortable lounge, furnished with leather couches and chairs. Reading lamps offered a soft glow in the dark wood-paneled room. The Wall Street Journal and Barron's were carefully laid out on the coffee tables. I felt as if I'd walked into an old man's exclusive club.

People milled around the hostess stand. To my right, I glanced into a large dining room with white tablecloths and fancy chandeliers. The robust smell of prime steaks, together with the scent of fine cigars insured an environment where deals got done. To my left, glass doors led into a crowded bar.

My stomach churned and it wasn't hunger. These people coming and going from the elevators to the bar or dining room knew each other. I got a good look at the class of the crowd and felt out of place. This wasn't the same crowd I served at O'Connell's Tavern back in Chicago.

I put myself in Mulholland's shoes. Why would he run so fast to Preston? Sure, it gave the attorney leverage, but was there something else?

People with gambling debts don't run off and broadcast it. Heck, I knew that from personal experience. Your first inclination is to hide it and try to get back to even, not showcase it.

Rudi said hello to several members at the hostess stand and headed toward the glass doors. She was filled to the brim with conversation, fully prepared to enter the bar where members would be in the midst of a raucous happy hour. Mingling, hobnobbing, and everyday bullshitting were Uncle Mike's territory, not mine.

When did we delineate this boundary between us? Our duties became defined by what came naturally. Uncle Mike, the saloon owner, and detective, easily adapted to making contacts and initiating interviews, while I assumed the physical duties like jumping off fire escapes, running down a fleeing suspect, or breaking into a home or office.

Inside, I gave the bar the once-over. It was a beauty. The shelves behind the bar were loaded with enough bottles of top brands to supply O'Connell's Tavern for a year. A mirror above the shelves reflected happy, animated faces chatting socially after a day of making big money. They wore casual clothes, but designer casual.

I sensed an economic divide the size of the Grand Canyon. The Ferrari stood out in my mind. Eighteen grand was a sizeable amount for the common wage earner, but what about an attorney who drove a Porsche? An eighteen thousand debt would be an embarrassment. When I compared it to the amount I rang up on sports, it seemed like a parking fine.

"Let's take a seat away from the bar," she said. "If I get beat up by Preston, I'd prefer it to be in private."

People glanced our way. I stared back and imagined their names on my debtor list. Rudi's presence labeled me as Zany's replacement. Their steely eyes lobbed a question my way. Could I be trusted?

I followed her to a corner table on the other side of the room where a wall-sized portrait of a thoroughbred and its jockey stood out. Rudi told me it was a photo of Kelso, the namesake of the establishment.

The frame below the picture held the title in bronze letters: "Kelso Stands Alone—Post Parade, Aqueduct, 1963."

Uncle Mike had brought up Kelso whenever the talk turned to great racehorses. The grainy black and white scene showed a crowd in motion, necks craned to obtain a good view of the legend. Ladies wore pillbox hats. Men wore fedoras and black ties.

The photo was taken from above, the camera lens angled down on Kelso. The masses squeezed up to the rail. Kelso stood in the stretch, perpendicular to the rail, his eyes fixed upon the photographer and the crowd, an air of confidence and defiance only a horseplayer like me could see.

A plaque to the left of the photograph of Kelso detailed the career:

With a record five consecutive Horse of the Year titles from 1960 through 1964, Kelso was one of racing's great stars. Owned by Richard C. DuPont's Bohemia Stable, the gelding was Horse of the Year as a three-year-old, despite not running in a Triple Crown race. He retired with 39 wins in 63 starts and an earnings record that would stand for 15 years.

Rudi tugged on my sleeve. A waiter stood over our table.

"Do you want anything?" she said. "I'm having a chardonnay."

I thought about a scotch but that wouldn't help me maintain restraint. I opted for an iced tea. Members streamed past us through another set of glass doors. Rudi told me it was the simulcast area where the customers bet on the horses and the dogs.

"I have to check it out."

"We don't have time." She reached for my arm. "Preston might be here any moment."

"I'll only be a minute." I got up and walked through the doors.

Inside, flat screens mounted around the room televised every track running at this time of day. Thoroughbred races, harness, dogs, it was all here. I felt like a kid on Christmas morning.

This was the main attraction. Everything else—the fitness area, dining room, and bar, was just window dressing.

This kind of place had been my refuge, my arena, where time slowed and life became a simple matter of picking horses. I once won twenty-one grand in one day. Overnight the O'Connell patrons crowned me the undisputed heavyweight champ and any and all questions concerning the horses were brought to me.

I lived up to my reputation. Another time I won a share of a Pick Six for forty-four grand. If you could win that much in one day, I reasoned, what did it matter if you needed to borrow or who you borrowed from? If I could win at the horses, why not sports? But those Vegas lines were set with the precision of the Norden bombsight. And I did get bombed.

Double the square footage of the bar, the simulcast area provided every amenity. Lush carpet. The clink of happy hour glasses. Members sat in high-backed leather chairs at desks, divided by wood panels similar to a library carrel. Somebody yelled encouragement as horses ran through the stretch on one of the many oversized flat screens. A waiter came by and asked if he could bring me something.

My neighborhood OTB facility had folding chairs and smelled like a bus depot.

Arlington was over but Del Mar was still running. I had a good streak of simulcast play at the San Diego track last summer. Caught a couple of trainers making all the right moves with some recent claims.

A member ran up to the windows to wager. It was legal to wager on horses in this facility but not on sports. To wager on sports, they'd have to use Zany's store or some other bookie. Rudi had mentioned how much action Zany took here during football season. A disguised survey of the crowd didn't reveal anyone holding court and taking bets. In response to my question, the waiter told me he hadn't seen Peter Leister today.

How many minutes to post for Del Mar? A stack of racing programs sat ready on a table near the entrance. I felt naked without a decent-sized bankroll and Burrascano's expense cash didn't count.

I could sit down unnoticed and get something down. I had time. No, I promised myself I would only take a few minutes.

I snatched a racing program on my way out, rolled it up in one hand and tucked it under my arm like a shoplifter, and went back into the bar.

A man sat with Rudi at the table. My heart skipped a beat.

"I didn't think you were coming back," Rudi said. "Eddie O'Connell, this is Preston Williston."

The man stood but not as a courtesy. I thought he might walk off. "Mr. O'Connell, how good of you to join us."

He was of medium height, the beginnings of a potbelly, probably in his fifties. Casual clothes perfectly pressed and tailored. Beard expertly trimmed. Beneath the open collar, a thin gold chain around his neck. The type who thought he knew lots of everything and could be counted on to wager big. Any bookie would salivate at the sight of him.

"Mr. Williston. Nice to meet you." I held out my hand.

Preston inspected me, sniffed, then sat back down. "Let's get started. I don't have much time."

I pulled my hand back and sat down. Anger rose inside me but I counted to ten. What would Uncle Mike do? "This is a great place. Kelso needs to be remembered."

Rudi shot me a look. I was supposed to shut up and listen. I got pissed off all over again and clamped a hand over my mouth.

Preston cleared his throat. "The reason I requested this meeting, Mr. O'Connell, is quite simple."

I wanted to tell him to call me "Eddie" but kept my mouth shut. I saw the way Rudi stared down into her empty wine glass.

"The Kelso Club maintains a certain reputation." Preston leaned over and spoke directly into my face. "Our membership makes this club and, in turn, the club looks out for its members. You can understand the point I'm making?"

I nodded like a dope.

"The club extends certain privileges to you based on certain parameters." Preston gestured with his hands, held vertical to form two walls. "It's a loose, unspoken relationship, but still the club respects your role and you must respect the club and its members."

"Where is Mulholland, my accuser?" I asked. Rudi glanced my way.

Preston pointed to his chest. "I have a vested interest in how the club is perceived and all the good things it does for the community. So naturally—"

"Naturally." I couldn't help myself.

Preston coughed. "It's a two-way street. When one party is out of line, steps must be taken."

I felt a droplet of sweat drip down under one arm. The thought of failure clouded my thoughts.

"As I told Rudi over the phone," Preston said. "Attorney Mulholland has been a longtime member and his wishes must be heard. I'll tell you quite frankly, Mr. O'Connell. You strike me as a young man who wants to get to the point. Attorney Mulholland has asked that you be banned from the club."

Rudi gasped.

"Give me a break," I said. "The guy owes money."

"He said you wrecked his Porsche?" Preston said.

"What?" Rudi asked.

Alarm bells went off. Mulholland had sprung some sort of trap and expected me to get pissed off and walk out. I had to be careful. "Bullshit," I said—not too careful.

"I was there," Rudi said.

"If you think you have grounds, the board might grant you a hearing," Preston said.

A woman came up to the table and gave Preston's shoulder a playful punch. She wore a low-cut, black blouse and stood with her hands on her hips. Her stylish long blond hair framed a well-preserved face. I guessed she was in her late forties but tried to pass for her mid-thirties. Her lips formed an angry pout.

"Where is he?" the woman said.

Preston rubbed his shoulder and looked up at her. "He said he'd be here."

Preston's low-key reaction to the shoulder swipe and the way he looked at the woman told me they were a couple, and that Preston was pussy-whipped.

With one hand, the woman patted Rudi's shoulder. "Hi, Rudi. How are you doing? Everything going okay?" The woman slurred her words.

"Hi, Crystal," Rudi said. "It could be better."

"Zany was a great guy. I'm still not over it." Crystal tugged on Preston's shoulder. "It's Zach's birthday and you said Allegro would be here. Where is he?"

Allegro Martin? The basketball player? I'd seen him in the twilight of his NBA career when he'd given a young Michael Jordan a run for his money. I could buy time and find out something about this board hearing Preston mentioned.

"I know, I know," Preston said. "We were having a meeting."

"Crystal," Rudi said. "This is Eddie O'Connell, my new boss."

For how long, I thought. "Nice to meet you." Preston's stern mood had softened.

Crystal gave me a warm smile then looked down at Rudi as if they shared some secret then back at me. "Nice to meet you, too. We'll have to talk. Right now, my son's birthday celebration is about to get underway. Zach is one of the best players on his college team and the whole conference. He should get into the NBA."

It was something every mother would say. "Is he one of those tall guys by the bar?" I wanted to keep the distraction going then try to talk sense to Preston.

"Yes, the one with the blond hair." Crystal pointed. "So, you can imagine what it's like for him to have Allegro at his birthday dinner."

I spotted Zach perched on a bar stool, a pair of crutches under one arm. He watched our table with a sly smile. "You mean Allegro Martin, right?" I asked.

"Yes," Crystal said. "It's a big deal for Zach. A really big deal."

"It would be a big deal for anybody," I said.

"Allegro's a close friend," Crystal said. "The club hosts a charity golf tournament in his name."

"Crystal, give us a minute. Please," Preston said.

Rudi touched Crystal's arm.

Crystal looked at Rudi then at Preston. "What did I miss?"

"Never mind." Preston stood up. "Mr. O'Connell, let's talk further about the remaining issues with the members tomorrow when I have more time. Twelve o'clock in the simulcast area."

"Sure," I said. I didn't like Preston's tone. It sounded as if I'd be executed at high noon.

As Preston dragged Crystal back toward the bar, I leaned over to Rudi. "I'm banned?"

"Keep your voice down. Maybe I can work on Crystal."

I resisted the urge to run after Preston and tell him off. "What is it with you and Crystal, are you friends?"

"We have become pretty tight," she said. "She referred me to Mulholland for my divorce."

"Great."

"Like I said, Preston is unpredictable. Maybe tomorrow—"

"Remaining issues? Does he want me to write off the debts? Let's get a photo of Mulholland's car," I said.

"Good idea. All you did was close the door of his Porsche."

My cell vibrated. I took it out without thinking.

A scratchy, gravel-like voice spoke. "Mags needs to see you."

"Now?" I asked.

"Yeah. Outside." The call ended.

I didn't need another distraction. "I've got to go—"

"What?" she said. "I don't think this is a good time. Preston—"

"I've got to meet Mags." I stood. Maybe he'd heard of my banishment. Maybe that was Mulholland's work as well.

6

OUTSIDE A GUY IN A WORN, MUD-COLORED OVERCOAT WITH fat cheeks and large round eyes waved to me. He stood next to a ten-year-old caddie double-parked beside the valet stand. I walked over.

His mouth hung open and his bottom lip quivered. "You O'Connell?" His face reminded me of a grouper fish.

I asked him what was going on and got a grunt in response. How did I manage to pop up on Vincent Scarlamaglia's radar?

The man scooped the fast-food cartons and newspapers off the front seat of the car and tossed them in back so I could sit down.

I got in. The cracked brown upholstery stank of stale cigars and body odor. An empty thermos rolled out between my feet as he pulled away into traffic.

I tried the buddy approach and told him my name and made a crack about the steaks at the Kelso Club. Tried to learn something. Prepare myself for whatever bombshell Mags might heave at me.

The man didn't answer. In fact, he turned up the volume on the sports talk station. A full analysis of the Broncos training camp and which third-string linebacker might make the team filled the void.

We drove east on Colfax, past the state capitol building. The good soldier drove with one arm slung over the wheel and snaked between cars at top speed. Not once did I flinch or second-guess a maneuver, the man was an artist with a motor vehicle.

The landscape changed after four or five miles. Cheap hotels, strip clubs, and dive bars lined the street, populated by the usual cast of street walkers, gang bangers, and winos. We skidded to a stop in a gravel alley beside a motel.

"Enjoyed the field trip," I said. "Does it come with a sack lunch?"

Again, no response. A man in a black leather coat stood watch on an iron staircase of the motel, which led to the outside walkway. The man waved me up but kept his eyes on the street. More men were camped at the stairwell and another outside a room. I followed their silent directions. Each one gestured toward the room. Common sense told me to run in the opposite direction.

A lean man in a sharp-pressed, gray suit, black tie, and thick glasses stood in the doorway. His salt and pepper hair leveled by a crew cut, vintage early 1960s. My car insurance salesman had the same look.

"I'm Vincent Scarlamaglia," he said.

"Eddie O'Connell." I reached out my hand but didn't get a handshake in return. The second time tonight. Good thing I wasn't running for office.

Mags stepped back inside and waved an arm toward the bed. "Take a look. What all your good work has done."

A woman in a black negligee with a gunshot wound to the head lay dead on the sheets. It was Amity.

The fact Mags had me brought here showed that he respected Chicago, Joey L, and Burrascano. That respect extended to Uncle Mike and then to me. I had been given the job as the investigator so I was brought to the scene.

Mags seemed at ease. I looked away—I couldn't give him the pleasure of any gut reaction to the tragedy.

Zany's killer must be responsible. The killer had probably been watching me last night at the ballpark. I'd looked into the crowd. The murderer had been looking back at me.

How had the killer been tipped off? It could've been Mags or one of his men. The Kelso Club had probably been buzzing with the news of Zany's murder.

Peter Leister would be interested in Zany's replacement. After Amity, I might be next on the killer's list.

Who did Amity bring to this shitty room with the mustard-colored stains on the ceiling?

I had told her to call if she heard from someone.

It was impossible to imagine this transformation. Last night she was full of life at the baseball game. She'd strutted off to her next appointment and now this . . .

I took a deep breath and inspected the body. Marks around the neck, signs of strangulation. Most likely the killer had questioned her before the shot to the head.

"Anybody call the police?" I asked.

Mags grunted. "Yeah, I thought we'd all stand around and take pictures. What the fuck?"

"Who found her?"

"Some drunk who manages the place. He works for us."

"I'll need his name."

"He can't remember what happened yesterday. But sure, get his name." Mags nodded to one of his boys on the walkway.

"Did anyone see anything?"

The mobster bent down and wiped dust off his shiny, black Florsheims. "A few hours ago? Who knows?"

Mags stood up again and placed his hands on his hips as I moved about the room. Probably took notes on my technique.

Amity's black sequin bag lay unopened on the dresser. I took out my handkerchief and used it to unsnap the bag. I found hundred-dollar bills, together with a driver's license, sunglasses, and makeup kit. I eliminated robbery as a motive.

I looked around the bed then stepped into the bathroom. The plugged toilet fit the motif.

No sign of Amity's cell phone or the slip of paper with my phone number. With a pen, I picked up Amity's little black dress off the floor but found nothing underneath. Her shoes were tossed beside the wall.

"Did anyone take anything?"

"Like what?" Mags said.

"Before you got here. Did anyone go through the room?"

"How should I know?"

The cheap motel didn't fit Amity's clientele. She must've been lured here by the killer. But she'd already talked to me.

What was the killer worried about? Or was it only a matter of vengeance? "Can you get me a list of the woman's regulars?"

"I can find out." Mags gave his man instructions.

"I've seen enough," I said. "Let's leave and call the police."

"You want to drag the cops into this?"

My uncle and I had a rule: don't make things too complicated and get all the help you could. The police had superior resources and could uncover something we couldn't.

"Give them an anonymous call," I said.

He pointed toward the bed. "What if she leads back to Zany?"

"It would be worse if one of your guys is found lugging a body around."

"Look Sherlock, all I care about is Zany and his operation. It throws off a lot of cash during football season."

The money was his chief concern and I'd managed to foul up that stream of revenue on my second day. It would only be a matter of time before he heard about my banishment from the Kelso Club. Maybe I should ask him for a loan to run the store.

"Don't worry. I'll run it the same way Zany did," I said.

"You're collecting on the gambling debts?"

"Right."

"Zany was soft on collections," Mags said. "No reason why all the deadbeats can't be turned over to me. They should be paying the street rate."

What would Preston say if I handed over the list of Kelso Club members to Mags? If I gave in to Mags on this, it would be a sign of weakness and his hard-nosed collection would undermine my investigation into the Kelso Club. I needed time.

"We don't want the debtors to run to the police," I said.

"I pay them off. How do you think you got those police reports?"

Mags had only delivered the police report after several calls this afternoon. He didn't deserve a gold star for cooperation.

"What about Peter Leister?"

"What about him? Like I don't run a smooth operation? Like I don't protect my people?"

"Take it easy," I said.

"Shit. I still don't understand why Burrascano thinks he has to send someone out here."

"I don't ask Burrascano what he thinks." I took out my cell. "Here, why don't you call him?"

He stuck a finger in my face. "Every month Burrascano gets his cut. The money I send him pays for his big house, the girlfriends, the boat."

I stared into the murky, dark eyes of Vincent Scarlamaglia. No facial scars, but thin, cruel lips. He had a reputation for violence. Denver made money. All the major sports represented. According to Joey L, Mags was old school. He kept every faction in its place—the Mexican cartels, the Asians, the Russians, the gangs—everybody within their prescribed territory.

Now he had a problem and didn't know where to strike. Having me poke and prod through the dirty laundry didn't help.

"You send Burrascano his cut," I said. "But don't forget who gave you what you've got."

He took off his glasses. I didn't back away as he came closer.

"You got some of your uncle's blood in you."

I'd touched a nerve with the old school gangster. Now was my chance to bargain. "I can't get anything done in a couple of days. Give me some time—"

"We don't have time. People wait to see what I do—Leister and others."

"I've stepped into Zany's shoes to make myself a target," I said. "Maybe we'll get this over quick."

"The murderer must be following you around."

"Maybe."

"You met the woman last night. I'll find you like this," Mags nodded toward the bed.

"Maybe the guy you assigned to follow me will spot the killer. He's camped out wherever I go." Grouper face, the artist with the caddie.

"You mean Charlie Grasso?" he snickered. "Don't count on old Grasso. He distrusts outsiders as much as I do."

I didn't like his sense of humor. I was the outsider.

7

FRIDAY

The next day, I stood by the elevators inside the lobby of the Kelso Club to meet with Preston at high noon. A tall young man on crutches swung gracefully across the marble floor from the fitness area. I recognized him from the night before, Crystal's son.

"Hi, Zach," I said. "Crystal told me about last night's party. Belated happy birthday."

He looked down through his shaggy, damp, blond hair, his eyes thin slits. "Oh, yeah." He smiled. "Eddie O'Connell, the bookie. I heard about you."

We shook hands. He had a good-sized grip and I suspected he could palm a basketball.

"How's the rehab going?"

"It's a bitch. They try to get you back on the court fast. I missed most of last season."

"I take it one more year and you'll go in the draft?"

The elevators opened, and I let him go first.

He maneuvered inside. "That's top secret. I'll need to show them that the knee isn't a problem." He punched buttons—the second floor for me and, I assumed, the penthouse suite for him.

"First round?"

He laughed. "I hope. Maybe late first round. I'd take that."

"Good luck."

We stopped at the second floor.

"Good luck to you, too," Zach said.

I held the elevator door open. "What do you mean?"

"I heard them arguing last night. Preston and Mom. She went to bat for you."

I could tell from his low voice the outcome wasn't good. "Want to join me? I could use an ally."

"I can't. But I'll be down later to place some wagers."

I walked into the simulcast area a bit early for my appointment. Preston Williston stood up from one of the handicapping carrels in the back row and waved me over.

I'd hoped for some time to get my bearings. Pretend these races on the big screens around the room didn't come with odds and action. As if the line of members at the windows might have been a lunch crowd waiting to order takeout instead of placing bets.

But Preston waved again. Rudi had talked with Crystal who promised to talk with Preston and "soften him up." Rudi thought it best that I approach Preston alone. That way I could crawl and beg for mercy without hurting my pride.

No way I would be begging. I didn't wreck Mulholland's Porsche, and I had a right to collect the money he owed. I looked for the attorney but didn't see him.

Preston's strong-arm tactic to ban me from the club struck me as a bluff. Maybe the guy fished for a bribe. Could that be? The place seemed too high class for such a cheap move.

These gamblers standing in line to make wagers on the horses would need an outlet for sports betting action when football started and Zany's store fulfilled that need. Preston couldn't afford to ban me or he'd have a revolt on his hands. Leister wanted to compete against Zany's store but it would require a big operation that could handle high volume action.

As I stepped up to Preston, I spied Saratoga, Monmouth, Delaware, and Gulfstream, tracks from the top of the eastern seaboard to the bottom, in full swing on the flat screens around the walls. A race call echoed throughout the room.

Preston's hand directed me to the adjacent carrel. "Mr. O'Connell, let me introduce you to Jim Arnold."

Arnold looked up and nodded from his chair. He was in his late thirties, rail-thin, and wore glasses. The pens clipped to the pocket of his wrinkled shirt branded him a computer geek. Arnold's name appeared at the top of the store's alphabetical list of debtors. He didn't get up to greet me.

"Mr. Arnold is a club member," Preston said. "He used to work for First United Bank but was laid off because of a buyout. He holds a degree in Statistical Analysis from an Ivy League school. But it didn't help him on the last race."

I peered inside Arnold's carrel. Stacks of notebooks, racing programs, and a laptop screen populated with figures jammed the three-foot square work area. A shot glass with a double shot of bourbon filled to the rim was positioned at his elbow. I could smell it.

"A race from Saratoga." Preston stroked his well-trimmed beard. "He's talked about this track all year. Couldn't wait for the meeting." He turned to Arnold. "Mr. O'Connell is in town to take Zany's place, Jim. You can't wait for football either."

"Nice to meet you," Arnold said as he eyed the glass of booze.

Preston cleared his throat and pointed at the small television screen inside Arnold's carrel. "The results have been posted. Go ahead, Jim, take a look. You see, Mr. O'Connell, Jim Arnold missed on this race. One more ticket and he'd have had it. The trifecta paid what?"

Arnold's glassy eyes turned from the screen to Preston. "Four thousand three-hundred-and-forty dollars."

"And one more ticket. One more ticket, only two dollars, and in order to save two dollars, you lost forty-three hundred." Preston shook his head and clicked his tongue.

Too bad. If Arnold had won, he could've made a dent in the balance owed to the store. If I could persuade Preston to not impose a ban, I could find some other members on the store's debtor list to coax repayment.

"Aren't you going to take that shot?" Preston reached over and flipped the page of the racing program in front of Arnold. "Plenty more races on the card."

Arnold reached for the glass with a trembling hand, picked it up, and brought it slowly to his lips. He got out of the chair and extended to his full height. The glass touched his bottom lip. He tipped the glass at an angle, hesitated, and then threw it back. Bourbon streamed down his chin and neck. He doubled over coughing and hacking.

The fiery liquid must've burned a trail down Arnold's throat. I'd had bad beats before too. It was the best medicine.

"Fuck you, Preston." Arnold wiped his mouth with the back of his hand. "You never worked a day in your life." He raised the glass up over his head as if to throw it.

Preston held up his hands. "Easy now."

I ducked.

Arnold smashed the glass down on the table top. The crash echoed throughout the room. Tiny shards of glass ricocheted. Some blood splattered across the notebooks and oozed from a nasty gash on Arnold's hand.

"What are you doing?" Preston said.

"Holy shit." I handed my handkerchief to Arnold. Waiters ran over. Members popped their heads up like prairie dogs out of their holes.

"Get a doctor," Preston said.

"I don't need a doctor." Arnold flicked his bloody hand to shake off chunks of glass and flung droplets of blood into the air.

"Look at that. All over the carpet." Preston waved to a waiter. "Let's go. Get this cleaned up."

Two waiters got down on their knees and scrambled around with rags in search of blood splatter.

"You're lucky, Jim, that you're a friend of mine," Preston said. "Or I'd—"

"You'd what?" Arnold wrapped his hand in my clean handkerchief.

Preston jabbed a finger at me. "Never mind. As for you, Mr. O'Connell, I need to follow up on our talk from yesterday."

"Go ahead." I grabbed a towel from one of the waiters and wiped blood off some of Arnold's notebooks and computer screen.

"Crystal can't help you," Preston said. "This is a board matter."

Arnold arranged the notebooks in meticulous order. I wiped some off and handed them over.

"She volunteered. I didn't make Crystal do anything," I said.

Preston pointed a waiter to some blood spots on the carpet. "Prior to the next board meeting and in the interim, I must advise you—"

"The board is a joke," Arnold said.

I looked down at Preston. "I don't need to wait for a board meeting, and I don't need to play any games. Your club needs me and the store."

Preston avoided my stare and looked at Arnold. "Quiet, Jim. This doesn't concern you. Haven't you caused enough trouble?" Preston turned to me. "You see, Mr. O'Connell, the club must protect members like Arnold from certain outsiders."

I understood what I'd witnessed. Arnold had tried to fight his way back to "even" and for a gambler, it could be a losing proposition to chase it.

"Every gambler gets burned now and then," I said. "But they have to own up. If they're into the store, they'll have to make good. Now if you want Chicago-style collection, just let me know." I didn't like the way Preston gritted his teeth. Maybe I'd gone too far.

"Mr. O'Connell," Preston said. "You act as if I don't have an alternative. This club—"

"I won't be quiet," Arnold interrupted. "I didn't like the taste of that cheap bourbon. Reardon serves a better brand like the one I had last night."

"What's that?" Preston asked.

Preston came to full attention at the mention of the name Reardon.

"Wes Reardon had a party last night." Arnold turned toward me as if to explain the situation at Preston's expense. "Reardon has great parties. Puts out great food, an open bar."

"Sorry I missed it," I said.

"Reardon had a party? Last night?" Preston stepped over and pulled on Arnold's sleeve. "Why didn't I hear about it?"

Preston's demeanor changed. This could work to my advantage.

"Everybody knew you had Zach's birthday party," Arnold said.

"What?" Preston asked.

"Sure, they talked about it," Arnold said.

"They did? Who?" Preston asked.

Preston's "holier than thou" attitude began to disintegrate. Arnold took obvious pleasure in Preston's pleading.

Arnold ignored Preston and pointed me toward the television screen inside his carrel. "I've got something good in this next race at Saratoga—the four horse. I'll get back to even in no time."

Under normal conditions, I'd stick my head into the race and question Arnold on his pick. The fact that he could recover so fast from a rough loss told me he was a veteran player with track savvy. But I had more pressing issues. Like how to keep Zany's store open for business.

"Jim, please." Preston wedged his way between Arnold and the television.

Arnold looked down at Preston. "The usual crowd was there."

"Was Allegro there?" Preston said. "Was he?"

I smiled. No one was immune to the allure of the celebrity athlete.

"Allegro?" Arnold said. "Sure, he was there. You should've seen the babe he brought with him. A gorgeous gal with platinum blond hair and a short, silver dress. Looked like a movie star or a stripper."

"Goddamnit," Preston said.

Preston's face turned a shade of purple. A vein stuck out of his forehead. Allegro must've been a no-show at Zach's birthday party. His obvious misery made Arnold smile.

"After all I've done for Allegro," Preston said.

I wanted to twist the knife in his fragile ego. "Was Mulholland there?"

Arnold nodded. "Yeah. He introduced this guy named Peter Leister to everyone. Do you know him? Says he'll take our action during football season."

"I've heard of him." It was not what I wanted to hear. Leister could offer Preston and the Kelso Club members an alternative to Zany's store. I'd lose all my leverage.

Things fit together neatly. Mulholland demanded I be banned from the club and, at the same time, he introduces Leister to the lucrative member base. Leister and Mulholland must be working together. It would make sense for Leister to kill Zany then steal his customers.

"Mulholland and Leister spent most of the night sucking up to Allegro," Arnold said. "Me? I would've been talking to Allegro's girl. But she didn't talk to anyone. Maybe she was from a foreign country or something because all she did was hang on Allegro's arm and pout."

Preston mumbled under his breath. "Allegro knew what this meant to Zach and his buddies. I spent all night apologizing. Son-of-a-bitch, everything I've done for that guy."

"You should meet Leister, Eddie. He's after your business." Arnold said. "I'm sure he'd like to meet you."

I didn't know if Arnold was teasing me about Leister or trying to help. "I can't wait."

"Eddie," Preston said, scratching his beard. "I'm having some members from the club out to the track tomorrow. My horse is running in the feature race."

"Yeah," Arnold said. "I'll introduce you around."

Preston had addressed me by my first name. "Does this mean I won't be banned?"

"That will be up to the members." Preston raised an index finger as if to make a point. "It's not my decision."

"Sounds like we'll have a choice," Arnold said. "Coke or Pepsi."

Me and Leister head-to-head in the fine art of mingling with the store's revenue at stake. No way I'd stand for it. Maybe I didn't go far enough with Preston. I should've threatened to turn the members over for collection to Mags.

But then I thought again. Maybe Leister would tip his hand. It seemed he had the most to gain from Zany's murder.

Still, mingling had never been my strong suit, and I had Mags looking over my shoulder.

8

As soon as Preston was called to address some administrative chore, I tore myself away from the Kelso Club action. No reason to tempt fate. If I took a seat, I'd be there until the last race on the west coast, handicapping with the veteran Arnold. Not exactly the best strategy to win over the membership and provide confidence in their choice of bookie. Not to mention Mags and my promise to Uncle Mike not to gamble.

I went back to the store. Rudi immediately cornered me inside Zany's old office and shut the door behind her.

She stood with her hands on her hips. "Well, are we in? Did Preston like you?"

It was a damn good question. One I wrestled with as I walked back. Where did I stand with the rich guy? I filled in Rudi on what had happened with Preston and that he invited me out to the track tomorrow. He wanted to put Zany's store and Leister's operation to a vote.

I tried to envision myself making small talk with doctors and lawyers.

"That weakling, that's total bullshit," Rudi said.

"You think he's playing me?"

"Preston wants to put on a show," she said. "Make it look like he's taking care of everyone. According to Crystal, Preston doesn't like Mulholland. He overcharges."

"Mulholland is Preston's attorney? Great."

I filled in Rudi about Reardon's party.

"Wait till I tell Crystal. She'll go ballistic." Rudi folded her arms. "Leister isn't wasting any time."

"Now we know Mulholland is working with Leister and the bullshit about the Porsche was simply bullshit. I also met a guy named Jim Arnold. Another one on our list of debtors. He was having a bad day playing the races." I didn't mention Arnold's meltdown and the way Preston seemed to enjoy it.

Rudi took a sip of coffee from her ubiquitous cup. "We cut Arnold off until he pays up. I think Zany had gotten the okay from Preston. Arnold owes Preston money as well."

I had a lot to catch up on. "Why don't you go with me to the track tomorrow? Another representative of the store will help." I needed Rudi to supply some conversation to make up for the dead air I'd provide.

"I wouldn't miss it. I'm sure Allegro will be there too. I can't believe he stood up Preston."

"It will be me against Leister in a battle for the members," I should track down Leister today and tell him to stay on his own side of the fence, or else. Better yet, let Mags and his soldier Grasso do it. But I needed to let things play out tomorrow—Leister had emerged as a possible suspect. I juggled two balls in the air—the welfare of the store and the investigation. Managing the store was the perfect cover.

"I can get Crystal to help us. I'm afraid to ask but what did Mags want last night?"

How should I handle this? If I told Rudi that Zany went off to meet a woman after the ballgame—would she up and quit?

The picture of Zany and Rudi on the desk showed that they'd been in love. Rudi had left everything in Zany's office and on his desk the way it was before his death as if she expected him to return. I hadn't said anything about the preserved office and hadn't moved a thing. I felt like an intruder on borrowed time.

According to Rudi, Zany's last surviving relative, his Aunt Mabel, had the body shipped back to Idaho for a private service. It didn't give Rudi much chance for closure. I don't know. There are so many ways to deal with grief.

And if she didn't leave after I told her about Zany and Amity, what would she say when I told her Amity ended up murdered?

I had to do it. I had to tell her. If I didn't, she wouldn't be a part of the investigation.

"When I first got here, I had an interview with a woman named Amity Seville," I said. "She was with Zany the night of the ballgame—before Zany was captured and killed."

"What?" Rudi stood up.

I decided to let the cards fall where they may. "Mags found Amity murdered last night."

Rudi's chin dropped. She brought her hands to her face. I didn't know whether to put an arm around her and console her or give her some time. "Do you want a minute?"

"No," she mumbled.

I braced myself for her decision.

She caught her breath. "Zany told me he was done with . . ." Her lips trembled as she looked over at one of Zany's winner's circle pictures on the wall.

"Some habits are hard to break."

"Was the woman part of it?"

"Part of Zany's murder? No, I don't think so. I questioned her."

Rudi nodded absently. There was that little town in Nebraska, her hometown.

"If it helps, Amity said that she and Zany just talked," I said.

She snorted. "He doesn't deserve any points for that. It's not horseshoes. But I guess in Zany's case maybe it does help. Zany had it rough. Injuries. No steady income or steady woman. Battled his demons alone over the years." She dabbed at her eyes with a tissue. "One hotel after the next. You don't end up behind *that* desk if you have a real life."

I noticed where I sat. I switched the subject.

"I got a copy of Amity's social calendar."

I took out the list of Amity's regulars written on the back of a hamburger wrapper that had been slipped under my hotel door in the middle of the night and handed it to her. Probably a delivery from Grasso.

Rudi looked at the greasy paper. "What about it?"

"Are any of Amity's regular customers members of the Kelso Club?"

This was how these investigations proceeded. My uncle and I tried things. We ran down blind alleys, we took chances, dug into people's lives. Made people, good people like Rudi, miserable.

"Zany, the pervert, may he rest in peace." Tears welled up in her eyes. She wiped her face, bent over, and stared at the list.

She shook her head. "Wait. Here's a familiar name. I know this one. Koransky—he's one of our subs."

A sub was another bookie operation that fed business to the store. The store also had a number of agents who brought in new customers in return for a slice of the losses. The slice was then applied to the gambling debt owed by the agent to the store.

I had a connection. I needed to keep moving, not sit in one spot and make a fat target. "Let's pay him a visit. Where is he?"

"I've got his number in my office." She stood up with coffee cup in hand. It was a good sign.

On her way out the door, she spoke to herself, but I overheard. "Why did I ever leave Nebraska?"

I pretended as if I didn't hear her comment and said: "While you get in touch with this guy, I've got to make a call."

I needed to update Uncle Mike.

9

Uncle Mike and I had always been a team. I needed to bounce stuff off him but, at the same time, I didn't want him to see it as a sign of weakness. I recalled how Joey L hesitated when we met at O'Connell's, and how the job assignment was not a "slam dunk." Most of all, I wanted to know if Burrascano had second thoughts.

Uncle Mike didn't answer, and I didn't leave a message. Maybe he spotted my burner phone number and would call back. Since my office door had been shut by Rudi on her way out, I went to work investigating the drawers of Zany's antique desk. Maybe Zany kept angry letters from a customer or a secret compartment with bank information. An investigator lets his imagination run wild. Zany may have grown careless over the years with Mags overseeing protection.

The first drawer on the right had a stack of documents from Team Player and outlined collection goals for the office.

It was the type of stuff Zany planted in case of a raid. If the Feds came calling about taxes, he'd need to have documents on hand.

My burner phone buzzed. I replaced the paperwork and answered.

"Eddie, my boy. How are you doing?" Uncle Mike asked.

I heard the afternoon clink of glasses and voices inside O'Connell's Tavern. I had to remind myself it was an hour later in Chicago. Lots of customers came in after the early shift. "Good."

"Wait a minute, and I'll get back to the office."

I heard the door slam and some more grunts and groans, then the familiar racket of my uncle's desk chair. It emitted a high-pitched squeak then a low creaking noise as if it begged for mercy. My uncle was a big man, sort of a beefed-up, oversized version of Fred Mertz from those *I Love Lucy* reruns. Heavy jowls, bald, sharp blue eyes. Sometimes I thought his face showed the toll of all these murder cases he'd taken over the years, and I hoped that he'd shift gears and slow down. But he lived for these cases, and there was no way he could change. It was a life that was contagious because I'd caught whatever it was.

"Okay, I'm back. These crutches are a bitch."

"How's the leg?" I asked.

"Itches like a motherfucker."

"You're taking care of yourself? No pills if you're drinking."

"Who are you, fucking Florence Nightingale? Don't worry—bourbon only." Uncle Mike laughed. "How's it going so far?"

I listened closely to hear if my uncle's voice changed now that he was alone. His voice could telegraph trouble. No change in my uncle's tone. No reason to shade the facts. I told him of Amity's death, my conversation with Mags, and how the body appeared. We discussed the ramifications and what this second murder could tell us.

Uncle Mike groaned. "Did we report the murder to the police?"

"I told Mags to report it anonymously but so far there's nothing in the paper or online."

"Shit. Makes me wonder if Mags is doing something."

"Doing something" translated to the Denver mobster disposing of the body on his own and running his own investigation. "I'll watch for it."

I told Uncle Mike what Amity had said about Zany and that he needed to go to the Kelso Club to work something out.

"The Kelso Club? Have we been there?"

"I went. It's a gambling simulcast club for the rich and famous. It's run by this fat cat named Preston Williston."

I didn't want to tell my uncle how I'd been banned and could lose the valuable customer base for the store. I had a chance to win the members back if I made a good showing tomorrow. What would be the line on doing that? With my prior performance on the social scene, I'd go off at odds of thirty-to-one at least.

"You kept to the straight and narrow?"

"Not even a two-dollar win ticket."

"Good lad. Remember, Eddie, no gambling. We can't lose any leverage with Burrascano. The last thing I want to do is ask him for any favor or he'll want to take care of the killer himself instead of turning Zany's killer over to the authorities. How are collections going?"

I told Uncle Mike how Preston had my hands tied on the Kelso Club debtors and about Peter Leister's effort to grab the Kelso Club business.

"You gotta keep things going," Uncle Mike said. "Everyone wants to keep the money flowing. Who's running the place?"

"The store manager is a girl named Rudi. She's great but I suspect she's thinking about quitting."

"Can we keep her in the fold?"

"I've tried to get her involved in the investigation, but she's got this shithead husband she's divorcing by the name of Warren Potts."

"What kind of shithead?"

"The harassing type," I said. "He's trying to drive her off."

Uncle Mike told me he'd try to dig up some information on Warren Potts. We discussed the financial end of the store. I'd send what Rudi was able to dig up. Uncle Mike had connections with an expert accountant who could reconstruct financials from almost nothing. The ability to follow the money had been a key angle on previous jobs.

"How about Zany's estate?" I stared at the stack of invoices on Zany's desk.

"Let me shift this leg. Goddamnit, that's better. So far, it's a dry hole. None of the usual accounts. Zany didn't use our bank contacts. Burrascano would like to get his hands on Zany's cash."

"So would I. The store needs a cash infusion. I'm going to Zany's place tonight. I'll see what I can find."

"Great. We would've heard if the men in blue had found anything." Ice cubes rattled and my uncle coughed. "This leg hurts like hell, and I'm running short of medicine."

I could use a slug of whiskey myself. Maybe when all this was over and I was back tending bar at O'Connell's.

"Be careful," The chair wheezed and creaked. "Got to go. Remember, we have to do this for Zany and Splendid Runner. Something tells me we were meant to solve this case."

A sudden hunch struck me at the core. If someone in the gambling world killed Zany, then it took somebody like me to find them.

"Wait. One more thing," I said, deciding to come clean. "I might be banned from the Kelso Club. But I'm working on it. It will work out."

"I heard," Uncle Mike said.

"You knew?"

"I wanted to hear it from you."

How many nights had I come back to O'Connell's dead broke but would say I'd broke even? My list of lies and stories to cover up my gambling stretched back years.

"Joey L said you wrecked some guy's Porsche?" he said.

What is it about a Porsche? Even a rumor of a scratch becomes nationwide news.

"I didn't. It's bullshit."

"Look, I'm glad you told me. We're a team, and if I'm going to be any help back here, I need to know everything. Besides, it seems like Burrascano knows everything before I do anyway. Thank God for Joey L. Get back on the good side of this Preston prima donna."

Joey L had always looked out for us. "I'll keep sucking up. I'm supposed to meet him and the members at the local track. His horse is running tomorrow."

"The track? Jeesus Christ."

"Don't worry."

"I'm not. Just find that goddamn money tonight. That will help."

"No problem."

But I did worry. And I did have a problem.

10

Rudi had changed from casual business attire to a pair of shorts and a T-shirt. We stepped from the office sauna into the summer sauna outside to meet with Koransky. I wished I'd changed too.

"How long has Koransky been a sub for Zany's store?" I asked her.

"He has a great setup at Mile High University. At first, he laid off business to Zany but then it got too big and now he works for us. He gets a nice piece."

It was a way for Zany to grow the business. Bookies got lazy and funneled action to another bigger store until they ended up as a go-between or subcontractor. Sometimes they faded from the picture entirely.

"Zany liked student-body action?" I asked.

"Loved it. It came with a pretty good guarantee—parents."

"But we've still got students?" I'd classified the debtor list into groups.

"Nothing's perfect. It was a sore spot for him," Rudi said.

She walked a step ahead of me down the alley and checked her phone. This bit of distance told me she needed time to come to terms with Zany and Amity, as well as Amity's murder. Maybe Rudi also kept me at arms-length to keep her options open.

A slight breeze made the outdoors bearable. The ninety-degree heat was good for one thing, the fact Rudi changed into those shorts. Her legs were tanned and finely tuned from the calves to her upper thighs. Clearly, someone who worked out.

Rudi stopped. "Shit." She bolted into the garage.

I ran after her toward the SUV. The dark blue Yukon had been washed and shined.

The tires were flat. "What the hell . . ."

She screamed and crouched down. "Oh, my God. Oh, my God. I can't believe this."

Her hands trembled as she touched the rim. She loved the vehicle. It was her most prized possession.

Rudi got down on one knee to examine the tires. "That fucking bastard."

Several dime-sized holes could be seen in the folds of rubber. Probably punctured with an ice pick.

"That son-of-a-bitch." Rudi stood up and took several steps. "Where are you?"

"Who?"

"My fucking husband, Warren." She trotted to the other side of the SUV. "Very funny, you—you loser."

I didn't see anyone but I liked the way she took a fighter's stance, her lips pursed and her chin out as if she'd take on all comers. My anger swelled. I wanted a piece of this guy. Let him try to fight me with an ice pick.

"See anybody?" I dodged between cars and checked down the aisles.

"Warren is here. I know it. He's spying on me right now."

All I saw were empty cars in the garage. Rudi swung a fist at the air. She battled ghosts. Her haunted face spoke of the years of trouble she'd had with the guy. I wanted to wipe the slate clean for her. I dropped to the concrete and checked under parked vehicles for any sign of Warren's shoes but saw nothing.

"What is it, Warren?" Rudi yelled. "You want to win me back? You think this will help? You bum." Her words echoed through the garage.

"I don't see anyone," I said.

"It's not like we ever had red-hot sex." Rudi turned to me and her voice dropped down to normal. "What does he want from me?"

It was a question I couldn't begin to answer. "Want to reschedule with Koransky?"

"No fucking way. That juvenile won't change my plans."

She looked away from me and her chest heaved but she didn't cry. I felt guilty. I'd seen Rudi at her worst and could do nothing.

"I'll flag a cab or get an Uber." I started toward the street.

"I've got Triple-A. I'll call them and the sheriff when I get back. Mulholland as well." Her voice rose in volume. "Who cares about the price of a set of tires if I'm free of that bastard husband?"

11

AFTER A SHORT WAIT, I MANAGED TO CATCH A RIDE. RUDI jumped in back and shouted instructions to Koransky's house.

I joined her in the back seat. "What is Warren trying to prove?" With my own divorce and all the domestic trouble that drove customers to drink at O'Connell's, I felt like an expert in the field. Slashed tires bordered upon physical violence. I recalled the fear I'd heard in Rudi's voice yesterday.

She rummaged through her purse. A tear ran down her cheek. "Who knows? He wants to make my life hell. Thinks he owns me." She went to work on her face with a makeup mirror.

"Do you have his social security number?"

She wiped her nose with a tissue. "What are you going to do?"

I didn't want to tell her how Uncle Mike would investigate. She might be insulted. "Find out where he lives. Talk to him." It was a partial truth. I didn't think we'd do much talking.

"Good luck. Zany tried but couldn't find anything and he had contacts all over town. I do have Warren's social security number back at the office. He worked for Zany part-time for a week but when a collection didn't show up, Zany fired him."

"Warren pocketed the money?"

"And he wanted me to cover for him."

"Has he done something like this before?"

"You mean puncture my tires? No, this is new. Another thing to add to the list."

We drove on in silence up I-25 north to Highway 36. So, Zany had a history of trouble with Warren. Then there were the harassing phone calls, the serious relationship between Zany and Rudi, the slashed tires—all the ingredients to make Warren an excellent suspect. If he'd murdered Zany, perhaps Amity became a loose end to clean up.

The driver pulled off the highway and headed up a side street toward the campus, the grounds framed by the surrounding foothills. Impressive museum-like structures dotted wide swathes of green lawns. White pillars fronted each building where wise old professors handed out the secrets. The price of each morsel went up every year. Without a degree, I'd better find a way to strike it rich. Maybe I'd have to go the free-agent detective route.

What would it have been like to graduate from college with a sizeable student loan? My uncle and the regulars at O'Connell's made fun of the college boys who didn't have the smarts to make it on their own. I should've gotten a college degree, but felt I'd gained more street smarts managing the bar and working with my uncle on these jobs for Burrascano than any school could teach.

The cab stopped at a light and several students, with books under their arms or backpacks slung over their shoulder, trudged past. "Don't the students have enough financial worries with tuition and books? Why gamble?" Rudi asked.

"They are the customers of the future. What do you want them to do—play chess?"

"Sometimes I think sports betting is harmless fun. But I don't know. We've gotten calls at the store from family members."

"Don't go there. Every state has lotto. Casinos pop up everywhere. A ball game is boring without some action." I should know. The last-minute field goal or basket, the change in the spread—who cared when you didn't have something down?

Rudi directed the driver to the house. I handed over a nice tip and followed her up the sidewalk. Burrascano would insist I add the tip to my expense account.

The house matched the size of the frat houses. Rudi walked around to a side door. She rang the bell; three long rings followed by one short ring.

"We get a lot of business from this hangout," she said.

Rudi had a way of parsing out advice. It meant Koransky pulled his weight and I should be careful not to piss him off.

The connection to campus through Koransky impressed me. Zany's operation spread its tentacles all over the front range. Sports bettors were easy to attract. Everybody thought they knew more than Vegas.

A computer geek in a long sleeve shirt and the pocket pencil set answered the door and led us up the back stairs to a room taking up the entire main level with high ceilings and heavy curtains across the windows. Rows of couches and recliners sat in the shadows before numerous flat screens. At the far end of the room stood a long, oak bar. I imagined a big crowd roaring on a fall Saturday afternoon whenever the favorite team scored.

The computer geek didn't offer conversation and led us into a back room.

A man I assumed to be Koransky got up from behind a desk and came around to us. He greeted Rudi warmly and then she introduced me.

Stephen Koransky was prematurely gray, in his early thirties, wore horn-rimmed glasses, and was a bit pudgy around the middle. He avoided my eyes. There was a tobacco pipe in the ashtray and an open, thick book on the desk. A scientific diagram of the human digestive tract hung on the wall.

Rudi and I sat in the chairs that fronted the desk while Koransky sat behind the desk and picked up the pipe out of the ashtray. He made a show out of filling his pipe and lighting it. The room soon filled with a cloud of perfumed, fruity tobacco smoke. I remained patient. It was best if I allowed him to continue to believe this was merely a social call.

"I guess I'm on edge with Zany's murder," Koransky said. "Football season is about to start and the students get back next week. They'll be ready for some action so I'm glad you stopped by. I was getting worried. I've got tuition to pay and equipment to buy."

I fished to find his hot button. "You have to buy equipment?"

"I'm in med school. Took me seven years to get in. I didn't have perfect grades so I had to do grad school after college and work for peanuts in the lab. Now, four years of med school and I've only got three semesters left. Then I start my internship. I'm going to be a gastroenterologist, so I need to buy equipment to start my practice."

I kept a straight face and didn't laugh out loud. What would the guys back at O'Connell's say to this—eleven years with your nose in a book? I dug out some bullshit. "That's quite an accomplishment."

Rudi leaned forward. "All this time we worked together, Steve, and you never told me what you planned to do. Is it the same as a proctologist?"

The professional student grinned as if he had the world by the tail. I hoped he wouldn't give us his life story all over again. "No, a gastroenterologist specializes in the study of the anus, rectum, and sigmoid colon. In short, assholes."

On cue, Rudi and I both looked up at the chart of the digestive system on the wall.

This time I did laugh. "Why? Did they cut cards and you lost?" I liked how he sat back in his leather desk chair.

"I know it sounds crazy but that's where the money is, and I plan to make lots of it," he said. "No low-budget family medicine for me. And thanks to this gambling gig, no student loans."

"Smart." My uncle and some regulars complained in vivid detail about their colonoscopies. Despite the medical importance,

I couldn't help but think that poetic justice would be served if this guy spent his entire life staring up the other end of the scope.

"You don't have much longer to go," Rudi said. "Congratulations."

"Thanks." He smiled and put his feet up on the desk as if he'd qualified for entry into the royal kingdom.

"About this fall," I said. I pulled out the debtor list. "I noticed quite a few students owe the store."

"I can't help it if Zany ran a sloppy operation." Koransky brought his feet down and leaned forward across the desk. "He told me to take whatever action I could."

Rudi glanced my way then back to Koransky. "Zany gave you a sweet deal. Most places would take these debts out of your cut."

I nodded at Rudi. She was a natural. "That's right. Just because Zany didn't put enough pressure on you is no reason not to do your job." It was the same story at the Kelso Club. Zany was too easy on collections.

"I know, I know," he said. "But Zany . . ."

"Tell the student body the fun ride is over," I said. "If their parents don't pay, cut them off. No more easy credit. I won't pay for keggers around campus and have freeloaders laugh behind my back."

"Sure, I-I-I, can play the enforcer," he said. "These kids get b-b-beers in them and lose control. I can babysit if that's what you want."

The stuttering told me he found this part of the job distasteful. Maybe it would hurt his big man on campus image.

"Your name came up lately. Connected to a young woman named Amity Seville."

He got busy with a pipe cleaner and inserted it into the stem of the lit pipe. "You know her?"

"I talked to her the other day," I said. The busy hands told me he had stuff to hide.

"You did?" he said.

I waited. He seemed to search for words.

Rudi touched my arm then leaned forward. "She's a prostitute."

He stopped with the pipe. He stared at Rudi as if the feminine sex were an exotic species. What did Amity mean to him? From his scared little boy expression, I'd say she meant more to him than sex.

"Yes, that's right," he said. "She is that. But . . ."

His hands started to fidget with the pipe once more. Rudi's presence seemed to make the man bashful.

He turned to me. "When did you talk with her?"

"Couple days ago," I said. Cracks emerged in the physician's armor.

"That's strange," he said.

"Why is that?" Rudi said.

"I've tried to get in touch with her and she hasn't called me back. She always called before," he said.

I glanced at Rudi. She waited for me to say something. Again, I waited him out.

He bit his lip as if upset. "We talk almost every day."

"When was the last time you saw her?" I asked.

He stopped and thought for a second. "Sunday. She stopped by on Sunday."

"And when was the last time you talked to her on the phone?"

He examined the bowl of the pipe. "Tuesday, I think. Why?"

"You and Zany have similar tastes in women," I said

His eyebrows shot up. He set down the pipe cleaner and started to puff on the pipe again. "How did you know?"

"What did Amity say to you about Zany's murder?"

"Nothing." He looked first at me and then at Rudi. "She was shocked, that's all. We all were."

"Did she tell you if she saw somebody? She was with Zany just before he was killed."

"What are you anyway? You want to do the cop's job?" He snickered.

I didn't like the evasive attitude. "You don't think it's important?"

Koransky held up one hand. "I didn't mean it like that. I liked Zany as much as anybody. She didn't say anything."

"You don't feel a bit frightened that you have so much in common with Zany—a murder victim?"

His mouth dropped open.

"Do I need to make a list? Same bookmaking business, same woman, what else?"

"I don't understand . . ."

"Let me tell you what I understand," I said. "They don't hand out those medical licenses. You need a lily-white record. No one wants the cops involved in any of this." I had to make this nerd sweat. He said he'd been worried—about what? I didn't like the fruity smell of the tobacco either. Could use a cigarette to clean out my lungs.

"Who said anything about the cops?" he said.

"You did," Rudi said.

Nice timing.

"I did?" He stuttered again.

"Zany paid to protect you, you know that," I said.

"Yes." He stared down into the open book on his desk.

I knew how Uncle Mike played the interview and set the hook.

"Do you know why Amity isn't calling you back?"

He looked up and barely shook his head. Sweat trickled down his temple.

"She's been murdered." I watched for his reaction. He kept his eyes glued toward me.

He slumped in his chair. "What? When? I didn't hear about it."

"I saw the body. Want to know how she died?"

He pulled off his glasses and rubbed his eyes. "No, no."

"So that leaves you right in the path of the cops." My words dripped with sympathy for Koransky and his shaky medical career. Tears welled up in his eyes. He seemed lost as if he wanted to ask a question but couldn't find the words. I wanted him to believe I knew the way out. "Maybe the cops will come in here and question you on a Saturday afternoon when the room is full of college students. You want that?"

He dropped the pipe into the ashtray. "You think they'd come here?"

"If I didn't show up here today, you had some other plan in mind, didn't you?" His brain was overloaded with smarts so it wasn't hard to guess what he might be up to. "You were going to send the college business over to Peter Leister."

Rudi grabbed my arm but said nothing.

"How?" Koransky said. "Maybe."

I pretended the "maybe" was, in fact, a "yes." "You know what Leister will do. He'll take your customers direct." Leister wouldn't pay him any piece of the revenue once he absorbed the customers. Koransky would be left high and dry.

"He will? Leister contacted me first." He wiped at sweat.

"You know he will," Rudi said.

I wasn't surprised Leister took the initiative. Koransky's dependence on Amity and his reaction to Rudi exposed an underlying weakness, one that Leister would make it his business to know.

Uncle Mike liked to explain consequences. "And Leister won't pay for protection. Don't worry, you can hock that asshole equipment to bond out of jail," I said.

His head dropped into the palm of his hand. He rubbed his forehead and then looked up. "Tell me what you want me to do."

It was what I wanted to hear. Now I'd be a step ahead of Leister for a change.

12

AT TWO IN THE MORNING, I TOOK THE CROWN VIC OUT OF the parking garage and drove toward the foothills to Zany's house. On the lookout for a possible tail, I checked the rearview mirror. No sign of the caddie. Mags's old soldier had to sleep sometime.

Uncle Mike's parting shot reverberated in my head—"Just find the goddamn money. That will help."

His words had cycled through my head a few hundred times since my afternoon call. Squeezed every last drop of meaning out of them. What did he mean: "that will help?" Did it mean I was on the ropes? Did Burrascano think about pulling me and sending in a sub? A quarterback controversy made me question every move.

Tomorrow would be a bitch. Maintaining the store's revenue stream seemed to matter more to Mags, Joey L, and Burrascano than the investigation, and that stream depended on the Kelso Club members. Leister had Mulholland as a member in his corner and who did I have? I'd have to enlist someone. Maybe Arnold, the rabid horseplayer. The things I'd learned about Leister from Koransky might help. Rudi worked on Crystal, so I could count on that too.

I backtracked and checked again for a tail—nothing. This part of the job was in my wheelhouse. I almost began to relax a little as I drove out to Zany's house, finding my way down unfamiliar back roads I'd mapped out. Thank God my mind could switch gears, get out of this rut about tomorrow or what Burrascano might be thinking. If I found the money, I'd be a hero again. I'd be able to breathe easy. The store's invoices would be paid. Finding the "goddamn money" was the insurance I needed to stay in the game.

As I drove into Zany's suburban neighborhood, I began to go through my pre-job routine. On my first couple of jobs Uncle Mike would question me before and after: How did it feel to be in another guy's house? Did you check each room, each door? How did you know if you fully shut down the security system? Were you afraid?

The houses I passed were big ranches with long front yards. Zany had good taste. I drove past his house, tucked back down a hill on the last curve of a winding road beside a large lake. I didn't slow down, even though it was difficult to see through the trees and shrubs. All I spotted was a lone porch light. My heart beat a little faster.

A half-mile down the road, a private swim area and boat dock at the far end of the lake offered a place to park. The Crown Vic slipped into a corner of the lot behind a stand of trees. I'd sit for a while. I even checked my watch. On these jobs time had a way of slowing down.

A cool night breeze flowed through the open car windows. I listened for dogs or loud neighbors. Watched for security or cops cruising past. Teenagers getting hammered on a six-pack. Anything.

This was the moment I'd typically smoke. I counted time by the number of cigarettes. I craved one now. In fact, I had the urge to scrounge through the nearby dumpster for a butt. Instead, I chewed on the end of a pen.

The neighborhood remained quiet. It was a clear night, hot. The stars and a quarter moon lit up the lake's surface. The breeze rustled the leaves overhead as a chorus of crickets sang. Rowboats and canoes bumped at the boat dock.

The plan was simple. Go to the house, check it out, and go inside. Find the stacks and stacks of money and the records. Go back, get the Crown Vic, pull it into the garage, and haul the booty away. How easy was that?

Oh yeah, I forgot about the possibility of a police presence or a grieving relative who'd taken up residence. On previous jobs, relatives had become a nuisance, especially if there might be money in the victim's estate.

I worked on the fear. Like Uncle Mike said over and over, fear will keep you alive and out of jail. Don't lose it.

It was time. I got out and closed the car door gently. A guy coughed. Then another cough. It came from the opposite shore. Every sound carried and the lake acted as a transmitter.

Down the road to Zany's place, I walked as if I belonged in this rich man's neighborhood. Just in case I didn't fit the part, I came up with a story. The Crown Vic played a starring role, complete with a long history of mechanical problems.

Uncle Mike's reminders gave me an edge. The fear stalked me. It could be a turn on of sorts.

I walked toward the empty house whose owner had been brutally murdered. I hadn't received any updated police reports from Mags but my uncle would've heard if they'd found the cash. Like any bookie, Zany kept his secrets well-hidden.

That's why the key that I'd found taped to the bottom of one of Zany's desk drawers would pay dividends. An internet search told me what this type of key was used for. It meant Zany had an underground bunker—something the cops wouldn't be able to find. This key would unlock some custom hatch manufactured to disguise the entryway. I had the advantage.

Loose stones from the shoulder of the road were strewn across the asphalt. Every inadvertent crunch of gravel seemed to blast throughout the neighborhood. I didn't need the dog patrol to start a howling match.

The neighbors, asleep and safe with their 401(k)'s tucked under the bed, probably had no idea what Zany did for a living. What story did he tell these bankers and corporate types? Did they even know he'd been murdered? He probably owned the house through a shell corporation and used an alias.

No sign of a police cruiser or any vehicle. It was a sprawling ranch house like the rest of the neighborhood. An oversized picture window faced the lake. The best cover was between the house and the lake, plenty of trees and shrubs. I took one last look up the road and darted across the driveway toward the side of the house.

The patio appeared abandoned. No ashtray with a used butt, an empty bottle, or forgotten glass. The grill was cold.

I became bolder. Checked windows and the sliding door with the touch of a safecracker. On a hot night like this you'd need to leave the windows open or turn on the air conditioner. I walked around the house until I found the air conditioner unit. It wasn't running.

It meant the house was vacant but hot. I could use a free sauna.

It struck me how I'd stepped into Zany's shoes and caught all the risk yet got none of the rewards. Sure, I'd be able to make my gambling debt go away, but I wouldn't mind a place like this instead of the two-bedroom down the street from O'Connell's Tavern. How much cash might be in that bunker? Untraceable, unaccounted for . . .

I circled back to the patio and found a side door to the laundry room. Before I started, I called Zany's residential number once more—again it rang through to voice mail. I could just hear the phone ring inside the house.

How fast could I open the door and find the security control panel? The security invoices on Zany's desk showed that the business security system and the residence were linked. I'd gotten the code to the office from Rudi and used that to get what I needed on Zany's house from the security company after I paid the bill with a credit card. Customer service and paid invoices always trumped security.

My penlight and tools were ready. I waited another few minutes. Sweat crawled down my back. Why didn't Zany launder the money through Burrascano's bank? Maybe his hidden records would hold a clue to his murder.

I jimmied open the lock, turned the knob, but didn't open the door. I pressed my ear near the door and listened for footsteps. Crickets kept up their racket, but I tuned them out. Finally, I stepped inside and walked straight toward the kitchen where the security panels were usually located, my eyes accustomed to the dark.

No warning sounds from the alarm. I didn't flash my light around but kept it focused on the wall where security companies positioned the controls. My foot struck something. I glanced down. A broken floor tile had been flipped over. I kept moving, found the security panel near the fridge, and entered the code, but it had already been dismantled.

That was odd. Maybe the cops didn't reset it. Uncle Mike would force me to circle through the house, check bedrooms, closets, and bathrooms before I headed to the basement. If the bunker was here, the entrance would most likely be found through the basement.

I went back into the kitchen and checked the refrigerator. No beer and no food. The light from the refrigerator allowed me to see the entire room more clearly. Somebody, probably the cops, had ripped up floor tiles. Punched a hole in the wall by the stove.

Down the hallway and into the dining room, I found a hutch had been emptied. Dishes piled up on the table. The ceiling was lower in this room. My head scuffed a piece of drywall hanging down.

A lot of damage even for the cops. They had only left this afternoon. Somebody else had gone through the house ahead of me, searching for Zany's cache.

I bypassed the other rooms and headed to the basement. Did they find the bunker? How would I explain to Burrascano that the cash was lost on my watch?

I opened the door to the basement and froze. No finished drywall encased the stairs and no carpet on the cement floor at the bottom. What if somebody was down here? I'd failed to check the basement windows from the outside. Anyone in the basement would've heard my footsteps overhead. Maybe they waited in the shadows.

I closed the door to the basement behind me to shut off any outside light and stood at the top of the stairs in pitch black. I could wait out a non-professional. Their inner clock was set on alarm mode while mine ticked on Uncle Mike time.

The steps to the basement of O'Connell's Tavern came to mind. When I was a kid, I would sit there all afternoon and read and be a part of a grown-up world with no one the wiser. In my own secret world where imagination made the time pass.

More time passed. I didn't make a move. I knew how to breathe.

Nothing.

Finally, I crept down the stairs. With my penlight, I walked over to one of the windows and pulled back the curtain an inch or two to let in some light. Then I searched the floor and the walls for the hatch to an underground bunker. The lock could be disguised as a sprinkler system clock or drain. Survivalists were a creative bunch. Like a junk dealer, I burrowed through dust-covered old lamps, chairs, and couches awaiting The Salvation Army.

It didn't look as if the previous intruder had done much work in the basement. The cobweb net remained. Maybe they figured that since it was unfinished with a concrete floor and walls that nothing could be hidden here. I continued around the furnace and got down on my hands and knees to pull up the cover of a drain. *Shit—nothing.* Zany must have another location.

Then I heard a sound. It didn't come from the basement. It was outside. One step, maybe two on that river rock that bordered the driveway. Almost imperceptible. A fast footstep as if caught in midstride. The first step to gain traction and run.

I hurried back upstairs then through the kitchen to the garage door and caught a whiff of the dead mouse smell of leaking gas.

I opened the door to the garage a crack. Fumes overwhelmed me. The tick-tock of a clock. The hair stood up on the back of my neck.

I bolted to the laundry room and through the exterior door, slipped down on the step, got up, and raced across the patio. Dodged shrubs then slipped on a grassy slope down to the lake. My face kissed the cool grass.

The explosion pounded in my ears.

I scrambled and rolled. Shattered wood rained down like knives and tore through branches. I sprinted and plunged into the lake.

Then I dared to look back. Orange flames shot up out of the house and into the black, star-studded night. My ears rang.

Water up to my knees and soft mud gave way underfoot as I struggled to shore. Sirens wailed from far off.

13

SATURDAY

My cell phone buzzed. I cranked open my eyelids. Found the glow of the clock in the artificial darkness. The hotel's iron curtain shielded me from the morning light. Eight o'clock.

The desk by the wall, together with the chair and reading lamp, were festooned with my dirty clothes. The television on the dresser and manufactured artwork didn't offer a clue as to the name of the hotel, the city or place. I should be relieved this wasn't a hospital room with tubes hanging out of my arm.

I recalled the explosion. How I ran through the trees and dove into the pond like a frightened animal. I felt lucky and pissed off at the same time, never a good combination.

I took inventory. I was groggy but not hung over. This was a plus. There was a benefit to sobriety. I could work my way through simple exhaustion.

But my left knee stung and my back ached. I hunted for the damn cell as it buzzed again.

Saturday morning. I bet it was my uncle. "Hello?" I croaked.

"Good morning, Prince Charming," Uncle Mike said. "How did it go last night?"

"Not too good. Somebody rigged Zany's house."

"What? Jeesus Christ! Wait a minute."

I heard some heavy breathing and the clink of the phone against metal, probably my uncle's crutches.

After a few moments, he returned. "Okay," Uncle Mike said. "I'm in another room Holy shit, what happened?"

"The house exploded."

"Shit. You weren't near it I hope."

I'd considered what to tell my uncle. A certain degree of danger was expected and I didn't want to whine. "I got out in time."

"Damn. You're okay. Did they get the money? How far did you get?"

"I don't think they found anything."

"You don't?"

"They were looking in the walls and floors. I found a key in Zany's desk meant for one of those underground bunkers. I didn't find anything in the basement."

It was the simple explanation. But I'd spent a good part of the night trying to figure out if somebody trapped me or if I just happened to be in the wrong place at the wrong time. I'd been careful not to tell anyone. The only one who knew I planned to go last night was Uncle Mike. Unless he told Joey L who told Burrascano who told Mags . . .

"Did you tell anyone I planned to go last night?" I looked through the curtain down on the alley. A Coors delivery truck backed up to a loading dock.

"Joey L, but he wouldn't tell anybody." Uncle Mike said. "I'll get our guys on it."

Not only did Uncle Mike have friends in accounting, he had friends who found things—property, accounts, people. But I did hear some disappointment in his voice. Uncle Mike had wanted to pass along good news to Joey L.

"Any luck so far on this Warren moron?"

"Not yet. You're okay, right?"

"Yeah." I felt like I'd bungled my specialty. Instead of the hero, I was the dope who almost got himself killed. "Find out what Joey L has heard. I don't like a coincidence."

"I'll find out. Zany must have some other place." I heard my aunt call out my uncle's name. "Got to go." Uncle Mike hung up.

I fell back into bed and switched on ESPN, my constant companion on the road. As the announcer flipped through the baseball scores, I thought how great it would be to simply count yesterday's take at the store, instead of dodging explosions. Zany didn't know how good he had it.

I met Rudi as planned at the store around noon so we could get to the track in plenty of time for my afternoon performance. I'd bought her a new set of tires for the SUV and she was eager to try them out. One problem solved. My other problem was how to tell her about Zany's house. Maybe one of Zany's neighbors was a member at the Kelso Club and might know it was the murdered bookie's house that got torched. Maybe they'd kept Zany's identity a secret as a favor to their personal bookie. Until now.

"Thanks again for the tires." She walked through the parking garage to the Yukon.

"No problem." The SUV had been washed and waxed. The investment of Burrascano's expense money could be justified; I had to keep her happy.

Rudi wore a multi-colored, V-neck, pleated sundress. "Nice dress." I tried not to stare.

"Thanks." She gave me a smile.

Her perfume struck me when we got into the Yukon. I wanted to compliment her, but I wasn't sure if she'd appreciate it. I kept up the small talk, an excuse to avoid the news from last night. "How about your husband? The usual calls last night?"

"I had to leave the phone off the hook."

"Any other contacts from him?" I thought about email or text messages. All that e-stuff I barely used except to check injury reports and race results.

"He isn't that creative. He's still in the Neanderthal age."

She tore out of the parking garage, around the corner, and down the street toward Coors Field. I didn't mind a test drive on the tires, but my head pounded from the night before, and my neck pain had worsened. Maybe if I kept up some conversation, she'd slow down.

I wanted to tell her about Zany's house. But what exactly should I tell her? I could say I saw the house in flames or I could tell her how it exploded as I jumped and ran out—how

I could've been killed and how someone may have waited to murder me. The whole truth and let the cards fall where they may.

"How far is the track?"

"It will take a while," she said. "They stuck it out east on the way to Kansas."

"By the airport?" I knew the airport was out east but I didn't see a track anywhere below as we circled to land.

"South of the airport. In the middle of nowhere."

"I don't get it." The light turned green and we turned left in front of the stadium toward the interstate. "They stick this historical-looking, brand new ballpark in the middle of town but dump the racetrack out there?"

"People don't like the smell of horse manure."

"I saw ads for a stock show and some rodeo. I thought this was Marlboro Country."

"You see any cowboy hats downtown?" Rudi said. "How about the Kelso Club? Every city wants to be cosmopolitan. No matter where you travel, you're in the same place."

"That's how I felt in my hotel when I woke up."

We headed north on I-25. "Aren't we going the wrong way?"

"It's longer but we avoid lots of traffic. I'll take this to I-70 and then C-470 south. Zany liked to drive through Denver and Aurora. He'd schedule collection calls or meet a new prospect. He was a go-getter."

I recalled the internet map I'd studied earlier. Rudi's route skirted downtown.

Her cell phone buzzed. She glanced at it. "I see my dear husband got my new cell number."

"Let me talk to him."

"No, he wants to laugh in my face. Tell me how useless my attorney is."

"My ex likes to gloat. Inside the courtroom, you'd think she moonlights as a nun."

"At least you get in the courtroom." She pulled on the shoulder strap of her seat belt.

She felt trapped. "Is Mulholland getting anywhere?"

"I called my lovely attorney this morning. He owes me a call. Until he gets Warren served, the court can't do jack. I need an address or I'm screwed."

"Mulholland is too busy working with Leister to call you back," I said. "Your attorney never sent over the cash." I wondered what Leister had promised the attorney.

"Wait until the members hear what Koransky had to say about Leister."

Before I could bash Leister, I'd need to get a feel for the members and what they thought about Zany's murder. Mulholland would have members lined up in Leister's camp, so I'd need a plan, or what I'd say could backfire.

Enough small talk. There was no other choice but to give it to Rudi straight.

"I went to Zany's place last night," I said.

She brushed back a wave of her auburn hair and glanced over. "You did? Is that why you were going over those invoices for the security system?"

I looked into those green eyes for a brief moment before she turned back to the road. "Yeah. That's right." She didn't let much get past her.

Every time Rudi got into a good mood, I was the one to bring her crashing down. "I thought there might be some records at his house that would help our investigation." I searched for the right words. "The house blew up."

She slapped the steering wheel. "What? I can't believe—"

"I made it out."

"Oh, my God, are you okay?" Rudi had open space on the interstate on a Saturday afternoon. But she didn't speed up. She kept to the traffic flow much to my relief.

"Some ringing in my ears."

"Shit. The killer wants to destroy every single thing. . ."

If the killer could go after me, he could go after Rudi. "You need to be careful."

Her voice rose an octave. "Damn it. Did you see anyone? Who else knew you were going?"

"Nobody. You didn't mention anything about those invoices to anybody, did you?"

She glanced my way again. "No, I didn't think anything about it until now."

She was in battle mode, the same expression she'd had when she found the tires slashed yesterday. Death grip on the steering wheel. We drove on in silence, south on C470 onto rolling plains. Sagebrush and endless horizon to the east. I thought a herd of buffalo might stampede past.

I broke the silence. "Zany didn't own any other homes?"

"No, he loved the place. We used to sit on his patio and look out on the lake and make plans." Her voice changed to soft and faraway. "He had this beat-up canoe we'd take out. Sometimes Zany would take some of the neighbor kids out on the lake."

"He was a great guy." I wondered what she'd do. If she'd fight for Zany or take the prudent course and avoid danger.

"One time we had a bunch of his old jockey buddies over for a cookout. What a bunch of characters. Zany showed them every room. Talked about his plans to remodel the place." She rubbed her forehead. Tears welled up in her eyes. "Damnit, Eddie. We both know the kind of people who blow up homes."

"Yeah."

"How can you work for them?"

"I can ask you the same question."

"Please. Zany's store is no comparison to those mobsters like Mags."

"But the ones in Chicago are the ones who sent me to find his killer."

"They knew you were at Zany's house." She slapped the steering wheel. "You're crazy. Why work for these people?"

"It's complicated," I said.

"Complicated? I hope so. Because from what I've seen you're not one of them."

"What's important is justice for Zany."

"If you want me to stay, I need to know."

"It's a long story." A low flying passenger jet flew past us headed north to the airport.

"Bullshit. I've got an ex-husband out of control. My boyfriend was horribly murdered. His house was blown up. Zany's poor sex worker murdered."

"It's just not something I tell anyone."

"Your secret is safe—"

"Fine. When I was a baby, my mom was pushing me in a stroller through a park. She was visiting relatives downstate. It was autumn. Leaves all piled up on the sidewalk." Imagined details popped into my head when I didn't need them. My throat turned dry. "She was taken, and I was left. They found her body in a culvert. She was raped and murdered."

"Holy hell."

"They caught the rapist-murderer and he confessed. The judge let him off on a technicality. A guy named Childress. His father had connections."

"I'm so sorry."

"There's more." I never met Childress or saw his face in newsprint, but his shit-eating, demon smile stalked my nightmares. "He took off. Uncle Mike and Joey L on the fucker's trail."

"Oh, Jesus."

14

Rudi parked and I stepped into the sweltering heat. One hundred degrees and climbing. Was it humane for horses to run in this heat? From my vantage point, I could view the mountains that ran down the horizon like exposed, ruptured vertebrae. Mount Evans, I had learned, was the highest peak directly before me. In Chicago, I'd see factories and smokestacks when I visited the track.

The crowd streamed inside and the track loudspeaker announced that the day's races would go off as scheduled. There was a lot at stake today for Zany's store versus Leister. No chance for a rain check. Maybe I should've practiced my speech in front of the mirror.

A couple of steps and the nagging pain in my neck knifed into the back of my skull. I dropped my chin to my chest. Pressure forced its way to the frontal lobe. If I stood for a minute . . .

"What's wrong?" Rudi asked.

I winced. "Nothing. I'm okay."

"Are you sure? What exactly happened last night? You said you made it out."

I felt her hand massage my neck. "I slipped down that hill beside the lake." Having Rudi fuss over me made the pain bearable.

"You're sure?"

I moved my head back and forth. The pain receded. If I could get a better handle on Preston, maybe I could schmooze my way into his good graces. "So, Preston uses the running of his horse as an excuse to throw a party for the Kelso Club?" I started to walk.

"I don't know. He's got some sort of popularity complex. Crystal thinks it might be all about his brother back east. He comes from big money, and his brother is a member of all these fancy clubs and runs the family charitable foundation."

"That is big money." This was out of my league. Foundations, taxes. Nobody at O'Connell's could afford to give serious money to charity, but they scraped up what they could when somebody was down on their luck.

"You don't know the half of it. Preston's great grandfather started it all with a shipping business. His grandfather was into oil, and his father made a bundle on Wall Street. Preston makes fun of his money-grubbing, greedy ancestors, but he's got this inferiority complex, too. Drives Crystal nuts."

I imagined portraits of Preston's ancestors strung on the wall of a winding staircase in some Long Island mansion. Stern faces that had counted money, fingered ticker tape, and trampled through history. Each more self-important than the last, each one with a lot to prove. What did Preston have to prove and could this be his hot button? If I pushed it at the right time, I might be able to persuade him to make a decision on behalf of Zany's store.

"You talked to Crystal about today? About our store versus Leister?" I dared twist my neck back and forth. No electric shock into my cranium. I could make it.

"She promised to do what she could. Crystal was pissed Allegro didn't show up for Zach's party. Maybe I should give you the inside story."

We stopped for a second between rows of parked cars so I could hear her clearly. The ringing in my ears remained.

"When Crystal got divorced a number of years ago, there was a big battle with the ex over custody. Preston's money helped fund that battle. She ended up with custody of Zach. I think it almost made her too rough around the edges, if you know what I mean. Sometimes I think we're friends and sometimes I think she could turn her back on me and walk away. It's weird to have a friend like that. Anyway, when she feels slighted or the least bit insulted, look out."

"I know the type." My ex needed a constant sparring partner.

"So, Crystal felt slighted when Allegro didn't show up for Zach's party. She worships that kid and so does Preston, maybe more. He never had his own kids, and he's the kind of guy who loves his sports. He brags to everyone how Allegro is a member of the Kelso Club. It's as if Allegro's membership is everything."

"Regular guys love to be pals with the pros," I said. A former third-string Bear's linebacker once patronized O'Connell's, and everyone wanted to buy him a beer.

"Zach has a good chance to make the NBA," Rudi said. "A great comeback year in college with good stats, and he'll probably go in the first round. Allegro has been sort of a mentor."

"Okay." I still wasn't quite sure how this all fit together. The hot sun beat down on my pounding head. I should've brought that bottle of aspirin with me.

"All Crystal talks about is Zach's NBA contract next year and then the draft. And then Allegro had the gall to blow off Zach's birthday party."

"Why should he feel obligated to attend?"

"That's the kicker," Rudi said. "He can't afford to piss off Preston. Not now. The Allegro Martin Charity Golf Outing starts next weekend and it's sponsored by the Kelso Club. Preston runs it."

"So, Allegro has to go to Preston's little event today or there will be more trouble." I began to get intrigued by this soap opera. But next weekend college football kicked off and the weekend after, the pros. I didn't have much time. My responsibilities at the store would multiply. "What about Zany, did he get along with Allegro?"

"Zany would never say Allegro gambled because you know how it is—athletes and gambling. It's a huge no-no. But Allegro would show up with Zany at some of our hotspots— a bowling alley or the Elk's Club. Allegro's appearance brought in customers for the store. Let's get into the air conditioning." Rudi began to walk toward the clubhouse.

Could I rely on Rudi's take? Maybe she was biased. Plus, I could hardly be expected to absorb everything she threw at me. My neck ached and my nerves were on edge.

At least a place like Aurora Downs would be familiar. If there was one place I felt at home besides O'Connell's, it was the track. From the lowliest grandstand fan playing two bucks to show to the upper crust guys pitching C-notes in the clubhouse, I knew my way around.

When the horses weren't running live at the track, we sat before banks of video monitors and played the horses at other tracks. Simulcast play cut into the handle at the local track and resulted in reduced purses and, in turn, the quality of the horses. I assumed Aurora Downs faced this problem.

It was a vicious cycle. Together with pressure for the betting dollar from casinos and lotto, the smaller tracks were quickly going the way of drive-ins, vanishing from the American landscape. They had to offer pony rides and concerts. Bigger tracks lobbied for slot machines. Others bitched and moaned about the inability of the horse racing industry to police itself and the use of drugs.

But what could I do? I couldn't go on strike. Nothing was lily-white perfect when money was involved. The stock market was an insider's playground so why grumble about the horses?

It got depressing if I thought about it too much. Sometimes I dwelled on the romance of the sport. The way Splendid Runner accelerated in the haze of an early morning workout. The grooms and jocks that got up at dawn because they loved the Sport of Kings.

Now no one knew who the kings were. Maybe this Preston snob. This guy was born with a silver spoon in his mouth while I walked up to the turnstile in fear of gambling away Burrascano's expense money before the day was through.

We walked into the lobby where patrons stood in line to purchase a racing program. "Do we need to buy a program?" I asked Rudi.

"No, Preston will have a stack upstairs, complements of the Kelso Club."

Some fans raced past. The announcer stirred up the crowd by ticking off the minutes to post. I couldn't see the track from the entrance but I knew the horses had left the paddock.

Inside the elevator, fans crammed into the tight space. This was no Chicago track. Several men and women wore cowboy hats, bolo ties, jeans, and boots.

When we got off the elevator on the clubhouse level, I nudged Rudi. "This is where the cowboys hang out."

"You're right. Lots of ranchers in Colorado. The horse industry is alive and well out west."

Rudi walked toward the clubhouse seating. Through a wall of glass to the track below, I spied the tote board that listed the odds on each horse in the current race. The infield contained a small pond and a flock of geese. Horses pranced in the aftermath of the post parade.

On a normal track day, I'd have a handle on the first race and the entire card. I'd have targeted my best bet of the day, what gimmicks I'd play to ensure the highest return on investment, and view the horses in the paddock. Listen for the late changes—the overweights, jockey and equipment changes—factors that might tip a trainer's hand. Instead, I ignored the odds blazing in hot yellow on the tote board, the bettors running to the windows, and everything else. My expression faded to a dopey smile. I could be an anonymous shopper walking down an aisle in Macy's.

Preston met us at the top of the stairs and pointed to a table at a lower level near the front. His feet danced and a bead of sweat lined his forehead. "I'll introduce you around when I can. Everybody arrived at the same time, and I have to fill these reserved tables." He ran off to greet others.

When we got to the table, Crystal hugged Rudi. Jim Arnold sat at another, smaller table, surrounded by his laptop and stacks of notebooks. My hands itched to join him in the handicapping trenches.

Crystal had a brief hug for me as well. Her fancy low-cut blouse, heavy perfume, gold chain necklaces, and bracelets made her appear overdressed for the occasion.

"You know my son, Zach?" Crystal pointed toward the end of the table. "Zach, you're not drinking, I hope?"

Zach wore a pressed, dark polo shirt and sat up straight with broad shoulders and blond hair. He nodded to me. "Yeah, we met." He sat with another man who nodded in my direction. Zach's friend with the unshaven face wore a gray, faded Miami Heat T-shirt.

Zach introduced me to his college buddy Cole.

We talked about Zach's knee and his rehab and that it had kept him on the sidelines last season. Not easy to shave points from the bench. Cole tossed out some of Zach's stats from the previous two years to confirm his star status. It seemed that Zach was a specialist from the three-point line, a valuable asset to any team in the college and pros. After we discussed Zach's team and its chances next year, I asked Zach what he thought of my chances today with Preston.

Zach shrugged. "Mom did what she could. But I wouldn't trust Moneybags if I were you." He stole a sip from Cole's beer.

"Eddie," Rudi called. "Eddie, come here."

I wanted to ask Zach if he knew a guy named Koransky but broke away to join Rudi.

Rudi's face was flushed. "Crystal said Leister talked with Preston a few minutes ago." Rudi was huddled up with Crystal. "He came right up to their table. You should hear what he said."

Rudi's mouth worked after her last words. Then she gritted her teeth and placed a hand on my shoulder. I huddled with them. I hoped somebody knew what play to call.

"That's right." Crystal kept her voice low so others couldn't overhear. "I'd never met this Peter Leister before but he's one smooth talker, let me tell you. He came up to me and Preston with Mulholland and apologized. The party at Wes Reardon's place was for Leister and his bookie operation. Reardon said he didn't know about Zach's party—a load of bullshit if I ever heard it."

Rudi grabbed my arm. "Listen to what Leister is telling everyone."

"He had this big smile when he told it," Crystal said. "Leister said that Zany had mob connections and everyone knows it. Leister says he isn't connected and the safe way to play sports this fall will be with him."

"What?" Maybe people who placed bets with a bookie were naïve or maybe they wore blinders, but they wanted to believe they placed a bet with a small-timer, a friend of a friend, or a bartender, and didn't want to think about connections. At a place like the Kelso Club, where the members nurtured a reputation, it made a go-between like good old Zany even more valuable for the mob.

Leister should know better. Certain lines could not be crossed without serious ramifications. Did he have a death wish? Or maybe he sensed a window of opportunity with my presence—a younger man he could steamroll.

"That's not all," Rudi said.

"Leister says Zany's murder is a mob killing. Then he says that you, Eddie—that you were sent out here to replace Zany, but you're only a straw man, and the mob isn't fooling anyone." Crystal bit her bottom lip and looked around. "Have you ever met Leister?"

"No." I didn't expect him to play hardball but after last night's explosion why should I think otherwise?

"He's up there a couple of levels in a blue suit." Rudi's head bobbed upward.

I turned and looked up. A man in a light blue suit sat among a crowd with Mulholland. The table roared with laughter as if on cue to mock me.

"Leister says Zany's house burned down," Rudi said. "He says that was the mob too."

I twisted back to Rudi and Crystal. The stakes of this game had been raised before it started.

15

I HAD BUILT UP LEISTER IN MY MIND AS A GUY WITH THE inherent ability to maneuver smoothly in a social atmosphere and sway the Kelso Club members. I'd done this to prepare myself and pick up my own game. Now, as I stole a glance Leister's way and saw how he moved with ease, joking and laughing with the crowd, he appeared to be everything I'd envisioned. I'd have my work cut out for me.

The second race ticked closer to post time. I needed to get a clear read on Preston's intentions.

Rudi placed a racing program in front of me. "You know much about playing the horses?"

"A little."

"It would help our cause if you'd give the members a few tips. Zany taught me. Maybe I can give you some pointers."

"I know a little." The understatement of the year.

"Let me know if you find anything."

I didn't turn the page. I knew Mag's old soldier watched from some hidden corner. I'd seen Grasso's old caddie skirt the parking lot. If I started to handicap, I might not be able to restrain old impulses.

"It's not part of the job description," I said. Zany, the ex-jockey, gave out complementary tips, but that didn't mean I had to.

Rudi shook her head. "Little favors will help."

Most of the members had arrived so Preston came over and sat beside Crystal, across from Rudi and me. At least I had that going for me. I glanced up at Leister and wondered what he thought of my spot with the head man of the Kelso Club. Then I thought about what Zach said: "Don't trust Moneybags."

Preston looked around the clubhouse with a wide smile. He told us it was the best crowd yet for one of these events. Crystal cut him off and demanded to know what he planned to do.

"About what?" Preston said.

Crystal ran her fingers through her shoulder-length blond hair and sighed. "About Leister and Eddie. You can't let the members decide for themselves. Leister is spreading all these lies. It's not fair."

Preston glanced around the table and pulled at the thin gold chain that hung around his neck below the expertly trimmed beard. "If people want to wager outside the legal confines of the club, it's . . ."

"C'mon," Crystal said.

I appreciated Crystal's efforts. Rudi said she'd been working on Crystal, and now I saw the result firsthand. "Zany's store is the one that has stood the test of time," I said. I felt like a used-car salesman.

"How can you trust the members to make the right choice?" Crystal asked.

Rudi leaned forward and spoke in a low voice. "Leister's bullshit about Zany makes me sick to my stomach."

"The club does not investigate such matters," Preston said.

"You don't know what Leister is like," Crystal said. "Zany and his crew are old friends. How can you turn your back on them? Did Reardon invite us to his party where Leister was introduced? No. There was a reason for that."

Preston sighed and folded his arms. "Reardon apologized. I can't endorse anyone. It's not my job."

"Good Lord. Be a leader." Crystal reached out and grabbed Preston's arm. "Don't be so spineless."

"Leister is not who he pretends to be." I leaned forward with Rudi. "We learned a few things."

"That's right," Rudi said. "Leister offered to put one of our people into his massage parlor business. He has them all over town. A front for prostitution and drugs."

"What?" Preston straightened and glanced up several levels. "Who told you that?"

"A reliable source," Rudi said.

It was what Rudi and I had learned from Koransky.

Preston cleared his throat. "That's an incredible allegation. We'll have to . . ."

"Do what?" Crystal said.

"What do you really know about Leister?" I asked. "Isn't that Reardon sitting with Leister and Mulholland?"

"That's right," Rudi said. "Why did they have that party on the same night as Zach's birthday party?"

Preston scratched his forehead and wiped at his mouth. "That's a matter of—"

"And how do we know Leister didn't burn down Zany's house," I said. Last night's explosion was still fresh in my mind and pounding in my ears.

As I watched Leister work the crowd, the possibility that he was the mastermind behind Zany's murder began to take hold. Leister had the most to gain. But without proof, I couldn't raise the allegation.

And what about Amity? The innocent bystander was strangled and finished with a headshot.

Preston glanced at me then back at Rudi. "Reardon's party was a simple coincidence. Sometimes it's a matter of social calendars. Schedules get mixed up."

Preston chose the easier subject to address. Ignore the arson of Zany's house and talk about screwed-up calendars.

"Allegro should be here any moment," Preston said.

It wasn't so much that Preston was weak, he was crafty. I recalled what Rudi had mentioned about his popularity complex. Like a master politician, he wanted to deflect disputed issues, avoid confrontations and keep everyone happy.

"Look, Preston," I said. "The Kelso Club is a classy place. The members can't take a chance on somebody like Leister. You told me yourself that the Kelso Club is all about reputation. That the club has to watch out for its members.

We've told you about Leister's little criminal operation with the massage parlors and you ignore us. Sure, maybe Zany had connections, but they've proven over time to be silent connections. The type you and your members don't need to worry about. Leister and his massage parlors might make a splash on the front page any day."

"You forget, Eddie, that you started all this with Mulholland," Preston said. He stood, excused himself, and ran off to meet some latecomers.

16

"Anybody got a good pick on this next race?" Zach called from the end of the table.

"I'm afraid we've been too busy," Rudi said. "Maybe the next one."

"What about Mr. Arnold?" Zach said. "Cole, see what horse Mr. Arnold likes and put a few bucks on it for me." He handed his friend some bills.

Rudi elbowed me. "We should handicap." She opened her racing program and began to work the third race.

If this were a typical day at my local track, my program would contain my trip notes and comments. Beside each horse, I'd have jotted notes from the previous races I'd watched and studied. Notes on whether the horse had stumbled, got bumped, or pushed wide. Other notes about the pace of the prior race, if a certain jockey was hot that day, if the track favored early speed—quick notes that would take me back to that day in the past and give me a "feel" for the race. Some of my notes could be found in the charts, but it was never enough. I had come to rely on my research footnotes.

At a foreign track like Aurora Downs, I'd start with a blank slate. So many questions. What about the jockeys and trainers, their records, their history? Some horses might take to this track, yet run poorly at other tracks or vice versa. Opening this racing program before me would be like opening the manual to a jet engine and then attempting to fly.

It didn't mean I hadn't caught a glimpse of that first race and how the odds board had changed at the last minute. It didn't mean the second race didn't come to my attention as well. I'd seen some things. I was tempted . . .

After the second race, Zach grabbed his crutches and stood. His buddy Cole stood with him. I followed their gaze and saw it was directed toward a tall man walking toward us from the elevators.

Preston jumped up and ran towards the man. Allegro Martin had arrived.

The former NBA star towered over Preston. Allegro's small waist and wide, out-of-proportion shoulders showed how his body had been molded for basketball. Each step a half-skip as if he could break out in a full gallop then stop on a dime and jump. The trademark smile with high cheekbones was a smile I'd memorized from all those years he stood at the free-throw line before a national television audience with the game on the line. Allegro could be counted on to score when it mattered.

"Crystal, I can't wait to talk with you." Allegro side-stepped up to our table and swept her into his arms. "When are you going to leave this chump, Preston, and give me a chance?"

Crystal melted in Allegro's arms. I'd expected her to berate him. Instead, she hugged back and cooed: "I shouldn't be nice to you. Where were you for Zach's party?"

Allegro cast his eyes down like a schoolboy caught in the act. "I'm sorry." He kept his arms tight around her and whispered something in her ear then spoke up. "You know how it is sometimes. Some lady friend and you lose track of time."

She gave his salt and pepper beard a playful slap. "You never change."

Then in a move that would make Houdini proud, Allegro slipped away and danced past Preston down the table to Zach.

"Zach, I'm sorry I messed up the other night. I'd planned to be there." He took the college star's hand with both of his and stared directly at him. "You'll score thirty a game next season without breaking a sweat."

Allegro had a way of capturing a person and taking them up to his higher plane of fame in spite of the onlookers. I glanced around and saw each face await their special moment.

In the next few seconds, Allegro had moved on. First to Zach's friend, Cole, then back down the table to Rudi.

"I'm going to miss the little guy." Allegro hugged Rudi. "It won't ever be the same without Zany."

Then it was my turn.

"Eddie? Eddie O'Connell? I've heard about you."

My hand was swallowed up by Allegro's.

I thought I was ready for him, but I stammered, no more immune to the star-power charm than everyone else.

"You're Zany's replacement, right? Making the rounds?"

I didn't know if I liked that he knew so much about me. Yet I glowed beneath the attention. "You heard about me at Reardon's party? From Leister?"

"Yeah. Your name came up."

"Don't believe everything you hear," I said.

"Officially, I don't know nothing about your line of work, but I hope today it includes the ponies."

"Maybe if we were at a track in Chicago, I'd be of some help," I said.

"Chicago's a great town," Allegro said. "Played there one season early in my career and loved it. Hated to be traded. But this is Denver and from what I hear, you'll have your work cut out for you to compete with Peter Leister."

And as quickly as Allegro said these words, he was gone and my hand was empty. He'd moved on to Arnold and then the next table and then the one after that.

Preston and the others at our table sipped their drinks in satisfaction and watched Allegro flow through the clubhouse like a fast-moving stream.

Maybe for a second, they believed as I did that we were inside Allegro's world, a world of fame and that our lives had attained some greater meaning. That we had some spot in history, some bookmark to tell our grandkids about. Never mind Allegro's playing days were in the past. Never mind those grandkids wouldn't have any idea who Allegro was. I felt what we all must've felt—that Allegro was the missing piece we'd been waiting for all afternoon.

When Allegro sat back down after his celebratory tour, directly across from me, I felt as if I enjoyed a special place in the ranks of the Kelso Club members. I was almost tempted to glance back at Leister to see his envious face.

Preston passed a rum and Coke to Allegro and another refill of iced tea to me. "Eddie, are you ready?"

"For what?" Ready for the afternoon? Ready to pick some winners?

Preston stood. "Please, everyone. Can I have your attention?" Since this was the lull between the second and third race—members stopped and listened. "Your attention everyone. Most of the members who signed up are now here. If not, I'll update them when they arrive."

Preston took a few steps back and then looked up. Multiple levels rose above him. Each level contained tables of members who could look down and obtain an unobstructed view through the glass partition to the track below. Some tables farther away, toward the elevators, contained the cowboy ranchers and other nonmembers. Crystal shook her head. Rudi grabbed my arm. We didn't know what Preston would say. I despised the fact I couldn't get a clear read on him.

"Let me say first of all a special thank you to each and every one of you who are in attendance today, including Allegro Martin," Preston said. "Not because my horse, Archive, will run in today's feature race . . ."

Some members laughed at the small joke, and Preston smiled. Would he tell the members he'd made a decision on their behalf and stick with Zany's store, or would I need to make my pitch?

"No, that's not the reason," Preston said. "My thank you is on behalf of horse racing itself. Because horse racing cannot survive without the customer seated in the clubhouse and grandstands. Despite the Kelso Club facility, racing cannot survive as a video game. So, allow me to encourage you to continue to patronize live racing whenever you have the opportunity or wherever you may travel."

"Can't hear you," some member called from the back.

I sat on the edge of my seat and held my breath. The store needed the revenue from these high rollers.

Preston cleared his throat and waved. He picked up a microphone and tested it out. Preston cleared his throat again and continued. "This is not a formal meeting of the Kelso Club. But we do have a less formal matter to decide today. It does not involve horse racing but involves matters within our club, the club rules, and regulations, as well as the needs and protection of our membership."

Something to decide? Uncle Mike had heard that I might be banned by the club. Joey L knew, Burrascano knew. My clue from Amity led to the Kelso Club, a clue proven by her murder. If I couldn't stop it, my investigation would end.

"As you all know we previously enjoyed the services of Zany, former jockey and entrepreneur. With his unfortunate passing, we must designate a new contact for these essential services. I have asked each proposed replacement to speak to you today so that you—the club members—can make an informed decision. Although I have taken on more administrative duties, I do not intend to run everything."

Preston held out his hands and looked at me. "Gentlemen, who will go first?"

My anger flared. Zany's store shouldn't be put up for a vote. I began to get up from my seat.

17

Before I could get around the table, Mulholland stood beside Preston, grabbed the microphone, and started talking to the crowd. I sat back down.

"I know a lot of you have met my good friend, Peter Leister," Mulholland said. He stood up on his tiptoes. "I'd like to introduce him at this time."

Leister ran down, shook Mulholland's hand, and waved to the crowd. He stretched to his full height of five foot four. "I'd just like to say how much I appreciate being asked to speak."

Leister's giggle reminded me of the old movie actor Peter Lorre who always played an immoral character. Made my skin crawl.

"I've met lots of you already," Leister continued. "My good friend, attorney Michael Mulholland, has been gracious enough to introduce me to many of you today and at Mr. Wes

Reardon's party the other night. It's a highlight for someone like me who has worked hard to build up my own business."

He took a quick breath and his lips turned down, revealing a hint of anger and resentment. I wondered how much of his presentation was an act.

"As you all know my family owns the Leister Steakhouse restaurants with locations in Denver and also Fort Collins and Colorado Springs. We have another branch to open at DIA in the near future. But enough about me and my family, I'm here to offer you certain services which shall we say . . ."

Leister broke off for a moment and gazed around the crowd. He laughed again like a sneaky little bastard who watered down drinks in his restaurants then continued.

"Services which we all find to be of priceless value during the football and basketball seasons. My partners and I have been in this business for many years serving the Denver community without complaint, and can offer you access via phone or over the internet with our new website. All the parlay bets you have come to expect."

Leister stopped and stared at me then snickered again.

"Getting paid on winning bets will be as quick and easy as a delivery from our restaurants. Our people come to you . . ."

As if he expected questions, Leister hesitated once more. I wanted to ask how much he charged at his massage parlors.

"Thank you, ladies and gentlemen." Leister bowed. "Now I'm advised by Mr. Mulholland that in honor of this occasion and your vote that he be allowed to say a few words."

Except for the yellow tie pulled askew to one side, Mulholland wore conservative clothes as if he'd come from the office. "Thank you, Peter," Mulholland said. I swore the attorney stared straight at me with an evil smile.

"Let's just say I want to throw in a little extra as an endorsement for my friend, Peter Leister." Mulholland slurred the word "endorsement," already inebriated. "Don't pass the word along to anyone. This is for you Kelso Club members exclusively. My handicapper experts say the six horse in this next race might be worth a look-see."

I got the point. Mulholland had given the members a hot tip on this next race on Leister's behalf. I had to give Leister credit—he'd made a powerful ally inside the club with Mulholland.

No doubt the attorney had told the members about the incident involving his Porsche. All the goodwill Zany had generated over the years might be lost.

Preston stepped forward and raised his arms. "As you all know, Mr. Mulholland's tips have been like money in the bank. But a word of warning to all members—use at your own risk."

The members grew solemn and studious and dove into the racing program. It seemed that this had all been planned to coincide with Allegro's entrance. Allegro had brought them all together.

I was the odd man out.

Allegro stared at me. "Eddie, why don't we hear from you?"

His smile matched Mulholland's previous evil smirk.

I walked past Leister and Mulholland who each made a point of ignoring me.

"Hey, everybody," Allegro called out. "Give Eddie a chance. You all remember Zany, right?"

I stumbled around the table to the spot where Preston still stood. From here, I got a good look at the levels where tables had been placed for today's event. A number of levels rose up and reminded me of a lecture hall. Heads bent over racing programs to search out Mulholland's hot tip. I tried to smile as if I was enjoying myself.

I cleared my throat and introduced myself again. Some people in the crowd nodded when they heard me recite my name. "Since I got out here, all I've heard from people is what a great guy Zany was," I said. "Well, the place he built and the employees like Rudi—they're all still here." Rudi turned in her seat and gave a quick wave to the crowd. Other quizzical faces looked up from their study of the next race, but maybe they were just checking out the odds on the tote board behind me. "I want you to know that I don't plan any changes." How many owed gambling debts to the store? None of them would vote for me.

I glanced at Rudi. She nodded and smiled encouragement. She wanted me to tell the crowd what we learned from Koransky.

"There are a lot of people here. I assume not everyone in the clubhouse today is a Kelso Club member. Some people might even be taking video with their cell phone." The members did a one-eighty inspection of the premises. I hesitated, to drive home the point.

Then in my best, matter-of-fact voice, without a hint of sarcasm, I stated something irrefutable and clear cut: "Where I come from, we don't talk about certain things in public."

Now I had the attention of the members. Even Jim Arnold straightened up from his handicapping fortress. One person clapped. Somebody else called out: "Here, here."

"Rudi and I look forward to talking with each of you one on one. Confidentially," I said. "Let's do that before any vote."

Preston stepped back up to the temporary speaker platform. "Thank you, Eddie. We appreciate your word of caution." His voice trembled and his face reddened. He cleared his throat again into the microphone. "I'll be moving through the crowd later. After you've had time to meet with Eddie and Rudi, we'll vote. Thank you to all the members."

Crystal stopped me on the way to my seat. "Very good, Eddie." She raised her voice so Preston could hear her. "At least someone has the welfare of the members in mind."

I wanted to tell the crowd that they were a bunch of ungrateful bastards if they considered Leister. Tell them what kind of person Zany had been and remind them how soft he'd been on collections. But I allowed the opportunity to slide.

When I sat down, Rudi leaned over to me and whispered, "Why didn't you say anything about Leister's massage parlors?"

I whispered back. "We have to take the high road. If I mentioned Leister's criminal activities, I'd sound like a snitch, but if we tell the members one on one, they'll think we're looking out for them."

She nodded and squeezed my arm. "You're right. Smart move."

Across from me, Allegro looked up briefly from his racing program and flashed a smile.

I sipped iced tea down my swollen throat and wondered how politicians had the stomach for public speaking.

18

Around me, everyone pored over the racing program. I knew what went through their mind. How can we use Leister's inside information to make the most money possible?

They could bet the six horse to win but they wouldn't want to pass up playing an exacta or trifecta that could provide an even bigger payday. What horse was likely to finish second and third to the Mulholland horse?

Rudi flipped pages of the racing program.

"You're playing the race?" I asked her.

"Yes," she said. "Preston wasn't kidding. Mulholland's horses have almost always won before. He must have some inside information."

I should've figured. Rudi was too practical not to play what sounded like a sure thing.

Crystal bent over in study. At the other end of the table, Zach and Cole exchanged whispers. Arnold was hard at work like a man with a deadline. Allegro made notes with a silver pen, probably used for autographs. The only member not handicapping was Preston, the spineless leader.

College football next weekend and then pros the weekend after. How could I explain the loss of revenue on my watch?

I stared down at the front page of the racing program and then past Allegro down below to the tote board. The six horse was being bet heavy. It made sense to look for another horse in the ten horse field. Try to make a decent score on an exacta or trifecta.

My fingers reached down and turned the pages of the racing program to the third race. "No gambling," my uncle had said. It wouldn't hurt to look, I argued. What harm would there be to check out the six? Find out what made the six horse such a hot commodity.

My mind clicked into handicapping gear as soon as I spied the past performances—previous races of each horse that contained information on where they'd run, the class of the race, and how they'd finished. Horses from other tracks I'd never played—New Mexico, Nebraska, Washington. Races run at Aurora Downs over the summer. Old claimers for a cheap price. Jockeys I didn't know and trainers I didn't know. Except one.

I knew the trainer on the two horse by the name of Joe Larsen. Good old Joe Larsen. What was he doing out here? He'd been suspended a couple of years ago in Chicago—the usual reason—his horses tested positive for a banned substance once too often.

Did Joe have other horses running today? Nope. The two horse had only run once at a small track in Southern Illinois a month ago and finished dead last. One workout last week listed. Joe's horse didn't fit with the field and appeared to be out for exercise—an easy toss out. Many trainers ran cheap horses into shape.

But the workout was decent. Joe would try to pull the same bullshit he'd done in Chicago.

The tote board showed Joe's horse, the number two, at odds of 29-1, the longest odds in the race.

Then I realized what I'd done. Exactly what I'd told myself not to do—I'd opened the program. Now what should I do? Close the program and pretend Joe didn't exist? Tell everyone to bet the two horse and look like a fool if Joe wasn't the same old Joe Larsen?

I turned the pages and closed my program as if it were the lid of Pandora's Box.

"Maybe give the two horse a look," I said. The words escaped as if I'd thought out loud.

Allegro glanced up at me then down at his form. "That horse looks like shit, Eddie."

The horses ambled down the track in the post parade. Joe's horse wouldn't catch any horseman's eye but I noticed some sheen to the coat, pricked-up ears, a certain alertness. The Mulholland horse, the six, pranced like a favorite but its back legs were wrapped.

"Are those bandages on the legs of the six horse?" I asked.

Allegro's head snapped around. "What?"

Preston stood. "Don't worry Allegro. According to my trainer, those types of bandages aren't a problem."

I didn't want to argue. But those bandages could mean trouble for the horse. Then again, a trainer might use them to make people nervous about a horse's chances. At the very least, it was worth investigating.

"Good. What are you trying to do, Eddie? Jinx me?" Allegro looked down at the closed racing program in front of me. "Aren't you betting on the six?"

"No."

"Why the hell not? Didn't you hear what everyone said about Mulholland's inside information?"

"I heard it. I've seen lots of hot tips lose over the years." I recited the classic racetrack warning but it wasn't so easy to follow. A hot tip got a horseplayer's blood boiling.

What did the lure of easy money mean to Allegro? Had the old pro stashed away a tidy portfolio from his playing days? I'd heard how many pros didn't plan for retirement, spent money during their playing days like an oil sheik, and ended up in bankruptcy. What about Allegro?

"Who ever heard of a bookie who doesn't bet?" Allegro said.

Time ticked down. Could I let Joe's horse go? It seemed as if providence had smiled down upon me and given me a longshot on a silver platter. How could I ignore such a gift?

19

IF I IGNORED EVERYTHING AND DID BET, WHAT WOULD I DO? I couldn't help but speculate. I could bet Joe's horse to win or I could play Joe's horse with Mulholland's six horse in an exacta box. What was the exacta paying? I stared at the probable exacta payoffs on a nearby monitor. The combination of the six-two had the highest payoff of any exacta involving the six horse—a hundred seventy-five dollars for a two-dollar bet.

Burrascano's expense money sat in a roll inside my pocket. More cash was hidden back in the hotel room and the Crown Vic. Burrascano didn't deal in plastic. But use cash from the gambling boss on the horses? I'd be on the next train back to Chicago or worse.

I could do something symbolic. Give Rudi a few bucks to take up to the windows. But that seemed anemic. Pull out a bankroll that could choke a horse and peel off a sawbuck? How would that look? And how would I feel?

It had been years since I played a penny-ante game. I invested—I didn't make action bets. Especially not here, today.

The track announcer warned the crowd: "Only three minutes to post."

It was decision time. "Those betting lines are long. Don't get shut out," I said.

Allegro bounced up. "Shit, you're right, Eddie. Preston, let's go."

Rudi stood up. "Aren't you going to bet this race?"

"No." But my insides churned with "decision time."

Rudi brushed my arm. "Don't you know what that will look like?"

What were the implications—a bookie who refused to play—too tight-fisted; a bad sport because it was a rival's hot tip; a guy who thought gambling was a fool's game and would take a guy's money but was too good to play himself? I could admit to my "problem" but that would make matters worse.

"There's always a hot tip at the track," I said.

Rudi sighed. "Fine. Don't mind me if I try to make some money. I might need it."

I knew what she meant by that comment.

Preston and Allegro almost ran up to the betting lines and talked back and forth like a well-oiled machine. A few autograph seekers were denied.

Jim Arnold pushed through another line; a notebook stuck under one arm. Zach and Cole looked over Arnold's shoulder. Rudi and Crystal in another line.

How long were the lines? The horses meandered toward the starting gate, perched near the start of the backstretch on the other side of the pond. Plenty of time remained to run up and get something down on Joe's horse or that exacta combination. I stood up and then sat back down. Squirmed in my seat like a rookie making his first play.

The odds didn't change on Joe's horse but they didn't go up either. The odds on Mulholland's six horse were down to 8-5. Not a bad return but the members in line would want more. Arnold would bet the trifecta, maybe the superfecta, backed up by the exacta.

Numbers played in my head—2-6, 6-2; trifecta boxes: 2-6-1. I'd hit a big payoff with the 2-6-1 once. About forty-five hundred dollars, the same as Arnold's missed trifecta yesterday. Always one more ticket, one more combination to unlock the future, it's what they all thought while standing in line, scribbling numbers, calculating bankroll.

Leister would look like a star if Mulholland's six horse came in. The members dribbled back from the windows in silence and took their seats around me. The others at my table returned. No one talked much about what they'd actually bet or what combinations they held. It might jinx their chances, and I didn't ask.

The horses were loaded into the gate. These were the last few seconds before the race when everything still remained possible. A moment later and one stumble could turn tickets into trash.

I could feel it, relished it. Saw it in Rudi's eyes. All those times I stood at attention as the bell rang and the horses left the gate.

Even practical Rudi, her hands clasped tight, was not immune. How had I lost the chance to live in the anticipation? Had I gone to the well once too often, used up all the old magic until the well became a deep, dangerous cavern that could swallow me in its bottomless darkness? Until this second, when I stood naked—wagerless—did I realize what I'd lost.

The race began almost before I could snap out of it. I stood back at my home track in Chicago with my buddies who even now played and replayed this anticipation, day in, day out, race after race, with no idea the well could ever run dry.

The horses stormed out of the gate and fanned out across the track in a six-furlong sprint. Difficult to see them on the other side of the infield but I checked the monitor. Mulholland's six horse came out strong but Joe's two horse knifed through on the rail. The rail had been smoking hot in the first two races. In short order, the six horse and the two horse ran together out front and opened up a lead on the pack.

A chorus of screams enveloped me. What the hell was wrong with me? Why did I let Joe's horse go? No wonder I'd suffered that long losing streak. Kicked providence in the teeth even when I had it on a silver platter. Absolutely stupid.

I didn't root openly. I needed Mulholland's horse to lose. Needed the six horse to drop out and disappoint all these screaming members so Zany's store could come out on top and maintain the stream of revenue. Stop Leister in his tracks. But inside, my gut screamed for Joe's horse to drop out.

I needed the two horse at 29-1 to give up. Jeesus Christ, 29-1 and I let it go. Sat squirming like a potty-training loser, instead of making a play.

C'mon two, give it up.

But the two horse continued to stalk the leader around the turn and into the stretch. The Mulholland horse and Joe's horse, two peas in a pod, seven lengths in front of the pack.

"Your goddamn two horse, Eddie," Allegro said.

Others around me screamed: "Go six, go six."

Inside I screamed: "Stop two, stop two."

I needed one of those old nags in the pack to wake up and cut into the seven-length lead and make a race out of it. At the same time, I needed the two and the six horse to get leg weary and let the pack catch up.

"Go six, go six."

Stop two, stop two.

Damn Joe Larsen. There should be some law to keep him out of racing. A sick, defunct industry.

No, it was my fault. Fell too far too fast. Asleep at the switch. I could've been jumping up and down inside—the savvy player, the veteran horseplayer. Not the sniveling wimp.

Down the stretch, the Mulholland horse and Joe's horse fought.

Allegro jumped up and down as if it were game seven of the NBA championship.

Rudi tugged on my arm. Ever practical, fully committed Rudi.

I had to pull myself out of this.

The six horse began to edge in front but Joe's horse fought back running past us to the wire directly below.

The track announcer's voice rose to a high-pitched, emotional level, lost in the screams.

Stride for stride, heads bobbing, my cold exacta threw dirt down the hole on top of me. I might be sick. The crowd around me irrational, uncontrollable.

"C'mon," they screamed.

The track announcer: "At the wire, too close to call—a photo finish."

My head couldn't take it. My legs wobbled. I wanted to fight somebody. Could I hold it together?

20

For one millisecond, total silence reigned. Like a note of jazz not played, it spoke volumes. The members stood transfixed in disbelief. They'd expected to hear the track announcer call Mulholland's six horse as the winner at the wire. The six was the hot pick, the sure thing, what the hell happened? I saw how their faces expected to win. They'd spent their lives in the winner's circle. Now they had to suffer through a photo.

"Where did that two horse come from?" Preston asked.

"Eddie had it," Allegro said. "Eddie told me about the two."

I stood stock-still as if I were a true track genius instead of a sniveling, reluctant rookie unable to wager.

Maybe I beat myself up too much inside, but I couldn't help it. It came with the territory. Based on what I knew of the horses, I felt that I should win and hated it when I lost. Usually,

I rectified the sour mood with the next race or the one after that. Not exactly a productive trait, and sometimes it could drag me into a dark place.

"That's right," Rudi said. "I heard him too." She talked in my ear. "You didn't tell me you knew anything about the horses."

"I said I knew a little," I whispered back.

"Maybe if you weren't talking on your damn phone," Allegro told Preston. "You would've heard him too, and we would've played Eddie's horse in the exacta instead of the others."

"We've still got the six horse to win," Preston said.

Allegro stomped his foot then cussed. He'd missed the big payoff with the 29-1 shot, and I could see it ate him up inside almost as much as it did me.

"I guess," Allegro said. "If we win this damn photo. Son-of-a-bitch. Damn two horse wouldn't give up."

"Mulholland hasn't missed before," Preston said.

"That Mulholland and his hot picks. I'm going to kill him," Allegro said.

I wanted to head for the exit. Allegro slurped from his rum and Coke. I stared at my iced tea. God, I needed a drink. Straight scotch, a double shot similar to the bracer Arnold slugged down yesterday.

"You've got this exacta, Eddie?" Preston asked.

"Fucker didn't bet," Allegro said. "Can you believe that? Had it cold and didn't play it. Refused the Mulholland horse because of Leister. Takes control."

My outer shell stayed cool but my insides boiled. I kept my mouth shut.

"Eddie is the only one in control," Rudi said. "I hate to say it but I need the six horse."

"You liked the two horse, Eddie?" Zach called from the end of the table. "Wish I'd known. That exacta will pay good, real good."

I pretended to smile. I wished I'd never said anything about Joe's horse to anyone. Kept my mouth shut. Allegro told anyone and everyone how I said to use the two horse. I wished he'd shut up. Every time somebody mentioned the two horse a knife twisted in my gut.

"Who do you think had it?" Allegro asked.

"This photo is taking forever," Preston said.

I glanced back at Leister and Mulholland. The attorney appeared pale and took a step or two back from the table as if he might take flight.

"Maybe a dead heat," I said. How many photos had I sat through? Usually, I knew immediately when I won. Whenever I couldn't tell, I lost. Nothing wagered on this race, and I still hated the wait. Get it over and post the two horse—end my agony. Insult added to injury as time dragged.

Allegro nodded. "I'll take that dead heat, Eddie. Damn right. At least I'll get some of my money back."

I heard a heartfelt squeal from a corner of the clubhouse. Instinctively, I looked down at the tote board. Everyone howled at once.

The number six stood first on the tote board. Mulholland could relax. Underneath, in second, sat Joe Larsen's horse—

the brave effort against the "sure thing" not enough. I'd have my work cut out for me to sway the members to stay with Zany's store.

Allegro shrieked, "I told you he won." The old pro slapped high fives around the table. Preston, out of sync, missed on the first try then connected.

Rudi gave me a hug. It lasted longer than might be considered appropriate for an 8-5 shot but I didn't mind. I liked the way her body fit snugly against mine.

I don't know how she did it. I leaned down to say something or she hopped up on her toes, but she managed to plant a kiss on my lips. Over before I knew it happened. But that's what winning can make happen.

Or, in my case, not winning. At least I didn't have to stare at boxcar payoffs on a 29-1 shot; about sixty dollars on a two-dollar win bet. But Rudi's surprise kiss sure helped.

I looked up behind me. Mulholland did a victory dance. A tray of shots arrived at Leister and Mulholland's table. Their celebration might be premature. I still had Leister's massage parlors to use as ammunition with the strait-laced membership.

"That's the way to start our day," Allegro said, as he reached for his drink and gulped. "Preston, how about another round?"

Preston immediately stood and waved toward the waitress. "An excellent idea, Allegro."

"Eddie, too bad you didn't bet," Allegro said.

I loved gambler euphoria. It was contagious and spread through me too. They say every racetrack is the same; all the horses are tired and all the horseplayers are broke. But today,

Aurora Downs had become a mystical place for everyone but me. For me, it was a haunted house. "The odds were eight-to-five and the horse only nosed out a twenty-nine to one shot," I said.

"Damn straight, by a head bob. Isn't that sweet?" Allegro did an abbreviated round of high fives from his seated position. "The jock on the six horse wanted to keep us guessing."

"He was in control all the time," Zach said.

Allegro nodded. "That's right. These jockeys are experts. They know where the wire is down to the last inch. How many times have they been around the track? Shit. How many horses they run six furlongs in their careers?"

"Every day. Workouts in the morning, too," Zach agreed.

Allegro nodded. "Like shooting free throws. If I had a penny for every one of those I shot, I'd be Rockefeller."

Zach laughed and raised his paper cup. "I'll drink to that. Coach never thinks I shoot enough of them."

Rudi and Crystal calculated payoffs while Preston got the waitress hopping. Zach's buddy, Cole, ran up to the windows to collect.

"Nothing keeps those fucking coaches happy," Allegro said. "You shoot all day, all night, they still think you're loafing."

Zach leaned in closer toward Allegro. "Not counting all the time you practice on your own."

Zach asked Allegro about everything NBA fame could offer. Zach and Allegro were the winners, while the rest of us were the losers. But with a year on the sidelines due to injury, Zach's NBA dreams would be a long shot at best.

"And the cars?" Zach asked.

"Do a lot of test drives, try them all. Me, I bought the first Mercedes I sat in. Shit—over twenty years ago. What a dope. My old teammate, Mancuso, tried to help, but I wish I had somebody to show me the ropes." Allegro's gaze moved from Zach and then over my shoulder. "Who do we have here? If it isn't our esteemed local counsel."

I turned to find that Mulholland and Peter Leister had walked up to our table.

Mulholland nodded to each one around the table as if he expected congratulations. He swayed slightly on his feet. "Hello, Allegro."

"I liked that tip on the last race," Allegro said. "Keep them coming."

Mulholland smiled a wide, shit-eating smile. "That wasn't too bad, was it?"

"Closer than I like," Allegro said.

The attorney rubbed his hands together. "A little extra excitement—no extra charge. We're on our way up to collect."

No one seemed happy to be reminded the six horse was the product of Mulholland's inside information. They wanted to make it their personal victory.

"Peter Leister, nice to see you again." Allegro reached out his hand. "Do you know Eddie here?"

"I haven't had the pleasure." Leister reached out a hand toward me, a flashy gold Rolex hanging on his wrist.

I shook Leister's hand. "Saw you sweating out that photo."

"It was a very close finish," he bowed slightly with the diplomatic air of a gracious winner. "I've been looking forward to meeting you. I hope we can get to know each other. You'll have to stop by my restaurant. The bone-in ribeye is excellent. You'll need to give me notice so I can fit you in. We're very busy."

"I'll give you plenty of notice." No reason to play the good loser—not yet. The guy wasn't stupid. Did Leister have the guts to commit murder?

"Your new friend is trying to move in on Zany's business," Allegro said with an evil grin. "You better watch him, Eddie."

"I won't let him out of my sight," I said.

Leister ignored me and nodded to Allegro. "I suppose you could say that, after all, business is business. I have long admired Zany's operation and how well it worked. I have also learned that where there is opportunity, one should not ignore it. I have to continue to think about expanding and growing."

"Expansion isn't always the smartest move," I said. "Sometimes you got to be satisfied with what you got." I did my best to stay under control.

"You just got into town." Leister pointed at his chest. "This is my backyard. Maybe the members will stay because of Zany's memory and maybe they won't. I've been around for years and will continue to be around. They can count on Peter Leister."

Rudi stood. "Bullshit. Your business wasn't enough for Zany to think twice about. The employees are still there. What Zany provided won't change. They know what kind of service they can expect."

Leister viewed Rudi up and down. "That is true. No one complained about a mixed-up order or a late payoff. Everything ran like clockwork. I know you were responsible for that."

"I hope that's not a job offer," Rudi shot back.

Leister held out his hands, palms up. "My door is always open to discuss terms."

I got up into Leister's face. "Is that how you charm those girls in your massage parlors?"

Leister's smile evaporated, replaced by a scowl. A number of members around us were glued to the exchange. I half-hoped Leister would take a swing at me.

"Now, everybody settle down," Allegro said. "I don't want any bickering to spoil my good mood." He reached out and put his hand on Leister's shoulder. "Sounds like you enjoy walking on thin ice, Mr. Leister. You and Eddie need to get along. You're sort of in the same league. I've got this charity event coming up this week. I hope you both can make it."

After a moment's hesitation, the salesman smile returned. "Thanks. I'll be sure to attend."

"Talk to Preston about the size of your donation." Allegro laughed and this got everyone else laughing, too. "Don't forget it's for charity."

As Leister and Mulholland walked toward the windows, I got up and followed. There was still Mulholland's unpaid gambling debt. The best time to collect is when a guy feels flush. I gave Mulholland a slight nudge and the lawyer twisted around, unsteady on his feet.

"Maybe you could pay down the debt you owe Zany's store with the cash you collect," I said.

"You are a pest." Mulholland smiled and pushed me in the chest. "In my own good time. You don't scare me."

This guy was right on the edge. It took all my self-control not to deck him. Instead, I shoved back and the drunken bum tipped over an empty chair. "Don't look for your Porsche in the parking lot, scumbag," I said.

"No one appreciates strong-arm tactics." Leister shouted at me as he helped Mulholland up.

"Fuck you, too, Leister. Stay away from Koransky and the rest of my staff or you'll find out about 'tactics.'"

I took my seat. My arms trembled. I'd wanted more than a little shoving match. Allegro stared at me, his mouth open.

21

A COUPLE OF RACES LATER, JIM ARNOLD CAME UP TO OUR table, racing program in hand. I almost laughed at Arnold's rumpled appearance. His ruffled hair stood on end as if he'd just gotten out of bed. He laid out the pages like an open newspaper between me and Rudi.

"I heard you liked this two horse, Eddie," Arnold said. "How'd you pick it?"

I got angry all over again about Joe's horse and the 29-1 shot that got away.

"Yeah, Eddie." Allegro laughed. "How did you get to that shitty-looking horse?"

Allegro was to blame. He continued to spread the word about how I'd picked the 29-1 shot. He seemed to have a sixth sense of how to needle someone. "You guys need a handicapping lesson? It will cost extra." I kidded back.

Allegro looked up at Arnold. "I've been trying to get Eddie's input on each of the last two races but he won't open the program."

"I'm sure he'll find the time on this next race," Rudi said. She elbowed me in the ribs. "For Zany," she whispered.

I winced. "I can take a look." What were my chances of finding another Joe Larsen-type horse?

"Thanks," Arnold said. "I'd like to know what handicapping factors you use."

I took a deep breath. I didn't like a lot of people around when I picked the horses. It was a sure recipe for losing. Too much distraction. Horseplayers at the track gave each other space to work. Handicapping took time and study, a lonely job. A lecture to Arnold about "factors" seemed laughable.

A couple approached Allegro's side of the table.

"Dr. Rutledge and Mrs. Rutledge, how are you?" Allegro reached out his hand to the doctor and began to stand.

"Please don't get up," Mrs. Rutledge apologized, a middle-aged beauty with long dark hair and bright red lipstick. "We hate to bother you, but my brother is a great fan, and we hoped we could get your autograph for his birthday next week."

Allegro smiled back. "Of course. Your brother? I remember when I signed autographs for somebody's kid."

"Thank you so much," Mrs. Rutledge said as she leaned over with her racing program.

Allegro went to work with his silver pen. I wondered how it felt to turn people on with your signature.

"What did you say your brother's name was?" Allegro said.

I couldn't hear what Mrs. Rutledge replied as I directed my attention to Arnold's program. Why did it take two races for Arnold to come over? Then I remembered the last couple of races at Saratoga had probably caught Arnold's full concentration. He played tracks in tandem, the lucky guy.

Was Arnold up or down? It would take some conversation to figure out, but he was definitely in better shape than yesterday when he stared down that double shot of bourbon. I read his program, a handicapping road map complete with all the circles and arrows and cryptic comments I employed. For a second, I followed his thinking and took in a fresh perspective.

"Eddie, hey Eddie." Allegro snapped his fingers. "Want to introduce you to Doctor and Mrs. Rutledge.

"Just one moment," I told Arnold. I got up and shook hands and said hello.

"Eddie took over for Zany," Allegro said.

"You did?" Mrs. Rutledge said. "Where are you from, Eddie?"

"Chicago."

"Oh, I'm originally from Minnesota. Moved here when the doctor was an intern. Isn't that right, Doctor?"

We both glanced at the doctor who stood as solid and useless as a set of encyclopedias awaiting the next garage sale.

"Yes, correct," the doctor said after an uncomfortable silence.

I swore his lips didn't move. "I've met more people here from the Midwest. Cold up there," I said.

I'd gotten better at the art of inane conversation. Allegro's introductions to Kelso Club members had gone on since the third race. At first, I didn't understand. I thought Allegro had connived with Leister, but then Allegro helped me. I had come to the conclusion that Allegro relished my skirmish with Leister and Mulholland. From what I could tell, Allegro's favorite hobby was to make trouble for anyone and everyone for his own amusement.

"I know you'll stay with us, Mrs. Rutledge," Rudi said. She'd stuck by me during the afternoon and took advantage of each Allegro introduction. I'd thought about that winning kiss and what it meant. Maybe nothing.

"And something else you should know." Rudi talked in a low voice and conveyed the information about Leister's massage parlors to Mrs. Rutledge, and how they were a front for prostitution and drugs. I thought the doctor's wife would have a coronary.

"Don't worry, dear," Mrs. Rutledge said, her face turning a deep shade of red. "The doctor and I aren't about to change."

So far this afternoon I'd discovered that, in addition to the massage parlor news, people simply hated change. The move from Minnesota was probably the biggest thing in Mrs. Rutledge's life—she still talked about it twenty years later.

I'd made some progress despite Mulholland's hot tip. Things were looking up. Now if I could only keep my head out of a racing program.

Crystal ran up to the table as the doctor and Mrs. Rutledge walked away. "I was outside on the balcony having a cigarette," Crystal said. "Rudi, it's your shithead husband. I saw him."

"What? Are you sure?" Rudi jostled past Arnold.

"Positive." Crystal handed her purse to Preston. "Here, hang on to this."

I nudged past Arnold. "Sorry, Jim." I joined Crystal and Rudi. "I'd like to have a talk with Warren." I tried to recall what the "talk" part was about—I knew how I'd end the conversation. I'd deflate Warren's face the way he'd flattened Rudi's tires.

Rudi rubbed her forehead. "Maybe we should let him be. Why can't he leave me alone? When will he stop messing with me and realize it's over?"

"C'mon, Rudi, you deserve answers," I said. Rudi's reluctance didn't make sense. But from my bartending experience, I recalled how complicated spousal abuse could be. So many sides to it, so much emotion. "Crystal, show me where he is."

Rudi grabbed my elbow. "Eddie, maybe you're right, but you don't know Warren. He's a big guy, and I don't want you to get hurt. He's not worth it."

I busted out laughing. I was touched that she worried about me, but there was no way he'd touch me. "Warren will get what he deserves."

Crystal led us up the stairs to a walkway lined with a bar and concessions. Cheap food like hot dogs and stale popcorn. One small grill fried hamburgers into black poker chips.

"Where did you see him?" I asked.

Crystal nodded toward a crowd trying to get the bartender's attention. "Near the bar."

"Did he see you?" Maybe Warren got scared off. Or maybe he ran out to puncture those new tires I just paid for.

"I think so," Crystal said.

Crystal and Rudi dodged back and forth to get a look at the faces congregated around the bar.

I got frustrated. "What does he look like?"

"A little taller than you." Rudi reached up one hand to indicate height. "Blond hair cut short."

"Brown T-shirt, square head," Crystal said.

"Sounds adorable," I told Rudi. "A Nazi farm boy."

"I don't see him." Rudi craned her neck from one corner of the clubhouse to the other.

"Why don't we go downstairs?" When I'd first entered the track earlier today most of the fans ran down the stairs to the grandstand area.

"Crystal, you go with Eddie and I'll catch up," Rudi stammered. "I have to use the restroom. Too many drinks."

Rudi seemed visibly shaken and almost relieved we hadn't found Warren. What was this guy capable of?

Crystal headed toward the stairs.

I hadn't thought about possible repercussions of a knock-down, drag-out fight in a public place. But talk of Joe's horse got my blood boiling. In Chicago, fights at the track were commonplace. It was like a hockey game—if both parties were willing, give them room and let them settle it. I hoped the same unwritten rule governed the Denver track.

I followed Crystal into a mob downstairs. People jammed into every nook and cranny probably to escape the heat and the dust I'd seen billow past the clubhouse windows from the gale force winds outside.

"Why don't you try over there?" I pointed Crystal toward the concessions. "And I'll check over by the betting windows."

I figured Warren had seen me while stalking Rudi. All I needed to do was find a big guy with a brown shirt and short blond hair with a look of recognition on his face and we could get to know each other better.

The betting lines in the grandstands snaked back from the windows in a tangle of bodies. Young people with kids in tow. Old people with walkers. Cowboys and cowgirls, Latinos, Asians, a melting pot of people who needed action.

No sign of any guy who matched Warren's description. I checked the men's room and circled back to the concession area on the other side. Checked into the nooks and crannies where bettors congregated in small groups around flat screens. Plenty of places to handicap and drop out like a slot player seated in a forgotten corner of a casino.

I went outside into a blast of heat and track dirt. A guy with a mask tended a grill with turkey legs. They didn't do those at my Chicago track.

Finally, I walked back up the stairs to the clubhouse. I thought about the elevator but didn't mind the exercise. I checked the smoker's balcony that overlooked the paddock. Cigarette smoke caught the wind and filled my lungs. I forgot how much I craved one. No Warren.

Back inside, I decided to check the clubhouse men's room and take a piss. I was ready to call it a wild goose chase and go back to the table.

The john was a busy place. Guys stood in line. But as I got closer, I saw how they talked in hushed voices and stood in clumps instead of a line. Maybe they had some inside dope on a race. Typically, I'd stand close by and listen or make conversation to pick up on rumors about the next race, but today I was in a hurry, and I really needed to use the facilities.

Someone ran out of the john as I pushed through the crowd. I thought maybe the toilets were plugged because more guys huddled inside. No one stood at the urinals so I ran up. I started to piss and overheard low voices.

A man mumbled: "He played his last race. A mess."

Another asked: "Did anyone see what happened?"

Somebody answered: "Must've happened during the running of the last race."

I stopped in midstream, zipped up my fly, and followed the collective focus of the men.

I looked toward the stalls and saw feet sticking out along the floor. "What the fuck?"

Maybe it was the elusive Warren, delivered on a silver platter. I looked back at the crowd then walked over and poked my head inside the stall. My foot kicked a loose shoe.

I studied the body. The toes pointed up but the upper torso was twisted downward. The head bent to one side and kissed the base of the toilet. I thought the man might jump up and laugh at me—as if I might be the butt of a bad joke.

The black pants and striped shirt were familiar. A stench of booze. Vomit on the floor and in the toilet bowl. Blood smeared the face. A glassy eye stared up.

A chunk of scalp torn away. Blood oozed and an ever-widening pool at my feet. On the toe of my shoe.

A security guard ran inside with a walkie-talkie. "Everybody out."

At first, I didn't recognize the face of the injured man. Like the moment I first saw Amity's body, difficult to decipher. Unexpected. Shock. At least Mags didn't stand behind me.

The guard yanked on my shirt. "Let's go."

"What?" The idea of first aid popped into my head but the guard kept pulling.

"We need everyone out now," he shouted.

More guards rushed inside as I stepped outside. A siren wailed. Walkie-talkies cackled back and forth like a flock of alarmed crows. Somebody shoved me into the crowd of gawkers.

Emergency personnel and paramedics in white coats exited the elevators and ran toward me. Guards pushed me back. A stretcher rolled past.

"Eddie, what happened?"

I turned. It was Allegro. I realized how fast my heart was beating. I couldn't help but think how this might change things.

Allegro gripped my shoulder. "Eddie, what is it?"

They'd all know soon enough. "It's Mulholland."

22

SUNDAY

At the Kelso Club the next day, I filled out the general information sheet with the intake sergeant at one of the tables set up in the lobby. Then he sent me upstairs to wait for the chance to give my statement on the Mulholland murder.

The members left the track quickly yesterday when they heard. Crystal told Rudi that Preston gave the cops a list of those in attendance as a tradeoff for holding interviews at the club, rather than at the police station. Since they shunned publicity, the members had agreed to these terms. My name was on the list.

Rudi sat inside the crowded bar on the second floor. The place turned quiet as I pushed my way through. I'd already been convicted in their collective minds.

I took an empty stool beside her. "How long have you been waiting?"

"Forever. Did you see this morning's paper?"

"Afraid so." The paper splashed all the gory details of the Mulholland murder across the front page. Robbery had been mentioned as a possible motive. Aurora Downs pledged tighter security. The article described Mulholland's sterling reputation among the bar, his pro bono service, well-known corporate clients, and his service to charitable and alumni organizations. Everybody had good things to say—civic leaders, judges, employees, law partners—I might be his single enemy in the world.

Somehow Preston or one of the well-connected club members had kept the Kelso Club name out of the article.

Rudi sat up and leaned into me and whispered. "I don't think we're too popular. Do you see the look on their faces?"

"I know."

The members had resumed talking with each other, but probably about me because they shot me sideways glances. I'd made friends with many of them yesterday thanks to Allegro's help, but after the Mulholland murder, that changed.

"What are we going to do, Eddie? None of them will wager at the store."

"I don't know. Didn't Crystal tell people I was in the grandstands?" There had been little time to discuss things yesterday. Most of the members left after they'd heard what happened to Mulholland. Since then, they'd probably gossiped about my public argument with the attorney over his gambling debt and connected dots. The stream of revenue would be choked to a trickle.

"Don't count on Crystal. I told you how unpredictable she can be. Do you want me to say I was with you?"

I wanted to pull Rudi close and give her a hug, but she should run a hundred miles in the opposite direction from me, not offer an alibi. Maybe that winning kiss did mean something.

"No, it will work out." There were too many people, too many witnesses, and probably too many cameras. I couldn't let Rudi take any chances on my account.

A uniformed police officer walked into the bar and called a name off a clipboard. In response, one of the members got up from his chair and followed the officer into the hall. The rest of the crowd groaned and complained.

"No one is happy to spend their Sunday afternoon here," Rudi said. "What a nightmare."

"How many have they called so far?" I was told to be here at one o'clock and the clock on the wall said five minutes after one.

"I heard they've got several investigators doing interviews in different rooms but they're behind schedule."

The wait softened people up. Made them nervous. Forced them to rely on the truth. Ask any top-notch investigator like Uncle Mike.

"And you've been waiting for an hour?" I asked.

"Some people have been waiting longer," Rudi said. "At first, they were excited. Now, they're just pissed. It doesn't help that they closed the bar."

"A drink would help my mood, too."

Rudi swept a hand through her auburn hair. "Now my divorce filing is really dead in the water."

I settled in for a long wait. Already I'd been summoned by Mags for a meeting this evening. Bad news traveled fast.

Whenever it came time to meet a police detective on one of Burrascano's jobs, Uncle Mike took over. As a former homicide detective, it was familiar territory for him.

Sometimes the key to one of our cases might come from a police detective Uncle Mike had managed to win over. Now it was up to me to establish a similar relationship, but without any of the fraternal connections my uncle could rely upon.

The uniform came into the room again and a hush came over the crowd. He flipped pages back and forth on his clipboard as if he couldn't find the next name, enjoying the drama he caused. I yawned. How far down the list was I? Maybe I'd need to reschedule my appointment at five-thirty with Mags.

"Eddie O'Connell," the uniform called out.

An electrical shock ran through my body. I jumped. People gave me a cold stare as I twisted my way back down the bar. Nobody shouted any encouragement.

The uniform led me out of the room, through glass doors, and into the hall.

"Wait here." The uniform raised his clipboard and then went into the dining room.

Why was I called out of order? I didn't ask for special treatment. I'd hoped to be lost in the sheer volume of witnesses, another anonymous innocent bystander telling his story.

In the dining room, the police had a few tables set up in opposite corners where Kelso Club members provided information to investigators. It looked innocent but I began to wonder if the undercurrent of their stories featured my name.

The uniform took forever to come back and then led me through the dining room to a private room in the back. A lone detective and a recorder sat near the end of the single long table. The uniform closed the door on his way out.

The detective stood up and reached out a hand. "Detective Tenorio. You're Eddie O'Connell, I take it."

"That's right." I took the chair across from him.

"Quite the circus out there," Tenorio said. "I thought we'd be more comfortable in here."

My antennae shot up. Tenorio had slicked-back, black hair and chewed spearmint gum like a guy who had lots of stuff on his mind. His shirt, sports coat, and pleated pants showed me he was one of the detectives at the top of the food chain.

Tenorio sat down and smiled at me. Arranged his notebook as if he planned to take lots of notes, a pen in his left hand, a pink eraser in his right hand. The eraser was one of those kids use to do their math—about four inches long and half an inch wide with a black smudge on one end.

"I hear you replaced Zany," Tenorio said.

This statement told me where I stood. "Came out from Chicago. It's on that form."

Tenorio made a display of pulling out my information sheet and reading it. "You got a time?"

"Wednesday. Want a flight number?"

Tenorio shook his head and bounced the eraser on the table like a rubber ball. "How do you like Denver?"

At the moment I hated it, but I dug up some of my inane chatter from yesterday. "Hotter than I thought."

"Plan to stay long?"

The detective used the tourist bullshit to make me feel comfortable as if we were old buddies. I'd seen Uncle Mike lead a witness down this path a hundred times.

"No return flight."

Tenorio read from the sheet. "Bartender?"

"Yeah."

Tenorio dropped the eraser on the table and held out the palm of his hand. "Look, it's no secret what Zany did. Most of the guys in town bet through somebody who lays off to Zany's shop. Even guys in the precinct. But don't tell nobody."

I didn't respond. Anything I said could be used against me—another one of my uncle's favorite sayings.

"You know why you got called ahead of others?" Tenorio picked up the eraser again.

"Better looking?"

Tenorio smiled as if he enjoyed himself. "Afraid not. You see, I'm the lucky guy who drew Zany's murder case."

He waited for this to sink in, but I didn't register surprise. I watched the bouncing eraser and didn't make eye contact.

"So," Tenorio hesitated, "I've got to decide if Zany's murder is connected to this Mulholland murder."

Tenorio probably knew full well the murders were related, but for the sake of drama, we both had to pretend we didn't know. Plus, the one who figured it out first could grab the mantle of genius. I decided it might be best to forfeit this one and shrugged.

"We've interviewed a lot of people," Tenorio said. "They tell us you and Mulholland didn't get along."

I knew better than to deny anything a hundred people saw. "We had an argument."

"What about?" The detective glanced down at his notebook, pen ready.

"He owed money."

Tenorio stopped chewing the gum. "I like a guy who lays his cards on the table. I won't ask how he owed you money. Now, where were you at the time Mulholland was killed?"

"Not sure when he was killed," I said.

"Was it after you walked into the john or before?" Tenorio's jaw set in stone.

"Before."

Tenorio turned a page of his notebook with his left hand. "Witnesses said you left the table in the clubhouse."

I tried not to squirm. I didn't have a witness who could account for my whereabouts leading up to the murder. The cops were better coordinated than I'd hoped. I didn't think I'd be in the crosshairs this fast.

"That's right," I said.

"Where did you go?"

"I left with Crystal and Rudi."

Tenorio flipped a page. "That is Crystal Rogers and Paula Rudinger? She goes by 'Rudi,' right?"

"Yeah."

"Why did you leave?"

"Crystal said she saw Rudi's husband."

"What's the husband's name?"

"Warren Potts."

"Good. So, you met with Warren Potts?" Tenorio's fingertips fiddled with the eraser the way a poker player stacks and restacks chips.

"No."

"Why not?"

"We couldn't find him."

"What were you going to talk about?"

What had Crystal told the investigator?

"I don't know."

"Were you going to," Tenorio flipped a page and read: "pound some sense into Warren."

I shrugged. It was never a good idea to admit intent to do bodily harm.

"Were you with Crystal and Rudi the entire time?"

The detective was smart. I couldn't deflect this question.

"No."

"Why not?"

"We split up."

"Is that when you went up and met Mulholland in the john?"

"He was dead already." No one could be expected to know the exact timing of events or faces. Maybe the track security guard or the guys huddled in the john would remember when I entered the john and maybe they wouldn't. If this line of questioning led down the road to my arrest, my investigation would be over. I'd need a lawyer and a bail bondsman. Headlines could intertwine the words "gambling debt" and "murder."

"Did Mulholland pay you what was owed?"

"No."

"Did you argue with Mulholland in the men's room, sir?"

I didn't like this "sir" bullshit. "No."

"You wanted to teach Mulholland a lesson? Things get out of hand?"

"No."

Tenorio turned a few more pages. "You know a Peter Leister?"

This question threw me off balance. Nothing Leister had said would help me.

"Yes. Met him yesterday."

"What do you know about him?"

"His family owns some restaurants."

"Did you argue with him, too?"

"I can't remember." It wasn't an actual argument. No need to admit to specifics. A lawyer at this point would protect my rights, but it could mean the end of the investigation.

"Did Mulholland give you a tip?"

Fuck that race. "I didn't bet."

Tenorio laughed. "Too bad. Lots of folks say they made money. How did you feel about Zany's murder?"

"I don't know."

"When did you meet Zany?"

"About fifteen years ago."

Tenorio stopped with the gum. "Where?"

"In Chicago. He was a jockey."

"Since then. When was the last time you met Zany?"

"That was the only time."

"Yet you took over his store?"

I shrugged. I wanted to grab Tenorio's eraser and throw it.

"You know how Zany was killed?"

"The newspaper said he fell off a stadium."

Tenorio looked down at the eraser in his hand. "Zany's pants were unzipped. There were cuts on the body, cigarette burns. A testicle lopped off. You should've seen the body. A drop from that height sure makes a mess. Found pieces of his brain across the street."

I shrugged again.

I felt sick for Zany. I had to extricate myself from this interrogation and find Zany's killer. Violence spawned more violence. Killers didn't have the patience to wait and didn't like to be ignored. The killer had brought a weapon to the track in anticipation of killing Mulholland despite the crowd. Although he couldn't execute the murder the way he'd done with Zany, he was satisfied with a quick kill. It meant the killer either grew bolder or more desperate.

From the police report on Zany's murder, Tenorio didn't have much. He didn't even have the name of the woman Zany took into the vacant concession stand.

"No response?" Tenorio held his pen to the paper. "If I were you, if I were filling in for Zany, I'd be worried." Tenorio snapped his gum. "Well?"

"Is that a question?"

Tenorio slapped the palm of his right hand flat on the desk. "Look, if I don't get to the bottom of this fast, nobody's going to be taking any action—you or Leister."

"What about your precinct guys? They can play pinochle?"

"You're this far." Tenorio began to stand and held out his thumb and forefinger an inch apart. "This far mister, from getting your ass hauled downtown and booked for murder."

"Fine. But when those security cameras pick up my ugly face wandering around the grandstand betting lines when Mulholland was killed, you'll need to release me. I didn't do it. Forensics will prove it."

"You can't bluff me." Tenorio stood up and moved to the door.

"Wait." I stood in Uncle Mike's shoes. What would he do to win this cop over? I had to take the chance.

"What? What have you got?"

"I got the name of the woman Zany was with."

23

I COULD'VE TAKEN THE 16TH STREET SHUTTLE BUS FROM LoDo toward Broadway to meet with Mags, but I needed to blow off steam. The walk down the 16th street mall helped. Bars and restaurants with their happy-hour crowds on full tilt. At each crosswalk, the homeless mixed with the corporate movers and shakers waiting for the light to change.

The hot westerly wind drove the forest fire smoke down the alleys and side streets at my back. I was a snitch. Giving out Amity's name to the police went against everything I stood for.

Uncle Mike would "trade" information with a homicide detective, and it was a smart move. Now that I tried the same thing, I got this queasy feeling in the pit of my stomach. Maybe I'd given out too much information with not enough in return. Or, maybe I wasn't able to trust a cop the way my uncle could.

Mags might not know I'd given Amity's name to the detective. But he had contacts on the force and would find out sooner or later. Should I tell him? I'd told him to call the police when we found Amity's body. But the Denver mobster was more concerned with the store's revenue than solving Zany's murder.

What could Tenorio learn from a dead woman, anyway? He'd probably never find a body or body parts, or learn that she'd been murdered. I'd given the detective a dead end. The same dead-end that stared back at me, but at least I could get to places and suspects Tenorio could never hope to access. Evidence of Uncle Mike's magic.

And what would Tenorio do then? He wasn't done with me by a long shot. I made too good a suspect—too many coincidences.

Of course, Amity was only one of my worries. What had Mags discussed with Burrascano? I'd been on thin ice before, but now where did I stand?

Down a dismal side street lined with strip joints and bars, I stopped outside a bail bonds office. Maybe I should grab a brochure.

The Night Court restaurant sat at the end of the street, a forgotten spot tucked between the restaurant scene on Larimer Square and the Convention Center. Rudi told me Mags had a financial interest in the place.

The parking lot was almost empty. Inside, the cold air conditioning and darkness felt like a tomb. As my eyes adjusted, an inviting dark wood bar with a fancy round mirror behind rows of bottles came into focus. A large room of white tablecloths and the smell of steaks and one lone table of four tucked in a corner.

The bartender smoked a cigarette and read the paper. He didn't look up as the hostess led me past. A few waiters stood by the kitchen entrance, but no sign of Mags's old soldier.

The hostess led me down a short hallway behind the bar. Mags sat alone in a small room at a round table. His starched white shirt and thin black tie reminded me again of an insurance salesman. The sour expression told me to forget about ordering the ribeye.

He pointed to a chair.

A baseball game on the overhead television. At one end of the room, a portable bar and a half-open door behind it. On the table a martini beside the Wall Street Journal and a lighted cigarette in the ashtray.

"I heard this ambulance chaser got whacked," Mags said. "I didn't approve it."

"What the fuck, I didn't do it. I tried to collect his gambling debt—that's all."

Mags shook his head as if he might be disappointed in me and sucked on the cigarette. "Everyone thinks you did."

"Who's everyone?" I stared at the ice crystals afloat in the martini glass and imagined the first cold sip. Followed by a long, deep drag on a cigarette.

"Doesn't matter. It's just as bad. I got business interests, Eddie. I put you in charge. I've got others who aren't as forgiving as me."

Forgiving? When did he cut me any slack? I knew it would be about money, Burrascano, and everyone else. Never mind my possible murder charges.

"The detective questioned me. You think I'd be walking around—"

"Never mind." He swatted the air with his hand.

My big speech all prepared and he didn't even want to hear it. All about how I'd finessed this difficult spot I was in with Tenorio. But the speech was more for my benefit than Mags. He didn't give a shit. What did he care if Tenorio was busy interviewing witnesses and digging up evidence to build a case against me?

"Tell me about the Kelso Club customers," he said through a cloud of smoke.

I inhaled the secondhand smoke. "They don't like Leister; they don't like change."

He jumped out of his chair. "Fuck this. C'mon Eddie, what does it take? Did you tell Leister to fuck off? You rough him up?"

I leaned forward. "Hell no. A war won't help us solve this."

"You're supposed to look after the operation. Christ. Why does Burrascano send some kid? What *have* you done?"

"Followed through on the plan. Done some collections. Kept the subs in line." I needed to make him understand the murders of Mulholland, Amity, and Zany were related. That the killer was growing bolder. "Mulholland's murder shows—"

"Fuck collections. Who refuses to pay when guys get killed?" He stamped out the butt and pulled out another in one motion, and lit it. "It's Leister I'm concerned about—stealing business."

"Leister isn't the one. Why would Leister kill Mulholland? They were asshole buddies."

He whipped off his glasses to reveal a killer's dark eyes. "Football season is almost here. I'm getting pressure. I've got a dead lawyer. Headlines. I look like a damn fool." His voice rose with his temper. "My ass is hanging out."

My voice rose as well. "I need time. My uncle and I—"

"Your uncle—your uncle isn't here. That's the problem. Maybe you need some help."

"What I need is no interference."

"What interference?" His voice rose another notch.

The door to the back room crept open a few more inches. The crew ready to handle me? I talked fast. "I told you to report the murder of Zany's woman to the cops."

"You? You give me orders? I ran things when you were in diapers."

"What about Zany's house?"

"What about it? I don't have Zany's cash," he said.

"I'm not talking about the cash."

"Then what?"

"I had to run when the house blew up."

Mags grunted. "Too fucking bad. Maybe it was your buddy, Leister. Why are you asking me?"

I almost said how I suspected him or one of his men. Information about my midnight visit might've seeped back through Joey L. But I needed solid facts for such an accusation, and then I'd have to go over his head to Burrascano.

He took a sip of his martini and looked up at the television. I waited out the silence.

He picked the cigarette out of the ashtray and took a deep drag then spoke as he exhaled. "I talked to Burrascano. He's not happy."

I didn't want to hear Burrascano's name. These guys talked behind closed doors and decisions weren't open to debate. At least Uncle Mike could give Burrascano my story. "We report to him too," I said.

"I hope it's more than what you've told me."

"Burrascano doesn't second-guess." I could only hope. I'd never been on a job that went south.

He tapped an ash off the tip of the cigarette as if to punctuate my status. "Results are all that matter."

It seemed some decision had been made and there was nothing I could do to change it. *Fuck it.* "If that's it, I've got to go."

He looked at me through murky lenses. His thin lips smirked. "You're in over your head, Eddie. Wake up. Bookies don't fall from the sky."

An image of Zany in mid-air as he dropped from the top railing of the stadium flashed in my head. I was up against it, but I didn't know it was this bad. I walked out.

I had to act and fast.

24

Frantic was the best word to describe my mood. After Mags's pep talk and with Detective Tenorio on my tail, my days were numbered.

Not the best of circumstances to venture out in the middle of the night. Too much adrenaline and not enough fear, enough patience. But I had to take my chances.

The Crown Vic rumbled down the vacant city streets. I kept watch for a tail, one of Detective Tenorio's flunkies or Mags's old soldier.

No sign of any vehicles. Mags must've cut me loose after our talk. I could only guess what he'd cooked up. I knew Tenorio had me in his sights.

Side streets brought me from LoDo to Speer Boulevard toward Cherry Creek. On previous jobs, I'd bounce things off Uncle Mike or he'd try ideas on me. This solo gig had pitfalls I never suspected.

Sure, I could've called Uncle Mike more often. Talked things through and got his take. But this was my job.

What would my uncle say about tonight's venture? My big idea involved a break-in of Mulholland's law office. The cool night breeze blew through the open car window, but I started to sweat. Tenorio could add breaking and entering to the murder charges.

The detective would theorize that I searched for cash inside Mulholland's law office to repay that gambling debt. Obvious I'd go to any lengths to get paid—murder, break-in, Porsche malfeasance.

The adrenaline made me grasp for quick answers, but I tried to remain objective. I started from the assumption that Zany and Mulholland were murdered by the same killer. Both were killed at Kelso Club events. One way to find Zany's killer would be to find clues to Mulholland's murder.

Those clues might lie on Mulholland's desk. I'd spent time in lawyers' offices and it was never pretty. Notes and files everywhere.

A loop around Mulholland's office building revealed no sign of any police car, no cleaning crew or other vehicles. A dead quiet Sunday night at two a.m. and a perfect time to monitor the neighborhood. Ten minutes passed and only a few cars.

I decided to walk up to the front door like a guy who might have business inside and had lost his keys. No building security guard on duty. The door was locked.

Mulholland's website had said suite 310. A walk around toward the parking garage showed no lights in any of the outside offices for the third floor. On other jobs, I'd have Uncle Mike as a lookout. A call from him on the cell would give me the time I needed if there was trouble. But tonight, I'd risk it without a net.

I could've recruited Rudi. She'd probably agree but I couldn't drag her into something like this. I'd rather do jail time than have her face charges because of me.

Inside the attached two-story parking garage, I planned my next step. If I went ahead with this, I had to get the thought of "charges" out of my head. Fear was productive, but paranoia wouldn't help. My footsteps echoed through the concrete walls of the parking garage. Too bad Denver was such a solemn place this time of night. The drumbeat of traffic would've helped.

I checked for cameras and security, found an ancient one, and disabled it. Then I jimmied the lock on the door into the office building, stepped through the brightly lit lobby into the stairwell, and waited.

The police shouldn't rule out the possibility that Mulholland was murdered by a client and that client might try to steal their file. I asked myself if Tenorio was smart enough to post a cop inside Mulholland's office. With no hint of a police presence outside—no squad car, no lights—I didn't think he had. The cops didn't have unlimited budgets and it wasn't a crime scene. People thought all cops were brilliant like on TV. Uncle Mike had taught me that wasn't the case. Tenorio was too busy grandstanding at the Kelso Club to worry about the attorney's office. I walked up the stairs to Mulholland's suite.

I listened outside the office door then jimmied open the lock and waited. The lawyers I knew didn't incur the extra cost of a security system. But I listened for an alarm.

Nothing. I waited, prepared to run. My uncle's instructions came back to me. I couldn't assume anything. Fear was good. Thanks, Uncle Mike, thanks a lot.

I thought through my measured steps when I broke into Zany's house. Those bits of extra time had served me well. I'd heard those footsteps outside on the river rock only because I'd remained on full alert. Because of it, my teeth didn't end up at the bottom of the lake.

I stepped inside the office and closed the door and waited in the dark office lobby. This was the point of no return. If a patient cop had been posted by Tenorio, this was the moment I'd make easy prey. I used my penlight to check for security cameras and found none.

Street light seeped through the outer offices into the hallway and paralegal stations. My eyes grew accustomed to the dark. No sounds. I was in luck. I put on my gloves.

The desks were littered with files, loose paper, coffee cups, and bowls of snacks. As I moved down the hall, I grabbed a small Baby Ruth candy bar. I'd forgotten about my hunger.

The nameplate outside the corner office read: Michael Mulholland. Unlike the other outer offices, the door was locked. I went to work on the lock but no luck after a couple of tries. I took a deep breath, stepped back a second, and tried to envision the lock. Patience and a clear head were required.

I tried a lighter touch. This time I was able to manipulate the pins. The knob turned. I went in and closed the door.

I swept the area with my pen light and made my way to the windows. I stuck my finger in one slat of the blinds and checked. I had to think in terms of a silent alarm or some witness I didn't see. A car eased down the street out front and my heart stopped. It was a patrol car.

I watched to see if he'd stop. Their procedure in response to an alarm required them to park nearby and then approach on foot. Instead, he drove off.

Maybe I was in the clear or maybe he'd circle back. My mind raced.

A half-filled coffee cup sat in front of the desk computer with the name "Mike." Evaporation rings and some floating mold told me it had been left one or two days ago. Untouched correspondence filled the "In" and "Out" baskets. A clip around some envelopes and a note that said: "Friday's mail" was left on the seat of the high-backed leather chair. It was evidence that the office had been preserved the way Zany's had.

Files were stacked everywhere, in corners, windowsills, the stuffed leather couch, the credenza, and on every square inch of the desk. A high-class lawyer would take extra minutes out of every billable day to keep a clean desk. Of course, high-class lawyers didn't owe gambling debts.

Tenorio would need to jump over hurdles to get a crack at these files. He'd get bogged down with attorney-client privilege and the need for a court order. Too bad.

Mulholland's diplomas were stacked against one wall. On the credenza a few awards, family photos, and a picture of the Porsche—the start of my troubles. Any ill will I harbored toward Mulholland began to dissipate. I'd seen the body. Like Zany, another victim. I channeled my anger toward the killer.

I didn't know where to start. I took a bite of the candy bar and got down on my hands and knees and examined each pile. One stack close to the desk was the same blue color and each file number had the prefix "Kel." I glanced at some of the names and recognized members of the Kelso Club. Did Mulholland examine these files in preparation for the event at Aurora Downs? He probably had to talk with clients about their files and update them.

The first file concerned Jim Arnold. Mulholland's scrawl on sheets torn from a legal pad contained a list of credit card debts and the amounts. The gambling debt to the store was not included. The credit card debts totaled nearly one hundred and fifty grand and Mulholland had scribbled notes on the possibility of a bankruptcy filing. I could guess what a bankruptcy filing would mean to Arnold's future in banking.

I raced back to the office window and lifted the slat and checked again for a patrol car. Nothing. No cop approaching on foot.

Several thin files in the stack involved Kelso Club business contracts with vendors for the Allegro Martin Charity Golf Tournament. A file on Preston contained a letter from a "Winston Williston" and referenced a trust. "Dear Useless Loser," it began. I wanted to read more but set it aside to study later. I picked up another file from the stack like a law clerk junky.

The entire Kelso Club membership seemed to be represented in this stack. A thick file was devoted to Crystal's divorce proceedings. I tried not to drop it on my toe; it was the size of two phone books. I skipped it because I had a similar one at home generated by my ex.

A file on Crystal's son, Zach, involved a hearing with school officials about grades. The kid had probably spent too much time in the gym and forgot about the classroom.

Rudi's divorce file. It was painfully thin.

A tiny piece of a peanut from the Baby Ruth candy bar had gotten lodged in the back of my throat. I must've eaten too fast. I couldn't cough or clear my throat with much force without making noise. I tried to swallow hard and ignore the irritation.

A group of files involved Allegro: a number of current collection suits by credit card companies, a dispute with a company that had bought rights to his summer camp, a recent DUI charge, and several women who claimed Allegro had fathered their child and threatened to go public.

It seemed that Allegro's tidy portfolio from his playing days had been squandered long ago, but these women still hoped to cash in. Mulholland had sent each of the women scathing letters of denial and demanded paternity tests. I had to give Mulholland credit—his letters would make me think twice about whether to proceed, but I felt sorry for the women.

I turned to Mulholland's desk and rifled through the mess. How must Mulholland have felt each day as he faced all these legal problems? I recalled how he dodged Rudi's calls. No wonder he escaped to play the horses.

I almost coughed on reflex. The damn peanut wouldn't slide down no matter how hard I swallowed. I stood up and leaned over. Tried to clear my throat in silence. If I could find a drink of water, it would help. I didn't want to go back into the inner office. I could drink some of the slime in Mulholland's coffee cup but the thought of it turned my stomach.

A door slammed somewhere in the building. In the dead of night, a sound could echo. It could be down on the first floor. It could be a cop or it could be another tenant.

I got up and peeked through the blinds. Nothing. A bead of sweat dripped down inside my shirt.

I went back to work. I found a file on Leister. The Feds had an ongoing investigation and supposedly one of Leister's massage parlor managers had supplied information. Leister wanted the rat's name. It made my night to know Leister had problems.

Beside Mulholland's computer in the fresh legal spillage, I found a report marked "Confidential." This could be the item I'd hoped to find.

I read the report greedily. It was an extensive investigation by a private agency on one "Edward O'Connell." Great. The louse had investigated me. I almost choked again on that damn peanut. I stood up and walked around and picked up the framed photo of the Porsche and thought about throwing it against a wall then set it back down on the desk.

I could see Tenorio's smile if he found this report. The murder victim, Mulholland, had investigated the suspect, me. Why? Because Mulholland had felt so threatened by Mr. O'Connell.

Shit.

I sat back in the dead lawyer's chair and read about myself and my uncle.

> "Subject is the nephew of Michael O'Connell, owner of O'Connell's Tavern located on the near north side of Chicago. This well-established neighborhood bar is a local meeting place for union organizers, newspapermen, political insiders, and the local criminal element.
>
> "Michael O'Connell is a former homicide detective for the Chicago Police Department. He was suspended after an internal investigation that has not been released to the public and was not available to this investigator."

How had Uncle Mike pulled that one off? Pension intact. It was how Chicago worked. I glanced at the rest of the report. It detailed my arrest record. I didn't have time to go through it in detail and set it to the side to take with me. What Tenorio didn't find wouldn't hurt him.

I laughed to myself and almost coughed. Without thinking, I picked up the cup and sipped the rancid brew. I almost puked as the sludge crept down my throat but at least the peanut had cleared.

I grabbed some loose papers from the desk and tossed them onto the empty spot to cover up my theft. As I did, I saw a draft letter to Preston.

I read it over twice. Mulholland apologized to Preston about some matter that had not gone as expected. Then Mulholland spent some time blaming everything and everybody for their lack of cooperation. I could tell he was more concerned with covering his ass than anything else, but what was this "legal matter" he referred to?

The letter went on to say how disappointed Mulholland had been to receive Preston's phone call. I concluded that Preston must've fired Mulholland. This letter was an attempt to smooth things over and win Preston back. Mulholland highlighted all his many years of priority service.

The last paragraph of the letter had been crossed off but it caught my interest:

> "You must agree your phone call was highly emotional. Perhaps you were not thinking rationally. You mentioned the medication you'd been taking and I must submit for your consideration the possibility you may have neglected to take it that day. You crazy fucker."

This letter could be the smoking gun my investigation needed. Each killing had been charged with emotion. I'd found a dispute between the murder victim and a client with emotional trouble. Perfect.

Should I have suspected Preston earlier? But then I recalled Uncle Mike's warning to remain patient—don't jump the gun when you've got some success and don't get too down when you find yourself up another blind alley.

I set the letter to the side in my theft pile. Maybe the legal secretary would mention the draft to Tenorio and maybe it would be forgotten in the confusion of Mulholland's murder.

Again, I heard a door slam somewhere in the building. I stopped and listened.

I needed more time. I needed to know the exact nature of this "legal matter." Maybe something dealing with Preston's trust? Maybe the money supply was about to be cut off.

But I was on borrowed time. I took the stuff I set aside. As I ran out, I tried to come up with a story I'd tell if a cop waited downstairs.

25

MONDAY

The next afternoon, I sat at Zany's desk with the door closed and reviewed the documents I'd taken from Mulholland's office the night before. I dug into the report marked "Confidential" from Mulholland's hired investigator who had investigated me.

The investigator's report described my altercation one summer night a couple of years ago. I'd gotten into a fight with a former third string linebacker for the Chicago Bears who'd been riding me because of some woman. People had warned the linebacker to back off, but he didn't, and he'd gotten the worst of it. A portion of the police report was attached:

"A crowd had formed outside the tavern, which officers were forced to disperse. Unclear how the fight started. No witnesses offered a statement. Victim, a former Chicago Bear, was taken to emergency. Medical reports included severe concussion, broken ribs, broken jaw, fracture of orbital cavity."

I stood up and paced around the desk. Somebody told me later what had happened. The whole fight was a blur. As usual, we'd stepped out back into the alley to settle things. The linebacker had slugged me in the back of the head as we walked out.

I'd simply lost control. I remembered the sirens and the lights. The crowd. The police fighting with the crowd. Somebody had to be charged with something and, since I was the one still standing, I was their guy.

If I lost control once, could I lose control again? A question Detective Tenorio would ask.

The criminal justice system hadn't given me an automatic pass on the battery charge even with Uncle Mike's connections. There wasn't just talk about the possibility of jail time but how much jail time I would receive. I didn't understand how I could do time when the other guy asked for it. The lawyer explained it to me over and over but to this day I still don't get it. Something about my training as a boxer.

I stepped around Zany's antique desk and glanced up at the sidewalk level window. The shadow of someone's legs walking past danced behind the faded curtains.

When someone gets seriously hurt, somebody has to pay. The judge had looked down on me as if I'd crawled out of the gutter. At the last minute before trial, my lawyer and the DA came to a plea bargain, so I got off with probation and ultimate dismissal if I kept out of trouble for a year. One minute I stared at prison time and the next minute I was free.

The whole point had been to instill fear. Even now, years later, the thought of this case made me want to hop into my car and drive to parts unknown, run from this office, run from the investigation, and keep running. That's how far the fear had crept down inside me.

This was a useless fear. Not the kind of fear I cultivated to safeguard me on late-night errands, but the kind of fear that could drop a net over me and drag me off without warning, without reason. I thought about my aunt and uncle and what it would mean for them if Tenorio dropped his net over me for Mulholland's murder.

I shelved my old criminal proceeding, sat back down at the desk, and moved on to the Mulholland letters involving Preston Williston. In addition to the draft letter from Mulholland to Preston that described Preston as a "crazy fucker," there was a letter from Preston's brother and trustee, Winston Williston, to Preston. It began: "Dear Useless Loser," and stated in detail how Preston had become an embarrassment to the family's good name, and that he should return home and take his place on the board of the charitable foundation to contribute his time to its good works.

If he didn't, Winston Williston warned, Preston would face court proceedings to cut him off permanently as a beneficiary of the trust. I sat back and read this letter over a couple times and imagined Preston's reaction when he read it. His face had probably turned the same shade of red that it had Saturday at the track when I'd told the members that there were certain things we shouldn't talk about in public. I assumed

Mulholland had been hired by Preston to respond to the letter and threaten the brother with counterclaims.

My cell buzzed. It was Uncle Mike.

"Eddie, have you got a minute?" Uncle Mike said. I didn't like the tone of his voice.

"Sure."

"I talked with Joey L. He talked with Burrascano."

"Yeah?" I bit my bottom lip.

"They don't like the fact you gave out the woman's name to the detective. Saying anything about anyone makes them nervous as hell. We don't know this detective."

I was caught between two vicious worlds—Tenorio's net and Burrascano's lifelong oath of silence. Did I let Detective Tenorio bluff me? No, I gave him meaningless information. He couldn't question a dead woman.

Before I could respond, Uncle Mike cleared his raspy throat. "Don't worry. No one is talking about pulling you off the job—yet." He exhaled into the receiver and I could almost smell the cigar smoke. "I want you to watch your back. Joey L doesn't know Mags all that well. He might do anything."

"No problem." Relief swept over me. I'd been given a reprieve, but how much time did I really have? There was worry in Uncle Mike's voice. How much goodwill had he been forced to use with Burrascano to keep me on the job?

"Watch your temper for one thing."

Uncle Mike knew me too well. It must be eating him up inside to sit at home on the sidelines unable to question witnesses face-to-face. "I'll watch it."

"Good. Let me tell you what I found out today. Maybe it will help."

I sat back and tried to focus. Joey L had warned Uncle Mike about Mags. What would the local mob boss do? My meeting with him last night had not gone well. I pushed it to one side and listened to my uncle.

Uncle Mike had talked with the sheriff back in Rudi's hometown. Her estranged and deranged husband, Warren, had not only committed petty crimes passing bad checks and stealing from his Nebraska employer, he'd gotten involved with a drug ring. Meth was the drug of choice. He hadn't been charged but there were some recent murders, and he was under suspicion. The sheriff had been glad when Warren left the town and the state.

I told my uncle that Warren knew about Zany's bookmaking operation and had worked briefly for the ex-jockey. The other question on my mind was why Rudi didn't tell me about Warren's extracurricular activity in the drug trade. Or did she even know?

My uncle didn't have an address on Warren, but he was working with some repo guys who'd financed Warren's Jeep. The loan was in default and he expected to hear something at any time.

The cigar lighter clicked and my uncle exhaled again into the phone. "My accountant has been working overtime for you."

Uncle Mike read me pieces of the report and then summarized it. His accountant contact, a fellow named Irv, had pieced together a series of large payouts last winter by Zany's store to Preston and Mulholland. It could've been on football or basketball or both or maybe something else, the accountant was still digging. This information fit nicely with the letter I'd found last night at Mulholland's office and the bickering between Preston and Mulholland as evidenced by the "crazy fucker" reference. I told my uncle about my late-night escapade to the lawyer's office and the attorney's draft letter.

"Damn." Uncle Mike chuckled. "Nice work. Seems you've got your arms wrapped around this investigation."

I chuckled with him, but my chuckle had a sarcastic edge. I wasn't sure what I had my arms wrapped around. "So, if Preston and Mulholland worked together and then got into an argument that included Zany, it could lead to murder. I'll follow up with Preston." I wondered how the "unsuccessful legal matter" mentioned in Mulholland's letter related to these oversized payouts by Zany, and then I wondered how I'd get into the Kelso Club to question Preston. Yesterday, the Kelso Club members had stared daggers at me.

Uncle Mike agreed that Preston seemed like a good lead. He told me he'd get back to me as soon as he heard more from the accountant or about Warren and hung up.

Maybe Rudi would know something about the oversized payments by Zany to Mulholland and Preston last winter. Then again, it might not be something Zany had shared with Rudi. Sports bettors did win, and despite my experience, a sports bettor could go on an extended winning streak. For the bookie, such payouts were nothing more than business as usual and could pay off in handsome dividends if the bookie kept their cool. A bettor who won would tell others and everyone would want to know the name of the bookie and how they could join up as if a certain bookie might be the difference between winning and losing. One friend would tell another who would tell another. The bookie would get paid back multiple times on what he'd paid out to the winning player in the form of new business. A few weeks later, the winner would most likely lose back all his winnings and the patient bookie would make out on both ends.

Rudi was in the process of interviewing new employee recruits for the onslaught of football season, so when she had a moment, I'd ask her to come into my office.

Rudi stood beside my desk and placed several pages on my desk. "Here are the resumes for several promising employees to take a look at."

It would increase the staff from seven to thirteen. Most bettors placed bets on the offshore website, but Zany's store still had bettors who liked to call in. We also needed staff for collections, distributions to subs like Koransky, and setting up new customers brought in by our agents. Being number one in Denver and parts of the front range meant a commitment to resources during football season. I skimmed over the resumes.

"You'll check the references?"

"Absolutely."

Despite Mags's protection money, an informer might try to slip into the store.

"I didn't have the chance to thank you for yesterday at the track," Rudi said. "You went after my crazy ex-husband, and now you're in trouble."

"Trouble? What did you hear?"

"Crystal told me about Detective Tenorio. Of course, Preston has gone off the rails again and wants you banned. Warren caused this mess. If you wouldn't have been trying to find Warren at the track, you would've had an alibi."

"I'll deal with Preston. Don't worry. Uncle Mike and his accountant took a look at Zany's accounting records. Do you know anything about large payouts to Preston and Mulholland last winter?"

Rudi brushed back her auburn hair, looked away lost in thought, and then shrugged. "No, can't think of any payments. Zany didn't always share everything."

"That's the kind of business we're in. Bookmakers like to keep secrets."

"Every football season has its tense times, but this year is something else. Sometimes I think I'm on the verge of a nervous breakdown."

"I'm on the verge of one myself."

She edged closer. "I thought you always stayed in control."

"I try." She wore those white shorts.

Rudi placed her hand on top of mine. "The way you talk about your ex I'd think you'd sworn off women."

"No, I like them fine. I just don't like them in court." I could smell her perfume.

"So, you're seeing someone back in Chicago?" She leaned back against the desk and crossed her bare legs at the ankles.

"No. Who said that?"

"You didn't say that?" she said.

I spotted her sly smile. "No, I didn't." I stood and took her in my arms. "I thought you liked short men."

She tilted her lips up toward me. "Not always. With taller men, I can wear my high heels."

I would've laughed, but I was focused on her lips and her body against me. I leaned down and kissed her, a long languid kiss with tongues probing. My hands tight around her waist and hers around my neck. This one followed by another.

I ran my hands down her back. "Why don't we . . ."

She caught her breath. "We'll have to wait. I've got lots to do."

"Like what?"

The receptionist buzzed me and told me I had a visitor.

My heart skipped a beat. No one had paid me a personal visit since I'd arrived.

"Who is it?"

The receptionist lowered her voice to a whisper. I imagined her cupping one hand over the receiver. "He says his name is Vic. Says you know him?"

"Yes, I know him."

"Who?" Rudi asked.

I covered the receiver so the receptionist wouldn't hear me. "Sorry, Rudi. I'll have to meet with the guy. The less you know about him, the better." I took my hand away. "Tell him I'll be right up," I told the receptionist.

"I hope it's not another problem," Rudi said.

"More like a catastrophe."

26

Vic DiNatale had just "dropped" by the store to visit me? Right. I walked up to the front of the office.

Uncle Mike had told me to watch my back and here on my doorstep sat the result.

DiNatale had become the mob's top relief pitcher when the game got out of control. He threw nothing but heat. His reputation included a string of murders. When informants turned up missing or when a Russian refused to play ball, DiNatale could be found on the fringes. It had gotten to the point where his mere presence on the scene had a way of resolving "differences."

It irked DiNatale no end that Uncle Mike and I continued to play a role solving murders for Burrascano. In his opinion, outsiders shouldn't be necessary to solve mob problems. End of story.

With his massive frame, Vic DiNatale took up most of the cramped, six by six foot reception area. The shine of his curly black hair and strong cologne complemented his "fuck you" smirk. Dressed in a perfectly tailored dark blue suit, his feet shuffling and shoulders swaying, he was the image of a man in control of his surroundings and in tune to a certain unpredictable rhythm.

"Eddie, Eddie O'Connell, good to see you." His husky garbled speech was difficult to decipher at first. Uncle Mike said it had been due to a broken windpipe. DiNatale reached out his hand.

I shook it. "Hello, Vic." The walk up through the office had helped. I kept my anger in check.

"Nice of Mags to invite me out. I can use a vacation."

So, it was Mags. He wasn't going to wait around to see if Eddie O'Connell could solve his first solo case. No, he was going to call in reinforcements to ensure things went his way. The invite must've been approved behind the scenes.

"I thought you had a place in Florida like the other guys."

He glanced around and winked at the receptionist. "Too damn hot in the summer."

"It's hot here, too."

"Not like Florida. It's dry heat out here. I kind of like it. You going to show me around? I want to see if the place can handle all the action."

"Sure." Play the game, I reminded myself. Don't let DiNatale cause you to lose your cool.

I led him into the office, past the row of workstations. Employees studied us; their faces contorted into a look of astonishment. Without Zany to offer protection, maybe they felt vulnerable.

Their faces told a story. They could guess who he was. Who else shows up at a bookie's store unannounced on a Monday other than a guy from the mob? He didn't need a name tag, his stock in trade was clear to anyone.

DiNatale stopped and made small talk which only seemed to add to the tension. He told them how he was an old friend of Zany, and how much he hated to hear what had happened.

"The guy had friends all over town," DiNatale lectured them. "Good friends back in Chicago, the Midwest, and all over the Rocky Mountain region. I'm going to look into it, don't worry." He pinpointed one of the staff, a lady who, Rudi had informed me, had worked for Zany since the beginning. "How long you been working here? You like it? Not easy work dealing with numbers. Takes a person with smarts upstairs, know what I mean?" The poor lady could only smile and nod, trembling slightly.

I herded DiNatale into Zany's office and shut the door. Rudi's door was closed.

"Hey, nice digs." DiNatale roamed around in Zany's office and studied the numerous framed winning circle photos of Zany seated upon a victorious mount, each with its crowd of co-owners, trainers, and grooms smiling in unison.

When I slipped past DiNatale and sat down in Zany's old chair, the mobster winced. Maybe DiNatale thought I'd offer it to him.

"This place is a cash cow." DiNatale drifted over to Zany's trophy case. "No wonder Leister wants to get his hands on it. This place has class. More than I usually see."

I squelched the impulse to ask what other stores he'd visited in the past and what he was doing here. He'd tell me soon enough. Let him dance around and inspect the place and act like a bigshot.

"Glad you could make time to stop by during your vacation. There's good fishing in the mountains."

"Right, fishing. I always wanted to try and test my luck. But before I do, I thought I'd do some fishing of a different kind." His voice deepened and his expression changed as he directed all his attention to me. "Like fishing for Zany's killer. Zany was protected, and they knew it."

I tightened the lid on my anger. "That's my job."

"They cut Zany's balls off or tried to. Guys are pissed. No more bullshit."

"What bullshit? I have to handle it my way. Like any other investigation—"

"Your uncle isn't here. You need help. Lots of help. Bodies are piling up."

"It means I'm getting closer. The killer is feeling the heat. Mags won't listen—"

"He won't listen because he doesn't need to." DiNatale moved closer and placed both hands on the edge of the antique desk. "Nobody does. We all see what Leister is doing. The fucker is taking our best customers from under your nose."

DiNatale didn't give a shit about who killed Zany. It was all about the money. He was trying to provoke me, force me to take a swing, a swing at a made man, and sign my death warrant in the process. I might have a temper, but I wasn't a complete idiot. DiNatale's other objective became clear as well. He wanted to start a war with Leister.

If war with Leister broke out, Tenorio would shut down all the action. Then Tenorio would come after me for the Mulholland murder. How could anyone expect me to operate with DiNatale breathing down my neck?

I was about to get up and kick DiNatale out of the office and get Uncle Mike on the phone when I caught sight of Zany's smile in one of those winning circle photographs. I didn't know the name of the horse or the racetrack where the photo was taken, but Zany's smile hit me.

It was as if Zany was smiling up at me as I handed him a beer during that summer long ago when he was temporarily disabled and giving me tips on playing the horses. One of his tips came rushing back to me at the moment. He'd always talked about "heart." How it was more important for a horse than anything else.

Zany had this authentic smile despite the hard life he led. So what if the pictured race he'd won wasn't the Kentucky Derby? Zany loved the sport. He had heart. The investigation wasn't about me or about DiNatale and his hatred of outsiders, the investigation was all about Zany, the guy smiling at me out of this old photograph.

What the fuck? The last thing I wanted was to give in to DiNatale. Maybe he hated me and Uncle Mike, but we hated DiNatale right back. Zany's sage advice slapped me across the face.

"Shut up for a goddamn minute, Vic." I stood up behind the desk and faced him. "You want in? You can either do what

I tell you or you'll fuck up the whole thing. You want that? You want the killer to get off and make a fool out of you? If not, then listen."

DiNatale's eyebrows came together in a scowl and his jaw worked hard. He took a deep breath and his shoulders rolled as if he might reach for that gun in his shoulder holster. "What the fuck you saying?"

"I'm saying we can work together." I wasn't sure if these were my words that came out of my mouth or if they were Zany's words. Handicapping tips twisted up in the back of my mind in such a convoluted knot I couldn't think straight. Zany used to say that sometimes horses find a soft spot they never expected and they run the race of their life and the horse player is left dumbfounded. Don't try to figure it out, he'd say, you'll drive yourself fucking nuts. It was that kind of moment.

"Yeah?" DiNatale cocked his head to one side and studied me as if I was pulling a trick on him.

I nodded. Better to not explain. Maybe Zany didn't have any more words for me. Plus, I sensed a strange shift in the balance of power—not between me and DiNatale, but between me and the investigation—as if the investigation had grown a personality of its own. I began to see things in a new light. I *could* use DiNatale to my advantage. It wasn't some hasty spontaneous decision but something of sheer genius.

"Fuck, Eddie. You're kidding, right?"

I shook my head. "I've got an idea. We can make this work."

27

I MUST'VE BEEN OUT OF MY MIND TO BRING DiNATALE INTO my investigation. But that's what you do when you investigate for the mob. Take one risk after the next until you've built yourself a lopsided house of cards. Risk piled on top of risk.

Our first order of business was to take a trip to the Kelso Club. It was where all of Zany's heavy hitters played, the customers Leister was after. I thought DiNatale might try to give me one of his bro-hugs. His demeanor flipped one-hundred-and-eighty degrees in an instant. I rocketed from an adversary to his best friend. He insisted we take his limo the four blocks from the store to the Kelso Club.

"I don't go nowhere without my guys. You'll learn."

Outside, DiNatale raised one arm and a long black limo raced up to the curb. A Neanderthal in the passenger seat who I could only describe as "muscle," jumped out, tucked one hand into his coat as if prepared to pull a gun, and took up a strategic position at the intersection of the alleyway and parking garage exit. The driver walked fast around the back end of the vehicle and opened the door for us.

"See, Eddie. Why walk when you can go in style?" DiNatale waited for me to duck inside then I heard him growl directions to the driver before he crawled in behind me.

We waited in a short line of cars outside the Kelso Club. I didn't expect this. On a Monday afternoon when most horse tracks were closed around the country, I expected a small crowd. A big crowd would only spotlight my current poor standing at the club.

If I got the same silent treatment from the members that I'd experienced yesterday, it wouldn't help my cause. DiNatale would pass the information back to Mags that I was a pariah and Mags would pass it up to Burrascano. It would only be one short logical step from there to the termination of my investigation, and I didn't expect severance pay.

The limo found a spot near the front and DiNatale and I walked up. The mobster checked out the people walking in after dropping off their late model BMWs and Porsches with the valet.

"One of these kinds of places," he said. "Bunch of snooty bastards with fat wallets. Don't worry. I'm used to dealing with tight-ass pricks."

We stood in a short line to check in at the security desk. Raymond, the friendly white-haired security guard I'd gotten to know, acted as if he had to check on my membership status and asked us to wait in the lobby while he called the office. He tried to cover it up by telling me it'd be a crazy week due to the Allegro Martin charity outing.

DiNatale didn't seem to notice. He examined the glass-enclosed fitness area and the numerous exercise machines as well as the modern art that reached up to the lobby's high ceiling. He turned to me, "Hey, they got a spa back there. You tried it?"

I shook my head. The itinerary of events leading up to the Allegro Martin Charity Tournament might mean an influx of new people into the club. Another complication I didn't need.

"You should try it," DiNatale said. "You need to relax."

How could I relax? Why was I forced to wait? Maybe Detective Tenorio had caused this. People I didn't recognize continued to be allowed admission and walked past us toward the elevators.

Preston exited one of the elevators and headed straight toward me like a man on a mission. I didn't like the look on his face. What I needed was a good argument why I should be admitted. The members still needed to choose between Zany's store and Leister's store. As far as I knew, I was still in the game, but maybe that had been decided with Mulholland's murder and my nomination by Tenorio as suspect number one.

Preston came within a few yards and began to say something when DiNatale leaned over to me.

"Eddie, I think I'm going to like this place. You say they've got a simulcast facility upstairs? Very cool."

Preston stopped. What was running through his mind? Maybe it could be the sight of DiNatale talking to me. Preston should stay far away from the poker table. The gears in his brain shifted and squealed like a semi climbing a steep mountain slope. He examined DiNatale the way one might view a wild zoo animal and probably took note of the bulge beneath his shyster lawyer suit. The obvious mobster was accompanied by me, the guy who took over the business of a murdered bookie.

Preston's facial expression was the same I'd seen on the store employees, the very human gut reaction of fear.

I jumped at the chance to introduce DiNatale to Preston. With his garbled speech that was nearly impossible to interpret at first in the crowded noise-filled lobby, DiNatale and his cologne were forced to wedge uncomfortably close to Preston.

"I said, 'it's quite the crowd.'" DiNatale said to Preston. "How you doing?"

Preston took a step back, rubbed his well-trimmed beard, and wiped away DiNatale's spit. "I'm fine." He hesitated and then said, "Today is Volunteer's Day." He studied DiNatale and then began to talk fast. "We couldn't put on the charity tournament without lots of help. People who volunteer to sell tickets, marshals on the golf course, and those who contribute prizes for the raffle—lots of people. All for charity. Today is their special day. Allegro and some of his old teammates stop by to show their appreciation."

DiNatale grinned. "Sorry if we got here on a bad day. My first time at your club, and I'm in awe of these pieces you've got hanging in the lobby."

"You like them?" A smile lit up Preston's face. "Your name is Vic, right?" Preston swooned like the ugly schoolgirl asked to dance. "Some of the members find them a bit gaudy."

I couldn't help but laugh to myself. By instinct, DiNatale knew he had to charm Preston. DiNatale probably kept the welfare of the store's customers in mind and the revenue Mags had told him about.

DiNatale took Preston under his wing and together they admired a huge piece that hung down between the elevators. Colors flowed into swirls and designs I couldn't follow. Jackson Pollock with a bad hair day. I hadn't paid attention to it before.

The mobster pointed. "Now I know. I saw this same guy at the Museum of Modern Art last month."

Preston began to breathe heavy as if he'd found his long-lost brother. "I haven't met anyone out here who recognizes the artist's talent."

I stood by like the guy who can't find his way to the betting windows. They mentioned the artist's name—Milo-check or Milo-checkowski—or something like that. Whatever it was about, this was better than getting kicked out.

Preston led us upstairs where he showed off more of these Milo-things hung on the walls in the empty dining room. DiNatale scrounged up more comments.

"This one is better than anything I saw last month at MoMA. Take a look at the depth and contrast."

The routine continued with each picture. I had to give DiNatale credit, he knew how to charm the hell out of Preston. When the inventory of pictures had been exhausted, the mobster leaned close to his new pal and asked for details about the club's charity event.

Preston threw out his chest. "It starts officially on Friday but there's so much involved. I've run myself ragged. The third floor of the club will be opened for the weeklong festivities where we have another bar and a ballroom."

I hadn't been to the third floor or heard much about the charity tournament schedule. DiNatale was learning more from one of my prime suspects than I'd managed to find out. I should've studied art in school.

"Friday night is reserved for the tournament attendees," Preston said. "It gives them a chance to blow off steam. Lots of card games in the back room of the Derby Bar upstairs."

DiNatale stopped in his tracks. "You've got card rooms, plus a simulcast area?"

"Oh, yeah. Zany organized the gin games year-round," Preston said.

The mobster's eyes rolled. "Gin games?"

I thought DiNatale might have a coronary. Gin games could attract more betting action than poker. Preston ticked off the Saturday schedule: golf in the morning followed by a formal charity dinner that evening. There was a laundry list of other items: silent auction, raffle drawings, speeches, awards, etc. He talked about the charity too—a hospital for sick kids.

The second-floor bar was crowded. Preston pushed through. "Let me show you the simulcast area, Vic."

DiNatale looked back at me and smiled. I didn't return the smile. Okay, he'd gotten us into the place but that didn't mean I'd be accepted by the members. Of course, if DiNatale replaced me, the store might have a better chance to retain the members as customers. Maybe that was the strategy.

We weaved our way through the bar to the simulcast area. Preston showed off the room to his new best friend. They walked over to the windows where the bettors put down cash. DiNatale wore a big, dumb grin.

I checked out the second-tier tracks running on a Monday—Aurora Downs, Saratoga, Delaware Park, Presque Isle Downs, Finger Lakes, Ruidoso Downs, Mountaineer—all in various stages of their respective cards. No telling what a sharp player might be able to make at some of these tracks.

Zach waved me over. He didn't stand because of the knee but shifted in his seat. He sat beside Jim Arnold in their customary place. Arnold's carrel was filled with notebooks and the laptop while Zach had the smile of a drunk plastered on his face. I'd be surprised if he'd kept his nose clean the way Allegro had told him to do. I walked over and asked Zach if he was having any luck.

"Jim has been on a hot streak, haven't you Jim?" Zach said. Arnold only grunted. "He wants you to join us."

An excellent handicapper like Jim Arnold had his nose stuck so deep into the racing program that a spokesman or interpreter, and sometimes even a ventriloquist, was required. Zach had adopted such a position on Arnold's behalf. I was tempted to take a seat. I recalled the intriguing notes written on Arnold's racing program, and knew I could learn a few things from him.

Zach studied DiNatale. "Who's the suit with Preston?"

"He's a friend of mine. Vic DiNatale from Chicago. He consults on artwork."

Zach laughed. "Doesn't look like an art consultant. He looks like—"

DiNatale called to me and waved. He and Preston had concluded their tour of the simulcast area and were headed back into the bar.

I told Zach and Arnold I'd see them later and rejoined Preston and DiNatale. As we sat down at a reserved table in the bar, I noticed how the crowd stared at me and DiNatale. I saw the wheels spin in their collective heads. Maybe I *was* capable of murder. Maybe they'd underestimated me. Perhaps the rumor was true.

This wasn't a popularity contest. The balance of power had shifted. If these people wanted to bet illegal and bet sports, then they'd have to deal with me and DiNatale.

I'm sure they would've appreciated it if I introduced them to DiNatale. Their interest in him could hardly be disguised.

What would it be like to stand in DiNatale's shoes? To have his connections and be able to kill with a certain degree of confidence that he would avoid arrest? DiNatale's freedom to act without borders generated a certain degree of fear along with the undivided attention. My association with the mobster allowed me to bask in the shadow of that fear and afforded me a certain celebrity aura by association.

I saw it in their eyes. They feared me as well. And I could use it.

The more pressure I could apply to the killer, the better the chances the killer would make a mistake. I was exactly where I needed to be, snuggled tight within the confines of another Kelso Club event.

My suspects roamed about the club, each with a file at Mulholland's law office. Preston had a dispute with his brother over the family trust. Jim Arnold, ex-banker, had a bankruptcy going and played the horses with Preston. Zach, the basketball phenom, forced to sit out last season, faced a suspension proceeding by the school for his lousy grades. Crystal, Zach's mother and Preston's live-in girlfriend, had a legendary divorce case. Rudi had a pencil-thin one. Allegro had a bushel-full of litigation and a charity outing in his name.

At the end of the bar, Crystal talked and laughed with a middle-age man that looked familiar. Maybe an old ballplayer. People continued to file into the bar and the noise level rose. I spotted Allegro near the entrance. How swell of all my suspects to be in attendance. Let me introduce you to my old buddy, Vic, everyone. My pet cobra. His fangs are sharp and real but don't let that stop the party.

I asked Preston how he came up with Kelso as the namesake for the club. DiNatale expressed interest and leaned forward, his elbows planted on the table.

Preston pulled at the gold chain around his neck as his gaze drifted off toward the blown-up photograph of Kelso and the plaque beneath it on the far wall. "I guess it's a personal thing with me. Nobody has ever objected once they saw the plaque. The horse won stakes at any distance—six furlongs, a mile, a mile and a quarter, even two miles. He almost always carried the highest weight and took on all comers. I wanted to keep Kelso's memory alive. It harkens back to a better and simpler time, a time of Camelot. The early 1960's."

"Kelso was a gelding, right?" DiNatale's gold bridgework gleamed. "The owner castrates him and throws his balls up on the barn roof for luck?"

I noted the coincidence. The murderer had attempted to snip Zany. Maybe it was a message.

Preston frowned and talked about his horse that had run last Saturday and finished fourth. DiNatale bragged about his string of harness horses back in Chicago. The two of them commiserated about the travails of horse ownership—stable bills, trainer bills, and the chance a horse might pull a tendon. I remained on the sidelines and waited for an opportunity to ask Preston about those large payouts from Zany.

Some members had congregated near the bar. I didn't like the way they talked together and looked at me. More members joined the conversation every minute.

The waitress brought our drinks and DiNatale asked if Preston had thought about franchises. In his opinion, a Kelso Club should be a fixture in every city.

Preston's face lit up, probably the way his ancestors must've a century ago when they sold convertible debentures of worthless railroad stock.

"I got contacts." DiNatale fished out his cell phone. "I got a name here. An investment banker that handles financing. You put one of these in New York, Miami, and LA, and you can think about going public."

"You think so?" Preston asked.

The club probably bled cash. So many of the members owed Zany's store, how could they afford monthly dues? How much of Preston's personal trust money had been diverted to keep the club functioning?

Maybe the trust had begun to run dry. Or maybe Zany had been a source of funds. Perhaps he provided a kickback to Preston in return for the exclusive right to the Kelso Club members.

Allegro walked up to our table and pulled up a chair. He was dressed in a white dress shirt, black slacks, and a suede sports coat. "Well, what've we got here? The twenty-nine to one shot."

I introduced Allegro to DiNatale as if their individual celebrity status was on a par. DiNatale had attracted so much attention the former basketball star couldn't resist an introduction.

"What's this twenty-nine to one shot?" DiNatale asked after the formalities.

"Eddie had this twenty-nine to one shot the other day at the track," Allegro said. "Mulholland gave everyone this short-priced hot tip and—"

"Eddie picked the horse?" DiNatale looked back from Allegro to me. "I thought you weren't gambling?"

"Don't jump to conclusions. I didn't bet." I thought DiNatale might call the Associated Press with the news—he still held the cell phone.

"That was the funny thing," Allegro said. "He found this horse at twenty-nine to one and it came in second in a close photo and yet he didn't play the exacta. Paid good, too."

"What the fuck?" DiNatale chuckled in my face. "That must've hurt."

I couldn't thank Allegro enough. I shrugged and smiled like a guy with more important matters than a crummy exacta.

"You guys going to be around long?" Allegro glanced at his Rolex. "I got some network VIP's coming by. When are they supposed to get here, Preston?"

Preston told Allegro that they would be here shortly. Allegro sat back and smiled. What was the relationship between these two? Preston seemed to cater to Allegro's every need.

"What's up?" I asked. "Do they televise the charity golf?"

Allegro laughed. "Hell, no. Too many old farts and not enough celebrities. I'm up for a broadcast job. Big money."

The old pro needed the money but acted as if the job wasn't a big deal.

The crowd at the bar had swollen to the point where they were within a few feet of our table. One of them nudged Preston's shoulder. From the way they looked at me, it didn't take an investigative journalist to know whose scalp they were after. I recognized some who had sat at Mulholland's table on Saturday.

One of the members pointed at me. "What's he doing here, Preston?"

Preston stood up and addressed the crowd. "Take it easy. The detective said—"

"We don't care what the police said," another member said.

DiNatale stood and held up his hands as if to calm people down. "Hey, everybody. I just got out here and want to help." He shot me a smug look.

"Please, everyone," Preston said.

It didn't matter what Preston told them. The damage was done. These members wouldn't wager with Zany's store while I was in charge. DiNatale would report back to Mags and I'd be out on my ass.

Allegro poked my arm. "How does it feel to attract a crowd, Eddie? Now you know how I feel."

"I don't think they want my autograph," I said.

"Hey, look over there, Eddie," Allegro said. "It's your competition."

I followed Allegro's gaze. Peter Leister leaned against the bar and stared directly at me. He flashed his middle finger. A challenge I couldn't ignore. I got up and twisted through the Kelso Club members. The unfriendly crowd closed in behind me.

I stopped a few feet short of Leister. "What are you doing here?"

Leister pointed. "Who's your friend?"

Before I could answer, I felt a hand on my shoulder. It was DiNatale.

"My name is Vic DiNatale," DiNatale shouted.

I felt DiNatale's hot breath. His shoulder jabbed my shoulder. Leister's henchmen, three on either side of their boss, took a step forward.

"You're Vic? You've been busy." Leister spoke loud enough so the entire crowd could hear.

The crowd grew silent. The guy to Leister's right reached a hand into his vest pocket.

"I'll do whatever I want," DiNatale shouted back.

"What's your problem, Leister?" I wasn't about to back down. If DiNatale could handle one, I'd handle the rest. Didn't bet the 29-1 shot, escorted DiNatale around, Zany's murder, then Amity and Mulholland—I was fed up.

"You visit my massage parlors today?" Leister asked DiNatale.

"So what?" DiNatale fired back. "You own those joints? I wouldn't be so proud. The girls are pigs."

A collective laugh rose from the crowd wound tight around us.

Leister folded his arms. "A matter of opinion. You roughed up one of my managers."

"You should teach them some manners." DiNatale stepped forward. "I asked around for you and the fucker refused."

DiNatale knew a lot about the situation here in Denver.

Preston had slipped behind the bar. "Vic, you were where? Today?" The trust funder appeared hurt. DiNatale, his new art buddy, liked to make trouble.

Leister's voice rose in volume so everyone could hear. "I was talking to the detective about Mulholland's murder. We were all at the track on Saturday. We all saw and heard Eddie threaten him."

I wasn't tongue-tied. I wanted to answer all the allegations with my fists. "Didn't you get my message before—expansion isn't a smart move." I edged closer.

DiNatale's men from the limo, including the Neanderthal muscle, stepped out of the shadows near the entrance. Mags's old soldier, Charlie Grasso, was with them, his grouper face expressionless.

Leister snickered. "Is that why your friend, Vic, is here? To kill me, too? Everybody knows you killed Mulholland and the Kelso Club members won't forget. They'll switch to me."

Leister's accusation that I killed Mulholland became an accusation that I killed Zany, too. It fed my rage.

DiNatale nodded toward his men then spoke to Leister. "First, I'll close down those shitboxes you call massage parlors, then your restaurants. You know who you're dealing with?"

I felt the crowd around me and saw the hunger in their faces. They couldn't wait for the floor show—a brawl to kick off the Allegro Martin Charity Tournament. The same hunger I saw in the faces that night years ago when I'd fought the linebacker at O'Connell's. My temper hit the boiling point.

"You killed Zany. If you want a war that's what you'll get." I lunged toward Leister with DiNatale behind me. No time for Leister's men to pull a weapon. DiNatale's men came up behind Leister's henchman. It was almost a fair fight with seven of them versus the five of us.

I slugged one of Leister's men and went after Leister.

28

TUESDAY

The next day, I sipped coffee in my hotel room and took stock of yesterday when I'd lunged at Leister.

It had been intense. Hands had grabbed at my shoulders and tore at my clothes. I'd felt as if I swam the breaststroke against a swift current. The mosh pit pulled and dragged me off Leister before I could inflict much damage.

The whole thing was a blur. It'd lasted only thirty seconds or a minute. The crowd refused to allow us to square off. Maybe I'd slugged Leister and one or two of his men before the members wrapped up my arms. Preston ordered me to vacate the premises.

I didn't sleep much. A few drinks at the hotel bar, expecting DiNatale or Leister to show up. If so, I'd have been ready. But they didn't.

After the skirmish, DiNatale had left the Kelso Club in his limo, strutting and swearing at Leister as he and his guys took off. I was left to walk back to my hotel.

The only good thing was that I didn't get arrested. Nobody did. At the Kelso Club, bad publicity was the number one concern. The fight I'd started wasn't something I was proud of, but it seemed impossible to avoid. If I'd thought first about the investigation, instead of losing control, I would've been better off.

What was DiNatale's next move? Not to mention Mags and his pipeline to Burrascano, and what that could mean for my investigation. I checked my cell once again to see if I missed a call from Uncle Mike.

My cell phone buzzed. It wasn't Uncle Mike. It was Rudi, and she was upset.

She told me to come quick. Koransky was in the office and there was a problem. The tension in her voice concerned me. I asked her to take a deep breath and explain. "I'll let Koransky do it. Come now." She hung up.

I raced out of the hotel and walked fast down the street. Our previous meeting had concluded on good terms. Koransky would continue to take action and funnel it through the store. He had a sweet deal. So, what was the problem?

My strategy had been to let Detective Tenorio stay busy hunting for Amity. If Koransky had told the detective that I said she'd been murdered, what I'd used to shake up Koransky would come back to haunt me.

What kind of criminal charge was I guilty of—obstruction? A law existed for spitting on the sidewalk. I couldn't afford to be charged. It would be enough to make Burrascano and his confederates think about a solution. Something DiNatale would execute upon.

I took a deep breath as I headed down the stairs to the store. No need to alarm the employees by racing past. Stop and say hello, smile, make them feel comfortable as if today was another Tuesday morning. No big deal.

Rudi met me as soon as I stepped into Zany's office and shut the door behind me. "I thought you should hear this," she said.

Koransky stood up. Unlike our previous meeting, his clothes were rumpled and his face unshaven. I asked him what all this was about and he sat back down on the edge of the chair. His legs bounced and his eyes squinted at me behind the thick horn-rimmed glasses. Sweat streamed down the side of his face.

"Eddie, I'm glad you're here," he stuttered.

I stepped around the antique desk to Zany's chair. The morning sun streamed through the basement window behind me into Koransky's face.

There was a sharp knock on the door. It flew open before I could say anything and DiNatale strode in.

The mobster studied me, Rudi, and then Koransky. He took a step closer to the desk. "I hope I didn't miss anything."

"Vic, what are you doing here?" My question hung in the air. He must've followed me, spotted my frantic walk up the street, and surmised something might be amiss.

"Checking in," the mobster said. "What's going on?"

"I was about to find out." I made the introductions then waited for Koransky's story. I feared the worst, and now DiNatale could report back the sordid details.

"I thought I should get down here right away." Koransky fumbled with one of his tobacco pipes. "I didn't know what else to do. This affects you as much as it does me."

"Go ahead," I said. His hands shook and his voice trembled. This wasn't the same guy I'd met before, full of himself, and ready to be enshrined in the royal kingdom of medicine.

"Yeah, go ahead," DiNatale repeated, his shoulders swayed and his feet danced as he stood by the wall.

Koransky blinked into the sunshine. "I was still asleep. He came to the house and shouted so we let him in. I thought he might bust down the door."

"Who?" I asked.

"Mancuso. Coach Mancuso. He works at the school."

Rudi, seated beside Koransky, patted his hand. "Mancuso used to play in the NBA years ago," she explained. "Now he's the school's weight coach."

"He was a teammate of Allegro, right?" I asked.

Koransky nodded. "He's a huge guy. Six-foot-nine, six-foot-ten. All muscle even if he is getting old."

"No shit," DiNatale said.

"Right," Koransky said. "He slammed the door. Came over to my desk, threw all my books and papers on the floor. I thought he might kill me. Then he tossed the letter on the desk and said: 'Open it, Doctor Asshole.'"

"He called you an asshole?" DiNatale looked at me, his lips tight.

"Take it easy, Vic," I said. "What letter?"

Koransky reached over and picked up a piece of paper off Zany's desk and held it up. "I did what he told me. I opened up the envelope and read this. I guess I made the mistake of asking him: 'What the fuck does this mean?'"

"Mistake?" I asked.

"Yeah, because Mancuso reached out, yanked one of my favorite pipes out of my mouth, and cracked it between the fingers of one hand. Almost chipped my tooth."

DiNatale's fingers drummed against the wall. "Read the fucking thing."

Rudi patted Koransky's hand again. "Go ahead, Steve."

"It's full of bullshit about this shitty little scholarship I get every year but then at the end of the form letter is this kicker." Koransky looked at me then DiNatale and read from the text. "Take notice your conduct in affairs outside school suggest you may not be a proper candidate for the degree in your chosen field. This matter is presently under review by the Dean. This could result in the cancellation of benefits under your scholarship, suspension from the program, or expulsion. You should govern your conduct accordingly."

"What conduct?" I asked.

"Mancuso told me the school heard what was going on in my house, and if I opened up my place this fall, he'd personally come over and stick one of my pipes up my ass so I could study it." Koransky crammed tobacco into the pipe.

I asked the obvious. "Has Leister continued to call?"

Koransky hesitated and again Rudi urged him to tell his story.

"Lately it's been every day. Like you told me, I refused to tell him anything."

"What did Leister say? Did he make threats?" DiNatale stepped away from the wall and hovered over the college bookie, a Broncos blue and orange striped tie hanging down in Koransky's face.

"Yeah, sort of."

"Let's not jump to conclusions, Vic." I saw where DiNatale's mind might lead. He wanted to blame Leister and start a war.

Koransky slid to the edge of his chair. "I don't need this. I've only got seventeen months to go. Somebody told the school. We never had a problem. I never pressured a kid to pay or anything."

All Koransky had going for him was this medical degree and without it, he was a thumb-sucking momma's boy who had to dial a sex worker to get laid.

DiNatale pounded his fist on the desk. "What did Leister say?"

I thought Koransky might cry.

"He told me Eddie killed this lawyer at the track. Unless I wanted trouble, I better work for him."

"Motherfucker," DiNatale rocked on his heels.

"Wait a minute, Vic. We need to talk with Mancuso." I had to defuse the situation.

The mobster had one hand on the doorknob and looked back, his face red. "You talk to Mancuso. You can suck Leister's dick, too, while you're at it."

"Let's call Mancuso. Be smart," I said.

"Nobody fucks with me." DiNatale pointed at Koransky. "And you keep your fucking mouth shut or I'll do more than stick a pipe up your ass."

DiNatale walked out and slammed the door behind him.

It was official. Things had spun out of control.

29

THE CRITICAL THING WAS TO GET IN TOUCH WITH COACH Mancuso. Maybe the school's warning had been in the works for some time, and its delivery the day after the confrontation with Leister was a mere coincidence, and not something engineered by him. If so, I still might be able to head off DiNatale by contacting Mags. It was a long shot but I had to try.

Koransky wiggled in his chair. "Can I smoke?"

"No. You got the only place on campus?" I asked.

"Yeah, why?"

I wondered why Leister would contact the school. He knew how lucrative student-body action could be as demonstrated by his repeated calls to Koransky, yet placed his future business in jeopardy by alerting the school. It didn't make sense. Leister was a businessman, first and foremost. Leister could set up his own house and compete with Koransky.

"You haven't heard of anybody else taking bets at the school?"

Koransky studied his unlit pipe. "There was this one guy last fall but he was small-time and got expelled."

Maybe Leister went to the school as a knee-jerk reaction in response to DiNatale's visit to the massage parlors. Was Leister that dumb or that smart? Smart by hitting us in a well-known location that would hurt business, and dumb because it would provide DiNatale with an excuse to retaliate. Maybe Leister wanted a showdown with DiNatale.

"I finally got a live person." Rudi swept back into the office, cell phone in hand. "The kid said he'd look for the coach."

"Good." I thought through the possible angles. Could Mancuso have acted alone?

"Let me see that letter." I took it from Koransky. It was a simple form letter probably sent to thousands of students on scholarship programs. The paragraph Koransky had read was added at the bottom of the page with a different font.

"Has Mancuso talked to you before today?" I asked.

He squirmed. "No, never."

I couldn't tell if he was lying or if he'd dipped into the med school medicine cabinet. "Mancuso didn't wager?"

"We had some professors and school personnel as customers, but I don't remember him."

Rudi talked into the cell phone. "It's urgent we talk with him."

"Tell the kid somebody died." I worried that somebody might die if DiNatale wasn't stopped.

She tried it and then shook her head. "He says that Coach Mancuso has a strict policy—no distractions when he's in the weight room."

"What is it, brain surgery?" At least I knew where I'd find Coach Mancuso. It was a delay I couldn't afford but it was the only option. "Let's go to the school."

Koransky pulled the unlit pipe from his mouth. "No way. I'm not going. No telling what Mancuso will do to me."

"Fine. Stay here. We may need to call you."

I followed Rudi out of the store past the waiting crowd of applicants for part-time employment during football season.

"I'll be back in an hour," Rudi told them.

There was a collective groan from the group.

We hustled out to the parking garage. I was relieved to see the tires of the SUV fully inflated.

I watched the traffic as she zipped from one lane to the next, past Coors Field, and then toward the interstate that led to Mile High University.

"Have you met Mancuso before?" I asked.

"Yeah. A few times at the Kelso Club. He'll be there this weekend for the charity event. He played on a couple of Allegro's basketball teams. Mancuso has always been a gentle giant. Doesn't drink. A health nut."

I recalled how Allegro mentioned that Mancuso watched his back when he first came into the league. "It doesn't make sense for Mancuso to be working with Leister."

"Vic thinks he's working with Leister. I'm worried about what Vic will do. Did you see him?" Rudi said.

"Yeah. He gets like that." I didn't know what else to say. Rudi would go NASCAR if I didn't play it down.

"He was so nice yesterday and then this morning I thought—"

"Vic will cool off."

"He's like two different people. Leister must've gotten under his skin yesterday," she said.

I didn't want to think back to yesterday. Maybe DiNatale instigated things by beating up one of Leister's massage parlor managers, but I was the one who lunged at Leister inside the Kelso Club.

"Vic reminds me of Warren." Rudi flipped the station on the radio. More sports talk. "Nice one minute and then violent the next over some little thing. Finally, I realized his anger boiled under the surface all the time. That's when I got scared. That's when I knew I had to leave."

Drugs could do that to a person. The need for drug money could do the same thing.

"Before you left Nebraska what did Warren do?"

She laughed. "Not much. Looked for a job and got drunk."

"They have a lot of meth back there?"

"Yeah, but not Warren. Are you kidding? He's the kind of guy who buys a six-pack of tall boys and a bag of pretzels."

She didn't know about her husband's criminal activity. I hated to be the one to tell her.

"My uncle has some experienced contacts here in town looking for the son-of-a-bitch," I said. "So far, no luck. That tells us one thing. Warren has some serious street smarts for a Nebraska hick."

She glanced toward me; her lips tight. "What are you saying?"

"Uncle Mike talked to the local sheriff in your hometown. Warren was dealing meth and under suspicion of murder."

Her grip tightened on the steering wheel, but the Yukon maintained a steady course down the interstate. "Damn him. Urgent to leave town because of a job offer in Denver, he said. Such bullshit. I'm so gullible."

"Don't be hard on yourself. Criminals know how to lie."

"Who was the murder victim?"

"I don't know. I can find out."

"My mom says I left Nebraska so I could divorce him," Rudi said. "As if I had this master plan and that I never should've left. Because if I stayed, everything would be perfect—happily ever after with kids." Her words dripped sarcasm. "What would she say if she knew the real story?"

"I'm sure your mom has your best interests in mind."

The interstate cut though some fields and vacant land primed for development. The scene stretched to the mountains. So much empty space compared to Chicago's endless urban sprawl. Fewer places to hide in Colorado, but plenty of room to run.

She screamed. "Shit."

I turned my attention from the scenic view to the interstate.

She pulled hard on the wheel. Out of the corner of my eye, I saw a car swerve. The SUV skidded onto the shoulder. Rudi pumped the brakes but the momentum caused the vehicle to fishtail on loose gravel.

I felt the tires lose contact and we went over the embankment down a steep hill. I held on for dear life. My seat strained in its moorings. She swore and fought the wheel. The SUV zig-zagged and bounced. I reached over and shoved the steering wheel hard-left to keep from tipping.

My stomach did a roller-coaster flip. The SUV dove sideways toward a ditch.

30

WE RAMMED INTO THE DITCH AND MY FOREHEAD SLAMMED into the airbag. The SUV hissed steam like an old-time locomotive.

"C'mon, Rudi. You okay?"

"I think so."

She moaned. She complained about a sharp pain in her left arm, but otherwise, she was fine. The SUV sat sideways in the ditch on the driver's side so I could climb up and out through the passenger door.

I pulled myself up and hung my legs out for leverage then reached down and took hold of her shoulders. I couldn't see much through the steam and airbags. She kicked and pushed herself free. Every few seconds I stopped to be sure she didn't feel any strange twinge of pain other than from her arm.

"No, keep going," she said.

Voices rose above the hiss of the engine. Good Samaritans. Somebody got hold of my legs and we made a human chain. My chest and stomach scraped against the running board but it allowed me to slip her out. The vehicle rocked and I hoped it wouldn't topple in the gravel ditch and crush us when we hit the ground.

We dropped down into a pile of bodies. Other Good Samaritans steadied the SUV in place. More volunteers dragged us clear. The engine continued to sputter but no flames. Sirens blared in the distance.

"What happened?" people asked.

The adrenaline rush made it hard to say much. "I don't know."

"Somebody cut us off," Rudi said.

The cops and the medical personnel and the Good Samaritans gathered around us.

One of the cops asked: "Did you get a make and model?"

"No," I said.

One of them said: "People text while they drive."

Another said: "Probably doesn't even realize what happened and kept driving."

I doubted it. But my fuzzy brain couldn't analyze all the possibilities.

"Surprised you didn't roll," a cop said.

They hauled us up the incline, past the line of gawkers, to the ambulance and, sirens blaring, to a hospital emergency room.

Inside the emergency room, after the usual wait and the paperwork, they took Rudi first. She blamed herself for overreacting, but I tried to convince her otherwise. I couldn't recall the make or model of the car that cut us off, but I was pretty sure it wasn't a limo.

They took me to a small exam room. A nurse came in and took my vital signs, determined I'd live, and then told me to wait for the doctor. I felt lucky to come out of it with airbag bruises, some neck pain, and a splitting headache that replaced the adrenaline buzz.

After ten minutes, an orderly came into the room. I looked up from a magazine in the hope he'd have news on Rudi.

He was a big man with a white coat and came up close to me. "Shut up or you're dead."

I stared into the barrel of a gun. I did a double take. The cloud in my head lifted.

"You don't know me? You're fucking my wife." The gun shook in the man's hand.

"What?" I wasn't fucking anybody except in my dreams.

"Don't move."

Then I realized who this guy was. Warren. "What rock did you crawl out from?"

"Shut up. Turn around. Face the wall."

He was almost my height but stockier, close-cropped hair, wide eyes, and a big nose. The guy looked like a farm boy, almost innocent—a quality that probably attracted Rudi once upon a time.

I thought about going for the gun before I turned my back, but I didn't like the way it shook in his hand. I also didn't like the sweat that had broken out on his forehead or the tremble in his voice. Maybe he'd taken a good dose of drugs today for courage.

I turned around. "Can't shoot a guy in the back." I thought it was a good rule for the occasion.

"Shut the fuck up. What about killing somebody when they're puking?"

Mulholland. "I didn't do it."

"They all say you killed Mulholland. I should thank you. Murder my divorce attorney anytime." He giggled.

The high-pitched giggle didn't add to my confidence. I could see the headline: "Jealous husband kills wife and boss then kills self in emergency room."

"How did you know we were here?" I asked.

He jammed the gun barrel into the back of my rib cage. "I'll ask the questions. Why wouldn't I be concerned about my wife, you dumbass?"

Had he run us off the road? I knew one thing—I had to keep my voice steady and concentrate on how to get this madman out of the room.

"I'm concerned, too," I said. "She's got a broken arm."

"She could be dead. I should break your skull. You got her into this mess."

"Don't blame me. She wants to find Zany's killer." And by the way, Warren, did you do it? The guy was off-kilter. The gun barrel jabbed over and over. Sweat trickled down under my arms.

"Zany," he snickered. "That fucker always had a wad of cash. Rudi loves money."

"Right."

"Fuck you. Did I ask you something? Keep your mouth shut. You think I'm an idiot? You think I don't care?"

I could try flattery. "You've been ahead of me every step of the way."

"That's right. I'm going to stay a step ahead of you, too. If you knew anything, you'd know."

I smelled his sour breath and body odor. Any closer and we'd be a couple. "What can I do?"

"Here's what I want you to do, smart guy." He shoved the gun under another rib. "Fire her."

I liked the fact he gave me a job to do. "It might take some time. Football season starts."

"You don't think I'll use this?"

The gun left my rib cage. I froze. Then everything went black.

———

When I regained consciousness in the exam room, I got up off the floor and thought of Rudi. My second thought was to ask for my money back—was the ER staff out to lunch?

I stumbled, unsure on my feet. Wetness on my neck and the back of my head. Some blood smeared on my face. Just my luck, survive being run off the road at seventy-five miles per hour then get mugged in the ER.

The nurse took one look at me and ordered me back to the waiting room.

"I've been in the exam room waiting for my release," I said. "I've been treated."

"Good Lord," she said. "Where are your bandages?"

I leaned over the counter in her face. "I want Paula Rudinger's room—now."

"Don't do anything rash." She checked the register then came around the counter and headed down the hall. "Did you tear off your bandages? Didn't they give you a sedative?"

"No, I wanted to bleed." I walked beside her to Rudi's room dripping blood.

"We have regulations," she said.

"Good."

I stepped in front of the nurse and cracked open the door to Rudi's exam room. I didn't want to surprise Warren and cause him to start shooting.

No sign of him. She lay on the exam table alone talking on her cell phone, her left arm in a cast. I knocked once and walked in.

She was in tears. "Okay, okay. Bye, Mom." She hung up. "Eddie, are you okay? You're bleeding."

"I met Warren. He had a gun."

"I know. He was here. He made me call mom. Eddie, I'm sorry. I have to quit. This is it. I'm done. Today."

I sat on the bed and gave her a partial hug, cautious of her arm. "I can't blame you."

She laughed and pulled me close with her one good arm. "Shit, I can't even hug you."

I kissed her. "It's good enough for me."

"You ever been loved, O'Connell?" she whispered. "I mean really loved—by a good woman?"

I pulled away from her and looked at her face. My aunt and uncle's long marriage came to mind, and I knew what I'd been missing. "No."

Tears welled up in her eyes. "Keep me in mind."

31

WEDNESDAY

I rolled out of bed the next morning thankful for the pain pills and a night's sleep. But then yesterday's events rushed back.

Now that I'd finally met Warren, I had more questions than answers. If he killed Zany and Mulholland, then why not kill me? I made the perfect target as Zany's replacement. Rudi had become my confidante, and in his eyes, my lover. The exam room gave Warren the opportunity. No witnesses. A serial killer wouldn't pass up such a chance.

Did he really want me to fire Rudi? If so, then why go to Rudi's room, force her to call her mother, and get her to quit? He needed me for something else.

And what did he mean when he said: "If you knew anything, you'd know?"

When Rudi said she would quit, I couldn't argue with her. She might catch a stray bullet just by standing next to me. It wouldn't be right to convince her to stay. I'd have to struggle along without her.

Before we'd parted, she warned me again about Warren as if she felt responsible for his actions. She made me promise I'd find Zany's killer for her. She was drugged up and one of the employees was on their way to give her a ride home. We each tried our best to say all the right things.

The cell phone buzzed as I made a cup of hotel room coffee. It was Uncle Mike.

"Hi, Eddie. You'll hear about it sooner or later so I thought I better tell you."

"What?" I didn't like his grave tone. I braced myself for the worst.

"You should know right away . . ."

"What?"

Ice cubes tinkled in the glass. "It's a rumor. Something Joey L just told me so don't hold me to it."

"I won't." This must be bad. I'd already filled him in on yesterday's events. I thought things couldn't get worse.

"Some guys raided one of Leister's massage parlors. Nobody got killed but one of the employees is in the hospital. Heard he's in a coma."

"No shit. DiNatale didn't waste any time." No need to talk with Mancuso now.

"It's not good." Uncle Mike exhaled into the receiver. He must've lit a stogie. "And they wanted to keep sports betting under the radar."

Too early for cigars and bourbon but not today. I'd thought what a war with Leister might mean on a hypothetical level, but now that it was reality, I had to think it through.

"Leister will take revenge," I said. "Detective Tenorio will need to act. I'm the sitting duck in the middle running the store. Tell me how DiNatale's action makes sense."

"They don't always think like businessmen, you know that."

The raid was merely step one. Mags and DiNatale didn't trust me. Leister could take me out as payback for the raid and the death of his good buddy, Mulholland. Detective Tenorio would call me in for questioning or charge me for Mulholland's murder. The store might hit a new record low with the loss of the Kelso Club customers. I held a busted flush.

"Maybe I should get out of the way," I said.

Uncle Mike cleared his throat. "That's another problem. I didn't tell you because I'd decided it would hurt more than help. I figured it would be better if you thought it was a discount."

"What are you saying?" My gambling debt had hung over me like a dark cloud for months and the fact it had been resolved through a discount applied by Burrascano in return for the Zany job had given me a second life. The idea that it could be resurrected struck at every fiber of my being. My heart raced; I could barely breathe. Bile welled up in the back of my throat.

Uncle Mike talked fast. "We need the money from this job. You can't leave. Burrascano didn't discount your gambling debt, he gave me great terms."

"Terms on what?"

"I had to mortgage the bar. If we don't get paid on this job, I'll have to sign it over."

"What the fuck?"

"C'mon, Eddie. You owed a lot and our fee for the job wouldn't cover it all. Maybe if you'd have found Zany's money—"

"Why mortgage the place?" My uncle's pride and joy. It would destroy him if he lost it. And for me and my gambling to be the cause—

The clink of a bottle on the edge of a glass came from my uncle's end. Then the trickle of liquid. "I'm your uncle. You do what you have to do."

"Oh, man." I knew what he had done for me. My gambling debt had grown to the size where one of three things happened: you scrape up the resources, run to a far-off land and change your name, or get intimate with your health insurance coverage.

"I told you over and over to stop," he said.

I didn't need to go down that road again. "Don't worry. I'll handle it. I took this solo, and I'll finish it."

I hung up, pounded the wall with my fist and took a cold shower. I needed a plan and needed my gun.

I went to Zany's store. I'd need to make the best use of what little breathing room I had, if any. Rudi's office remained cluttered. She hadn't come in to clear off the desk. The employees had gotten wind of the fact she'd quit and pestered me to choose who would get her office.

The part-timers were back for the third day in a row and still, nobody had been hired. I designated one of the veteran staff members to finish the interviews Rudi had started. This decision pissed off some other veteran staffers so the entire store became a hate-fest.

I sat in Zany's chair and looked down at the photos on the desk. One of Zany and Rudi in happier times. One of Zany and his aunt. This was what it boiled down to—family and a few friends. I called Rudi on the cell but no answer. I didn't leave a message.

An employee knocked on the open door.

"What is it now?" I barked.

"A Jim Arnold is on the phone. He insists on talking to you."

"What does he want?" I asked.

The employee looked down at her shoes. "I guess he wants his credit limit raised again."

Arnold hadn't yet paid the store on his old balance. This got me pissed off. "I'll talk to him."

The employee nodded and shut the door.

"Hello, Jim?" I thought I'd wait about two seconds before I lit into him.

"Eddie? You're not an easy man to reach," Arnold said.

"Yeah." I didn't bother to apologize.

"I want you to come by the club. I've been meaning to talk with you, but you know how things get nuts around here with this Allegro Martin clambake."

"What's it about?"

"I was impressed by that horse you picked last Saturday," he said.

"The twenty-nine to one shot Allegro razzes me about every chance he gets?"

"Yeah. We didn't get a chance to talk at the track."

Arnold explained that what he wanted was my handicapping expertise. Like any good handicapper he looked for any and every edge he could find and wasn't too proud to ask. He wanted me to sit with him side-by-side through today's races so he could pick my brain.

I brought up my current status with the members. "They almost tarred and feathered me on Monday."

"They can go fuck themselves," he said. "You're my guest."

What did I have to lose? I was exactly in the frame of mind I needed to take my rightful place in one of the handicapping carrels at the Kelso Club. I agreed to meet him in the lobby when the eastern tracks got underway in an hour.

Once I'd made the decision, the bell rang in my head and I drooled like Pavlov's dog. I took care of some business at the store then raced over to the Crown Vic and got the remainder of the cash stake I'd received from Burrascano. Fuck him, he could add it to the mortgage balance on my uncle's bar.

I had lots of excuses to gamble but I didn't exactly study them to see if they were good ones.

32

I FOLLOWED A CIRCUITOUS ROUTE FROM THE STORE TO THE parking garage in case DiNatale tracked me. I retrieved Burrascano's cash from the hiding place in the spare tire compartment of the Crown Vic and stuffed it in my pocket. I almost ran to the Kelso Club, my gun secured under my shirt in the belt holster at the small of my back, on watch for Warren, DiNatale, Leister, and the bogeyman, Tenorio.

Who was I kidding? I was the punch-drunk boxer, who plans one last bout in the hope to dance nine rounds before taking a fall, but instead, the old training takes over, and he slugs it out, getting his brain pummeled into mashed potatoes.

No, I argued, I felt good. I wouldn't be chasing it the way I had at the end of my last gambling binge. I could start off fresh. But I hadn't kept up to date. I had no idea which trainers were hot, how certain tracks played—if they favored speed or if the rail was hot—nothing. No more than I did that day at Aurora Downs.

So maybe it was good to walk in with a clear head, a blank slate. See things I wouldn't have noticed before. Find some 29-1 shot.

Raymond manned the security counter in the Kelso Club lobby. He stood up as soon as he saw me. "I'm sorry, Eddie. You can't come in here."

Arnold ran up from the elevator to the security guard. "Raymond, it's okay."

"But I've been given strict orders by Preston Williston himself. Please, Mr. Arnold," Raymond said.

"I'll explain everything to Preston." He slipped Raymond some cash. "I sit beside him every day. You don't need to worry."

The guard scratched his white hair. With the other hand he pocketed the money. "I like my job. Except for this week, it's a piece of cake."

"I'll take full responsibility." Arnold took a pen from his pocket and wrote something on the back of a card and handed it to Raymond.

"Okay," Raymond said. "But you talk to Mr. Williston."

I shook Arnold's hand then followed him to the elevators. He seemed even thinner than last week. "Are you sure about this?"

"No problem." Arnold pressed the button to the second floor. "I haven't pissed off Preston since yesterday."

I wanted to clear the air on the big issue. "You don't think I killed Mulholland?"

"Over a gambling debt? Fuck no. How do you get paid when he's dead? Mulholland had a hundred enemies at the club alone."

What was Arnold's relationship to Mulholland? He'd consulted with the attorney about a bankruptcy. Was it only attorney-client or something more?

We exited the elevator and made our way through the bar to the simulcast area. At least it was still early. A few members sat at the bar after power breakfast meetings in the dining room. I saw one of them point me out to the bartender. Arnold had taken quite a chance, and I couldn't help but wonder if he had some other reason to invite me than to obtain handicapping tips. I'd learned that sometimes a killer tries to keep his hunter close and find out what they know.

Arnold led the way to the back row of carrels. "Take the carrel next to mine. I've got you all set up."

The workstation he provided had all the tools of the trade laid out in precision-like order—a laptop, the racing program, notebooks, several pens, and a calculator. The closed-circuit television perched on the top shelf at eye level displayed the odds at Saratoga Racetrack, the track back east in progress.

I could still leave. This thought raised my temperature to the boiling point.

Maybe I should stand around and play with myself the way I did Saturday at Aurora Downs. Let providence and 29-1 shots escape. Play the chump.

Burrascano and I had a deal, goddamnit. Burrascano got paid and, in part, I received a discount in return for this job and others. He'd gotten what he'd bargained for. I'd sucked it up and paid the agreed amount.

But he'd gone behind my back. Made another deal with Uncle Mike. Fine. So, I gambled again. What did they expect?

I sat down and flipped the page. Fuck them.

Arnold patted my shoulder. "No pressure."

Did I look like a guy under pressure? "My strong suit will be the Arlington card."

"Lots of races. Not a bad lineup for a Wednesday." Arnold clicked keys on his laptop.

I dove back into the past performances of the horses in the first race at Saratoga. My old lifestyle that I'd tried so hard to let go. I'd lose everything I'd gained these past months.

I'd sworn to change for Uncle Mike and here I was back again. I told myself how the only way to find Zany's killer was through the Kelso Club. Why did Preston fire Mulholland? Why was Preston, in Mulholland's words, a "crazy fucker?"

But did I tell myself all this as a way to get into the Kelso Club to gamble?

Before I could think through the second-guessing and the shame of making excuses, the handicapping gears swung into action like the fine movements of a Swiss timepiece. A checklist of items ticked off—the type of race, the comparative class of each horse, the trainers and jockeys, the condition of each horse coming into today's race, and other factors.

Today was Wednesday. I'd been in Denver a week. Rudi had quit. Amity's murder. I found Mulholland in a pool of blood and vomit.

How low I'd sunk.

The number one horse by the name of Bud's Charleton had the kind of speed to dominate this field. Not much other speed to challenge him on the front end. Could get loose on the lead and control the pace. A second-tier jockey who wouldn't attract a lot of action. I might get five to one.

I cautioned myself to go slow. No way I could jump back in and pick winners. I needed to watch some races and get a feel.

Arnold looked around from the side wall of the carrel, his glasses down on the tip of his nose. "Let me know if something leaps off the page at you."

I sat and watched Bud's Charleton win by six lengths, wire to wire. I felt sick. What was I doing? Had I lost the will to win? Could I make the old connection?

I needed to find my way back. Relight the fire. I refused to believe my insides had turned into a deep, bottomless well, empty and cavernous. I could get it back.

Play again like the old days. Feel the glow of anticipation just before the race. Sprint up to the windows with confidence. I knew I could get it back. I needed to find the old magic almost as much as I needed to find Zany's murderer.

In my mind, the two had become intertwined. As Mags said, bookies don't fall from the sky, but bookies don't get murdered by somebody who doesn't have a thirst for the action. When a bookie takes a dive off a stadium, nine times out of ten, a gambler gives him a push.

I handicapped the next race. Thirty minutes between races but longer in case of an inquiry or long photo—an eternity in casino time. People wanted constant action, constant feedback, check for another email, another text, another tweet. But it took time to saddle horses, groom the track, and pay off winners. It was ritual and tradition.

I dug through the next race. I reviewed charts of previous races and other handicapping databases on the internet. I could use up every second of the time between races with an in-depth review of the handicapping puzzle.

With only a few minutes to post Arnold leaned out of the carrel. "I like the three horse in this race."

I liked another horse named Mabel's Fable coming off a layoff. But what did I know? Arnold had all those notebooks. Plus, Arnold's three horse was one of my other top selections.

I had to start somewhere. "Here's twenty bucks," I said. "Put it on the three horse for me?"

Arnold took the twenty-dollar bill but gave me a strange look. I knew what he was thinking. Only widows and orphans asked somebody to place bets for them. Was I some rookie? Injured? An anemic bet for a big-time bookie.

But I knew what I was scared of. A trip to the windows would make it official. Plus, I wasn't too sure what degree of self-control I could muster with a pocket full of cash and the lure of exacta and trifecta combinations.

The bets were made and the horses loaded into the gate. I felt some of the old "zing." Maybe I'd begun to make the connection—some sparks flew as the race started. Arnold screamed and yelled for his three horse but it finished second. Of course, the horse I liked—Mabel's Fable—ran past the three horse in deep stretch as if it stood still. The track was playing *me*.

I went after the next race with a vengeance, a cheap claiming race with a big field and many possible candidates at attractive odds. This time I didn't listen to Arnold. I decided to bet two horses each at 10 to1 odds, twenty bucks each. A conservative wager.

I made my own way to the windows. It had been so easy last Saturday to imagine what the Kelso Club members thought as they stood in line to wager. How they calculated the amount to bet versus the number of different combinations to make the most money possible. But now that I stood in line myself, it was not so simple.

My head buzzed. My fingers rifled through Burrascano's cash—twenties, hundreds. Pure heroin for the gambler. Twenty bucks to win was not enough. But I'd steer clear of the gimmicks—exacta boxes and trifecta boxes which required a greater outlay of cash to cover various combinations.

As I stepped to the window, I pulled out cash. I bet one hundred dollars to win on one of my choices and fifty bucks to win on the other. The actual exchange of money for a chance to make fifty or twenty-five times the 10 to1 odds, reignited the old sense of power. It dated back through a maze of winners all the way back to Splendid Runner and summers long ago.

I felt a surge of confidence as I sat back down. A win under my belt would bring me back.

My two horses finished second and third, beaten by Arnold's horse.

"I used your two horses with my pick," Arnold said. "Caught the trifecta. It will pay good—thanks."

I plastered a fake smile on my face. Damn, why didn't I have that trifecta? It would pay well over five hundred dollars for a two-dollar combination while I lost one hundred and fifty. How much more money had I lost already by playing cautious and failing to bet? I had to either get into the game or stay out. I couldn't afford to stand in the ring with one arm tied behind my back.

"There's something I need to ask you." Arnold jabbed at me with his rolled-up racing program.

I pulled my head out of the next race. "What?" It was what I'd figured. He did have some other reason for inviting me to the Kelso Club.

33

ARNOLD SAT UP AND LOOKED OUT OVER THE HANDICAPPING carrel. I did the same. The simulcast area had begun to fill up. A lot of new faces. The Allegro Martin charity golf event had brought in a "B" list of retired pro athletes for the week's festivities. No sign of Preston.

He leaned in close. "Can you keep a secret?"

I wasn't all that happy to be pulled away from my racing program. I checked the minutes to post. "Sure, that's a bookie's job." A bookie owed a special relationship to the customer, similar to a priest and the sinner.

He clasped his hands in his lap. "I filed bankruptcy."

"You did?" I was somewhat surprised. Based on my review of the notes in Mulholland's office, the filing appeared to be in the early stages. Maybe Arnold's meeting with Mulholland had been some time ago. I hadn't had the time to check every detail.

But I couldn't tell Arnold about my late-night break-in at the attorney's office.

"I had another attorney stalling my creditors, but I couldn't afford to keep doing that," he said.

"Is it a relief?" I recalled all the debts listed in the file at the dead lawyer's office.

"It makes me sick. I can write off my career in banking. How can I handle other people's money when I can't handle my own?"

"There are other jobs."

"My wife and her divorce attorney pressured me. I was behind on child support. Now everything—my marriage, my career, my bills—all rolled up in a ball and flushed down the toilet."

"That's rough." I saw the deep lines in his face. "Your work experience—"

"Thanks. Maybe I get a fresh start. The slate wiped clean. But here's the part I'm grappling with."

"What?"

"I don't want to dig myself another hole."

"Yeah." I got it. Arnold's problem wasn't his career path. It was the effect of the bankruptcy on his gambling.

"I keep second-guessing. Horses I used to pick slip past me. A trainer I like ran this horse yesterday. With the move from a route back to a sprint, I should've been all over the horse at ten to one. Instead, all I do is study it and study it, until I talked myself out of it."

"Maybe you need to give it some time." The kind of trouble Arnold described was the kiss of death. What success the odds allowed depended on guts. Without it, he was just another bum. Like me.

"I don't know. I guess that's one reason I wanted your expertise with the horses. A new perspective. Tonight is another test. See all these fresh faces around us? All these retired pros? They're getting primed for a nice fat poker game where each tries to out-brag and out-play the other. And you know who rakes in the money every year?"

"You?"

"Every year they need a local guy like me. One guy they don't have to impress. They got these deals going—car dealerships, restaurants, you name it. They've tried to score in the real world but the business flopped. They've got to win and losing to me is better than losing to one of their old teammates."

"So, you take advantage?"

He snickered. "It's part of my annual income. But here's the other part I wanted to talk to you about."

I knew there must be something else.

"I had this problem with Zany and the amount I owed," he said.

My ears pricked up.

He talked fast. "I didn't think the amount was right. Zany wouldn't listen to anything I had to say." He sat up straight as his voice rose in frustration. "We dealt with bankruptcy quite often at the bank. All my debts are discharged—wiped out. Even ones I didn't list. I was pissed Zany cut me off. But now..."

I got it. Arnold wanted me to give him a clean bill of health, wipe out his sizeable gambling debt to the store due to bankruptcy and give him credit to bet sports again. Why didn't he go to Chase Bank or American Express and ask them for credit, why ask me?

"What?" I quickly composed myself. I recalled that Arnold was my benefactor today, and I should extend mercy.

"I don't want to go to Leister, I don't trust him," he said. "There's a reason I come to this Disneyland Preston built. First, it's the office mentality—I can concentrate. Second, I know I'll get paid. Offshore internet sites can go out of business and steal your money. Zany did a lot for us."

"But you had an argument with Zany?" A dispute over a gambling debt was what I'd been looking for and here it was. Was it enough to result in murder?

"We argued over whether I'd made a bet on this one game or not. Then he cut me off without notice. But I've got this game tonight that I'd really like to bet. The pitcher for the Rockies."

What would Mags and Burrascano say about wiping out a balance due to bankruptcy? I still felt the sting of my own gambling debt so why should I cut Arnold any slack? But then I thought about Burrascano's back door deal.

"Sure, Jim. I can't wipe out the debt, but I'll let you place bets. I'll call the store right now." I almost laughed out loud. I must be certifiable. I could hear DiNatale: "Discharge his debt? I'll give him a discharge—both barrels." But what the hell. By the time DiNatale found out I'd either be the hero or doing time.

"Don't worry. I do real good at college football." Arnold leaned back and wiped his glasses with a handkerchief.

It was plain to see. Arnold's true passion revolved around betting sports. The horses were just a pleasant diversion, a way to stay in shape for the real thing. "How did you get into debt?"

He shook his head. The gambler always felt stupid looking back.

"Fuck, I don't know. The end of college basketball," he said. "Couple of bad picks."

Digging into the past was something gamblers rarely did. I had to go for it. "So, what about those big payouts Zany made last winter to Preston and Mulholland?" If anyone at the club knew or sensed what Preston might be up to, it would be his handicapping buddy, Arnold, a statistician, former bank executive, and compulsive handicapper. I figured him as my ace in the hole.

He shot me the classic deer in the headlights look. "Yeah, I know."

34

Arnold's gaze moved above me. A hand clamped down on my shoulder.

"Hey, Eddie, you're in my spot."

I didn't recognize the gruff voice at first. I turned around and looked up at a tall, youthful man with crutches. Zach.

"You're not giving my winners away are you, Jim?" Zach dropped a computer satchel into the empty carrel beside me and juggled the crutches.

"Hi, Zach. You seen Preston?" Arnold asked.

"Why? Need somebody to write a check?" Zach laughed hard at his own joke, his straight blond hair, matted from a recent shower, flopped into his eyes as he bent over. He raised himself back up and regained his composure. "I don't know for certain. I've been down in physical therapy all morning, but he mentioned something about some lunch."

Zach had been doing more than PT. His eyes were glassy and the smirk on his face came from alcohol or drugs. I got a big whiff of locker room Right Guard and cologne, plus mouthwash.

"Lunch here at the club or somewhere else?" Arnold asked.

I didn't like Arnold's concern over Preston. It told me Arnold had committed a serious infraction of the rules by bringing me in. What did he write on that card he'd handed to Raymond?

"Shit, I don't know. Oh, yeah, Preston wasn't happy. Allegro and those network executives went to a spot downtown." Zach set his crutches to one side and dropped into the chair.

"Good," Arnold said. "That will take a couple hours or more."

"Just a second, Zach," I said, turning back to Arnold. I kept my voice low. "So, Jim, you were going to tell me about those payouts by Zany last winter?"

Arnold kept his head down inside his carrel. "I need to wager on this race from Monmouth." He got up and walked over to the betting windows, his program in hand.

It was an obvious brushoff. After the way we'd bonded over his bankruptcy and my willingness to extend credit at the store, it wasn't what I expected. He must want to keep it secret. Maybe Zach would tell Preston or let something slip. Arnold depended upon Preston and couldn't afford to be banned from the club. Arnold had that poker game with the old pros tonight.

The brushoff brought my investigation back to the forefront and changed my mood. The handicapping and the races were a diversion I had to set aside. For Uncle Mike.

Maybe Zach could tell me something about those payouts to Preston and Mulholland. Arnold and Zach were close. But it must be a sensitive subject and I'd need to approach Zach in a roundabout way.

"Too bad about Mulholland," I said to Zach.

"The members think you did it."

"Bullshit."

Zach laughed and slapped the table. "I know, I know. I like to get a rise out of you that's all. Mulholland was a putz. One good thing about it—"

He stared over the carrel toward the big screen on the far wall with a race in progress. It didn't seem as if he had a stake in the outcome.

"What's that?" I prompted.

Zach took a moment to refocus. "I got this fucked up hearing at the school. They're trying to suspend me. I'm not exactly Dean's List material, you know? Mulholland handled it so now everything is on hold."

It confirmed what I'd seen in Zach's file in Mulholland's office, but why tell me about it? Legal troubles had a way of eating you up inside and the next thing you know, you're confiding in strangers. I'd been there. "I guess you've got to pay another attorney to get up to speed."

"Yeah. Costs a shitload. Thank God for old Moneybags. Preston pays the bill because of mom."

"No money problems for Preston? The Kelso Club is quite the operation." I thought of that letter by Preston's brother.

"No," Zach said with a shake of his head. "No way. See the way the members drink? The bar bills alone help the club pay for itself. Moneybags loves playing the bigshot. We've got these two guards on the team from inner-city LA that are for real, you know? We got pretty close on the road and they don't have much. Moneybags gave them part-time jobs at the club for spending money." Zach laughed and tapped my shoulder. "They drop by once a month to pick up a check."

I nodded and shared in Zach's laughter. The practice of paying athletes on the side for a phantom job had become a common corrupt way to flaunt NCAA rules. "Nice of Preston to help them out. Preston told me he wasn't happy with Mulholland's services."

Zach had gotten lost in the big screen again and seemed to almost nod off. He turned back to me. "He did?" He swept a hand through his hair. "That's news to me. Mulholland seemed to work part-time in Preston's office, you know? I think those two were close. Well, as close as anyone can get to a guy like Preston."

From Zach's inebriated state, it wasn't easy to tell how reliable he might be. I needed to shake him up. "Your mom has been with Preston a long time."

Zach's face reddened. "It's like we're fucking trapped. Me and mom. She's done so much for me. Got custody from my dad who never showed up for games. She wants me to get to the NBA as much as I do. It's not a pipe dream. Coaches all wanted me."

I'd looked back at Zach's team from two years ago when they made the NCAA tournament. Zach and those two guards from LA tore up the league.

Zach clutched my forearm. "You gotta dream or what've you got? Nothing. Mom has sacrificed so much. When I sign that NBA contract, the first thing I'm gonna do is buy her a house and get her out of that damn penthouse. See all these old pros around here? Let me tell you their secret. They all had a dream, too. Didn't let no one stand in their way. Not once did I feel I wouldn't get my points. Fuck no. I couldn't wait for each game so I could put on a show for the scouts. I'll be back. You watch."

I glanced around at the crowd. "Is Coach Mancuso here?"

"I haven't seen him. He's not much of a gambler, but he shows up for the dinners and the golf. The kids all love him."

"Hey, guys," Arnold said. "I got a sixteen to one shot coming up in the next race."

It was a call to action. I did a sixty-second job of handicapping. Not much time before post. Arnold's four horse did have potential. Plus, I liked the eight horse with two straight wins since he'd been claimed by a hot barn. I bounced up to the windows and decided to box the 4-8 in the exacta and hit it hard. No reason to use caution or stay conservative. Preston could be back from lunch any time.

I barely sat back down and the race started. My adrenaline kicked in like the old days as the horses came down the stretch. Arnold's four horse and my eight horse battled in deep stretch. I had the exacta either way, but Arnold's horse had the greater odds, so if it won my exacta would pay more. I rooted for the four horse with Arnold and Zach. The four horse extended fully at the wire and got his nose in front of the eight.

My twenty-dollar exacta wager would yield almost a thousand dollars. It was the breakthrough I needed.

"Not as good as that twenty-nine to one shot you had last Saturday, Eddie, but I'll take sixteen to one," Zach said. "Good work, Jim."

Arnold waved and then dug back into the next race. He didn't celebrate much. I didn't have the time to give him my eight horse so I stayed mute about my exacta win. The track tried hard to suck me back in. Those upcoming races at the Chicago track came to mind. It would be easy pickings for me compared to these east coast tracks.

Zach stood and rubbed his knee. "This damn knee. I'm not sure the latest surgery did any good. Moneybags got me this specialist."

With the win under his belt, it was the perfect opportunity to question Zach. I stood as well. "I heard about those payouts by Zany to Mulholland and Preston last winter."

Zach's face froze. I could see the gears working. After a moment's hesitation, he blurted out: "Never heard about those. I've got to hit the head." He grabbed his crutches and made a fast exit.

Arnold whacked me on the shoulder. "I missed Raymond's call because of the last race."

We both turned. Preston stood at the back of the room.

35

I now knew what Arnold had written on the back of the card he'd handed to Raymond—"call me when Preston arrives"—or something similar. But Arnold missed the call.

Preston stood at the back of the simulcast room with three guys in dark suits—the network execs here to evaluate Allegro. But where was Allegro?

Preston didn't waste time. He marched toward me. His arms swung in cadence like a toy soldier, face red. "Eddie, I thought I made myself clear."

I was pissed. I had track money in my pocket. I needed to stay in the Kelso Club to pursue my investigation with what little time I had left.

"No, you didn't make anything clear." I stood face-to-face with one of my star suspects.

Preston kept his voice low and leaned forward. "From day one I've told you the club has rules and regulations which must be abided by—"

"Yeah. And you've either banned me from the club or threatened to ban me since day one and I'm sick of it." I stood and nodded in the direction of the execs. "Who are your friends?"

"That's none of your business. This is a private club. I ordered you off the premises due to your unwarranted attack on Peter Leister. If you force me to remove you physically from the premises then I will, but I'd hoped to save you the embarrassment."

"I don't embarrass easily. Why don't we go over and explain all this to your friends?"

Preston looked at Arnold. "Jim, I've been told you are responsible for Eddie's presence here today. You know as well as anyone—"

Arnold stood and placed his hands on his hips. "I'm tired of all these rules. Eddie's my guest. He didn't kill anybody and you know it."

"Don't blame him. I'm the problem," I said.

"Give me a break," Arnold said to Preston. "You built this place. Face it, Preston. You want to be a gambler. You want to place bets and talk about the odds but your heart isn't in it."

I recalled the day at Aurora Downs and how Preston was the one person who didn't dive into the racing program to make the most of Mulholland's hot tip.

Preston pulled a walkie-talkie out of his breast pocket. "Raymond, I need security now."

"You and your rules," Arnold continued. "How do you come up with them? You're always judging us but who judges you?"

"Mr. Arnold, the board will deal with you. Right now, I'd say there's a good chance your privileges will be revoked," Preston said.

"You are the board," Arnold said. "Who are you kidding?"

I'd managed to light the fuse on some smoldering fires. I stayed silent.

Other members had begun to congregate from the betting lines and handicap carrels, drawn by all the excitement. The execs had moved up several steps.

Preston studied the faces around him and grabbed the lapels of his sports coat with each hand. "Someone has to remain focused on how the club is perceived and its contribution to the community and charitable endeavors."

I looked around at the crowd. People didn't buy it.

Arnold shook his head and laughed. "Bullshit. Another speech. You know what I had to do, Preston? I filed bankruptcy. Hear that everybody?" He waved his arms and turned to the betting windows then back. "I said 'bankruptcy.' Chapter 7. You've all heard of it. And you know who relished every minute of my downward spiral to financial ruin—my buddy, Preston here. Stood by me every step of the way, even loaned me a few bucks so he could torture me with his lectures."

I knew how painful this admission must be for Arnold. A hint of despair in his voice. I had the feeling Arnold had run on a lifelong treadmill and even this disclosure wouldn't let him jump off.

"Your failure to exercise self-control is not the club's responsibility," Preston said. "What *is* my concern is that undesirables are not admitted into the club."

Undesirable? I'd been charged with a lot of stuff before but "undesirable" almost made me laugh out loud. Then I remembered to act outraged. "What the fuck?"

"I'll tell you why you loved to watch me go down the drain," Arnold said. "Because you can't do it yourself. Yes, Preston, it's something you can't begin to understand. Money handed to you all your life. Everything given to you. Your crappy little C-note bets can't put a dent in the interest on your trust fund allowance."

The crowd laughed, and Preston took a step back. I almost felt sorry for him—Mr. Popularity Complex. The rich were vulnerable when accused of being different.

"I've contributed more to this club than all of you combined," Preston sputtered.

"For what," I said. "What do you get out of it? The chance to suck up to Allegro and these other has-beens?"

Some of the old pros booed.

"I'll tell you why Preston does it." Arnold paced about as if he campaigned for their vote. "Preston runs this place as his private science lab so he can see how people *feel* when they lose. Some idea of what life is about."

Preston placed a hand on Arnold's shoulder. "It's the money that eats at you, doesn't it, Jim. I can see why it would under your circumstances. We'll see what we can do. But money has no effect on my efforts to establish a worthwhile meeting place to support the community."

Arnold broke away from Preston. "See what *we* can do? Who are you kidding? You really don't have a clue, do you?

Don't you see? That's what you're missing. Money means everything."

Preston withdrew his outreached hand. His mouth moved but words didn't come out.

What could he say? Money did mean everything and none of the people in this room would believe a word to the contrary.

I saw the faces and the crowd, the hunger. They looked down with anger at this man who held the purse strings, made the rules, and tried to enforce them. Preston, a man who'd built something he couldn't control. They needed Preston but hated him for it.

Raymond ran up with a couple extra security men. "I warned you, Mr. Arnold."

Preston threw up his hands. "This is hopeless. Raymond, escort Eddie out of the building." He turned to the execs. "A little misunderstanding, gentlemen."

I would never give poor old Raymond a hard time or the other security guys. "Thanks, Jim." I shook Arnold's hand. "We'll have to play the races again some other time."

"Sure," Arnold said.

Preston watched me go and then turned to the execs. "Gentlemen, let's take a break from these handicappers and tour the rest of the facility.

"You can't get rid of me this easily," I said as I passed Preston and the execs. "You fired Mulholland, but you can't fire me. I don't work for you."

"Go, Eddie. Go now," Preston called after me.

Preston's jaw twitched. My Mulholland comment had struck a nerve.

36

I EXITED THE ELEVATOR ON THE FIRST FLOOR WITH MY security guard entourage in tow. I tried to think of what my next move could be.

"Hey, Eddie," a voice called from the direction of the spa.

I turned to see Allegro come up toward me, his broad shoulders and slim waist guided his still-youthful body in a gliding motion along the marble floor.

"Hey, the twenty-nine to one shot, how you doing?" Allegro reached out his hand. "Where's Rudi, your better half?"

I shook his hand, somewhat surprised by the warm greeting after being kicked out upstairs. "Hi, Allegro. Rudi's not here." I'd tried her several times on the cell. I couldn't help but worry if everything was all right. Maybe she'd changed cell numbers again.

I leaned over to Raymond. "Can you give us a minute? I swear I'll stay right here."

"It's okay, Raymond," Allegro said. "I'll watch him." He busted out laughing.

I couldn't help but smile along with the contagious Allegro smile. "How was lunch?"

Allegro rubbed his stomach beneath the expensive suit coat and pressed white shirt. "Not too good. I had to run into the john as soon as we got here. How you doing? I thought you'd be busy with Leister. What are you doing upstairs?"

"Playing the ponies." I didn't like the Leister reference or being referred to as the 29-1 shot. Allegro knew the teasing got under my skin.

"No shit, I thought you were too cool to bet. How did you do?"

"I won." I thought of the track money in my pocket and the Chicago races I could've carved up if I'd had more time.

"And I thought you were a bookie who doesn't bet—you fooled us." Allegro rubbed his salt and pepper beard. "Preston kicked your ass out?"

"Yeah. The network execs were with him."

"Shit. What did they do? They say anything?"

I enjoyed getting a rise out of Allegro for a change. "No. They stood by while Arnold and Preston got into it."

"Goddamnit. I told Preston to forget about you, but he wouldn't listen."

"I thought Preston always did what you say."

Allegro took a step back, his expression faked mild surprise. "What do you mean?"

"C'mon, Preston runs around and does errands for you, buys drinks, and puts on this charity event."

Allegro smiled. "I know, I know. He's my biggest fan, and I appreciate him. But sometimes he can be a royal pain in the ass. Then I realize how I need every fan I can get."

I saw Allegro's head drop for a moment. "What?"

"You know what happened on the way back from lunch?" he said. "Me and my network execs walk down the sidewalk, a power team, right through downtown Denver—a great sports town—and not one person recognizes me. Not one. Me, Allegro Martin. I look people right in the eye—right in the eye—and they look past me like I'm nobody. Can you believe that shit?"

I acted as if I'd never heard such tragic news. "No way."

"I'm another old guy in the crowd with gray in his beard. A nobody. If I was a seven-footer then I'd stand out. But I was a jump-shooter. It's been a long time since I put up one of those forty-point nights and got my name in the paper."

I wanted to move things past Allegro's bruised ego. Raymond was looking at his watch. "They offer you the job?"

"No, not yet," he said. "It doesn't help your bargaining position when no one recognizes you in your hometown."

"You don't need the money, right?" I knew how much Allegro needed the money to pay all the ex-wives and child support, but I wanted to find out what he might say.

"Everybody needs the network's kind of money and possible endorsement deals," he said.

"This charity event should impress those network execs." Beneath the glow of fame from Allegro, I felt a strange need to keep him pumped.

"I don't know. It used to work out so well. I'd get endorsements from the outing's backers, and the corporate fat cats got to play golf with the old pros. Now we get fewer corporate guys every year. It's Father Time. The corporate reps get younger, and I get older. My face isn't out there the way it used to be."

"I'm sure the charity tournament will be a huge success. A lot of the old pros are here and the volunteer night was well attended. Maybe you can talk to Preston and get me back into the club. I'd like to attend." It was Allegro's event. If anyone had the pull to get me back inside, it was him.

"These network execs don't like bookies or sports gambling."

"That's bullshit. The reason people watch their twenty-four-hour sports channel is to know everything they can before they bet on the game. Why else would a national audience watch some game from West Virginia or New Mexico on a Thursday night?"

"You're not telling me anything I don't know. It's this unspoken thing. They pretend there is some office pool out there and it's good clean fun. Fantasy leagues and stuff—it's nuts. But when your charity event is sponsored by a gambling club, you got to be careful."

I saw how invested Allegro was in this broadcast job, but I still needed him to persuade Preston. "Let me back inside with you. I'll stay in the background. I don't want people to wager with Leister, that's all."

Allegro's eyes narrowed. "I'd like to Eddie, believe me. But you know how Preston and some of these members can be. They were big fans of Mulholland and want you out."

"Preston wasn't a fan. He fired Mulholland."

"He told you about that?"

I saw the surprise on Allegro's face. Maybe I shouldn't have said anything. It was something I learned about from my break-in. "I didn't kill the lawyer."

"I understand a Detective Tenorio questioned you?" Allegro said.

I shrugged. "You saw how I happened to be in the men's room when they found Mulholland. You were there. I was simply in the wrong place at the wrong time."

Allegro squinted. "You haven't been called in again?"

A wave of fear swept up my back. "No."

"That's odd."

I fought off a rush of paranoia.

"Eddie, please," Raymond called from the other end of the lobby. "Preston might come down."

"Okay, okay," I called back. "Too bad. I had some horses running today in Chicago. Arnold, Zach, and I made a great team." I hoped Allegro might want to ask me to go upstairs and we'd all play the races.

"You were up there with Zach? What did he say?" Allegro moved an inch closer.

It was a definite *tell*. I was touched. Allegro had this special concern for his protégé and maybe knew of Zach's bad habits. I was concerned about him as well. "He's worried about playing this year and getting in the NBA."

"I know. He sees other players signing big deals and he's on the sidelines. Zach lost a whole year. He's so close." Allegro shook his head.

Raymond walked over. "Eddie, please." He poked my arm. "You have to go."

Allegro shook my hand. "I'll see what I can do, Eddie."

I walked away feeling discouraged.

This could be the end.

37

That night I decided to crash the charity outing at the Kelso Club. It was late. I anticipated a shift change for the security guards and that Raymond wouldn't be on duty. Arnold would be winning at poker. He'd already won those sports bets with the store so he'd be in a super mood. I'd be his best buddy. I'd text him when I got outside the club and he'd come down and authorize my admittance. Members that were still around would be partying. It would give me the opportunity to question Preston.

I ran back to my hotel from the store for a change of clothes. No way I'd fit in without a sports coat. I'd spent the day in screaming matches with the store's employees. Rudi's absence had left a void and each employee wanted her job and her office.

Preston seemed like my prime suspect. Mullholland's letter to Preston called him a "crazy fucker," and I couldn't agree more. The two of them had fought over something. Those payouts by Zany to Mulholland and Preston had become a sensitive subject. Both Arnold and Zach refused to explain the payouts.

I ran up the stairs to my hotel room. Preston stood at the epicenter of the Kelso Club. Maybe the club was his own science lab like Arnold said. An exclusive LoDo gambling parlor for the city's high rollers, dedicated to the memory of a great racehorse and celebrating old pros. A place for faded dreams and one last night of bragging. Preston was the board, decided who was an undesirable, and maybe his experiments included murder.

My hotel room was dark. The maid usually left the curtains open or a light on. The door closed behind me as I hunted for the switch.

Someone stepped out of the john. "Leave it."

The man held a gun. It was Grasso. Another man came up and pulled me down the hall, DiNatale's muscle. He also pointed a gun at my gut. I couldn't go for my gun.

"What the hell?" I couldn't believe this. Burrascano had sanctioned my presence here in Denver. A figure lay on the bed.

"Eddie, where you been?" DiNatale swung his legs and sat upright on the edge of the bed.

"Vic, what is this?"

"I asked where you been?"

I looked into the sad, vacant expression of grouper face. "You do Vic's laundry, too?"

No answer.

I turned to DiNatale's bodyguard. "Do they ever let you drive the limo?" I asked.

Not a muscle moved on his dark face.

DiNatale's feet danced on the floor. "I asked a simple question. We've been waiting."

"You should've called first. I'd have ordered room service." DiNatale was taking a chance with this move. What would Burrascano say?

"You must've been somewhere, right?" DiNatale held out his hands, palms up. "Because you haven't been in your room, so where've you been?"

I wanted to see DiNatale's face. "Flip on the lights."

"No, I like it dark. You've been out here all week. You must've found out stuff about Zany's murder. So, tell me."

"Why?"

"I think Mags and Burrascano deserve a little status report."

"I report to Burrascano direct."

His voice changed from friendly to cynical. "And if you don't have anything that says a lot."

The guns within inches had a purpose. "Like what?"

"Like maybe you aren't doing nothing."

"Are you Mags's errand boy?"

DiNatale stood up. "You've been talking to the cops. I got a right to know."

"Mags gets the police reports with his daily Wall Street Journal, talk to him."

I couldn't show a hint of weakness. But this resolution didn't keep me from breaking out in a sweat.

"Something happens to you, somebody has to carry the ball." He took a step forward.

"I tell you, and you'll fuck it up."

"What?"

"Like that raid on Leister," I said.

"Bullshit. You're working with Leister."

This was beyond reason. "Bullshit."

"Where is this Warren cocksucker?"

"You heard about him?"

DiNatale took another step. "I heard you're gambling. Gambling Burrascano's money." He gave a slight nod.

I felt the blow to my solar plexus, deep in my side under the rib cage. It came from Grasso. The air burst from my lungs, and I collapsed in a heap.

Before I could catch my breath, another blow hit me in the same spot.

DiNatale bent down, his face close. "Burrascano's money. Get out. You're done. I'm taking over."

I heard some of the words, but I was too busy dodging kicks. I squirmed and rolled into a ball the way a nightcrawler tries to evade the prick of the fishhook. A kick to the ribs, my back. Better than my gut.

"Get the money," DiNatale said.

I felt hands in my pockets. My track money, Burrascano's stake.

"You should've thought of this before you gambled. It could be worse," DiNatale said.

A kick to my head and things turned black.

38

THURSDAY

I spent the night rolling around the floor. I'd wake up, roll on one side, feel a jab of pain in my ribs, then roll in the other direction. My body suspended between each breath. No position worked for long. Constant movement was required to find a few minutes of sleep every hour.

On the bed I'd be unable to twist and turn freely. The mattress would pull me down, and I feared suffocation.

I became intimate with hotel solvents and disinfectants imbedded in the nap of the tightly woven carpet, inhaled carpet fibers, and viewed my place in the world from my true perspective—from the dregs looking up.

I thought about what I'd do to DiNatale. They didn't take my gun.

I spent time on my investigation—Mulholland and Leister, Preston and Mulholland, Preston and Arnold, Allegro and each of them. Not sure if it was real or a black and white noir movie. Sounds of night traffic, sirens, gave way to the steady morning traffic. Doors slammed as guests left for the mountains, business, or returned home.

I struggled to my feet, bounced off the bed, and hit the door jamb of the john. I made it into the shower without falling and let the water ride over my head and body until steam filled the space and cloaked me in wickedness.

I should leave. Go back to the Chicago tracks. Yesterday showed I still had it. Some of the old magic came back. But if I'd been able to get it back then I could solve Zany's murder. The two were twisted up.

I needed to get DiNatale off my back. Do something to stave off the net Tenorio had thrown over me. I swam in less and less square footage.

I sat in the shower until my skin wrinkled. Some blood floated down the drain. Did I swim with chum? Would it attract sharks? I thought of Childress, my mom's killer, and the way he must've smiled walking out of the courtroom.

I craved vengeance. I imagined what I'd tell DiNatale, Clint Eastwood style, before I shot him in the face. After I kicked the shit out of him.

A super-human effort to stand upright. I steadied myself, shut off the shower, and toweled off. I was on a mission.

My cell phone buzzed. I stumbled through the room and searched around my clothes on the floor, found the cell, and answered without checking to see the number or who it might be.

"Yeah?" I stood naked.

"Eddie, what the hell is going on out there?" Uncle Mike yelled. "Joey L tells me you've been gambling, gambling Burrascano's money."

My head pounded but I heard some of what my uncle said. "I'm going to kill him."

"What?"

"I got a visit from DiNatale and the boys last night. In my hotel room."

"Take it easy."

"One of them sucker punched me. Kicked my ass. I'm going to kill him."

"No, you're not." Uncle Mike's voice became businesslike.

"Yes, I am. I'm going to beat the shit out of him and then put a bullet in his head."

"Wait a minute. Calm down. Get control of that temper of yours. You'll play right into his hands if you do something stupid."

I understood. DiNatale was a made man. I'd sign my own death warrant if I took revenge. "I'm pissed. Let me talk to Burrascano direct."

Uncle Mike talked in a low and level voice and explained how this was my first solo job and DiNatale wanted to take advantage. *Don't let him get to you.* Burrascano didn't say I had to leave, so let's think about the next step, make a plan. I took a deep breath. My hands were shaking.

I found my self-control and went through yesterday step by step and how it had been necessary to get back into the Kelso Club to gain information. How Arnold invited me as his guest, and then Preston kicked me out. Uncle Mike was on my side. But what about Leister, he argued. Was there some reason I avoided the logical conclusion?

This got me pissed off all over again and we went back and forth. In retrospect, I felt this had been Uncle Mike's strategy all along. Get me talking and blow off steam.

We talked about Warren. My uncle said how he'd seen this kind of domestic violence his entire career on the force. Warren wanted only one thing—to make his wife's life a living hell. I wasn't so sure if Warren wanted something else.

"Why don't you come home? We'll make it with what we've got."

"No." I didn't need to think about my answer.

Maybe I needed a good old-fashioned ass-kicking to wake me up. The payments by Zany to Mulholland and Preston. There was something about this war with Leister. The way he'd conveniently showed up at the Kelso Club shortly after DiNatale and I had arrived. Why Leister would target Koransky and notify the school. Mancuso's delivery of the letter. The whole thing struck a sour note. This war was trumped-up.

I'd also thought about the killer's next move. "I think things are coming to a head. The killer will strike again. He's growing bolder and this club charity event is the perfect opportunity."

"Maybe," Uncle Mike said.

"Both killings were at Kelso Club events. The killer can't resist. The Mulholland murder was done on the spur of the moment. The killer plans to do what he did with Zany in honor of the big club event."

"You mean extended torture?"

"Exactly."

"But what are you going to do?" Uncle Mike exhaled into the phone. "You're banned from the club. DiNatale and Tenorio are after you. Don't forget about Leister or Warren."

"I got friends all over, don't I?" I liked the sarcastic touch. I wanted a fight. "This is still my investigation. Tell Burrascano I've got a hot lead. Tell him something."

It was better than nothing.

39

I PACKED UP A WEEK'S WORTH OF STUFF SCATTERED ALL OVER the hotel room—laptop, socks, underwear, clothes in drawers and the closet, phone charger, shaving kit—and tossed it all into a suitcase and lit out. Too bad about the hotel bill—the credit card already over its limit, and I'd been robbed of my cash. Maybe if the hotel offered better security.

I took the long route down a back alley, checked to see if I was followed, then skulked into the parking garage. I dumped my stuff into the Crown Vic, dug out my laptop, and walked to a diner a few blocks away. At least I found a small stack of twenty-dollar bills stashed in the suitcase—enough for meals.

The name of the diner in LoDo was Nixon's. Assuming Richard Nixon hadn't found a second life behind the grill, it seemed a good spot to regroup. I found a seat in a back booth with a good view of the intersection of two streets out front. It also gave me an angle on who came in the front door and afforded a good escape avenue past the restrooms and into an alley.

I had to find a way to get DiNatale off my back. After I tried Rudi's cell again, I called one of Uncle Mike's old friends, Smily Anderson, at the FBI. We had worked together on past jobs, and I felt he owed me a favor. We didn't call him "Smily" to his face. As a southern gentleman he insisted on being called Bertram, an old family name. I left word on the answering machine to please have "Bertram" get back to me, in the hope he could look up some information for me on the status of the war between Mags and Leister. Something didn't smell right—or maybe it was those carpet fibers.

I set up the laptop and got a newspaper. I didn't dwell on headlines. My automatic reflex with my first cup of black coffee required a scan of the sports pages. A substitute for a cigarette.

On page three, stuck behind the Bronco's exhibition game and the Rockies' latest loss, was a story about Zach. A school regent announced late yesterday that Zach Rogers, high scoring, all-conference forward on the basketball team, had been suspended due to grades. The article was short and sweet. The regent was quoted that he "hoped that Zach could perhaps one day rejoin the team if his scholastic record could be brought up to the satisfaction of the committee."

Here I was feeling sorry for myself due to my late-night ass-kicking—and my ass still felt sore even in the vinyl cushioned booth—but I didn't face what Zach had to confront: the end of a lifelong dream. I felt sorry for him.

It had taken my breath away when Zach talked about the dream. How "you gotta dream." He said that he could score against anybody and coaches wanted him. The NBA pot of gold contract so close.

And how would Crystal take it? She'd spent all those years taking him from one camp to the next. She'd probably fought all night with Preston.

I sipped the coffee. Since when did a star player get suspended over grades? They had players teach Ping Pong or something. Maybe it was Zach's knee. The grades were used as an excuse by the school to free up another scholarship. Maybe he'd gotten stoned or drunk yesterday because he knew his fate. The reason he didn't care about PT or that tutor.

I flipped on the laptop and researched more about the story as I ate my eggs, and bacon, and wheat toast—as if I had a reason to worry about white bread.

There wasn't much more on the story, but I got into an internet groove in tandem with my caffeine buzz. I glanced at articles on Zach's short college career and games from two years ago. It seemed he'd been able to score at will. Then I switched to stories about Preston's family and all the charity the Williston family did back east. Preston's efforts at the Kelso Club not even worthy of an honorable mention.

I called the store to check up on things and one of the employees answered.

"This is awful," the employee said. "Some men came in this morning and said they were in charge and you weren't coming back."

"I guess not. Good luck." I hung up. DiNatale didn't waste time—he coveted Zany's big chair since day one.

The store had begun to mean more to me than cover for the Zany investigation. Maybe I should be relieved to be rid of the burden, but I felt the pang of defeat. I'd hoped to run the store when it was in full battle mode during pro football season. I might not know what I was doing and would make a mess of it, but I wanted the chance. I wanted to see what it would be like to be the House.

I no longer walked in Zany's shoes. I no longer held the power. Guys like Arnold wouldn't suck up to me and ask for credit.

DiNatale had won. My back and ribs ached and breakfast demanded a return trip as bile rose in my throat. I held onto the edge of the table in hope the nausea would pass, then slipped the waitress a few bucks to watch the laptop and went outside for some fresh air.

Of course, I stood with the smokers. Should I bum a smoke? My lungs wheezed beneath bruised ribs so I didn't dare. But I watched each drag and smoked vicariously.

Despite all this, what stuck in my craw more than DiNatale, Mags, Warren, Preston, and everybody, was my wimp-like failure to bet those winning horses yesterday. How the track played *me*. The last thing I should think about.

I went back inside and checked the Chicago horse racing result charts from yesterday. Some of the winners were very pickable. What a waste.

I thought again about Mabel's Fable and Bud's Charleton—two horses I didn't bet. Then I thought of Zany's Aunt Mabel so I looked up Zany on the internet again. Then I looked up Aunt Mabel and searched databases for her last names—she'd been married three times. In a stroke of pure genius, I looked up Denver real estate records to see if I had a match. Somehow it made sense. My gambling and Zany's murder coiled together like two snakes in ecstasy.

I found a house in the suburbs under Aunt Mabel's second married name, Mabel Lowery. Maybe it was a coincidence, another Mabel Lowery in Colorado.

What else did I have to do this afternoon? I'd check it out.

40

I BEGAN TO GET EXCITED WHEN I PULLED UP THE STREET MAP to the suburban home on my laptop and found it sat on a direct line between downtown and Aurora Downs. Rudi said that Zany's preferred route from the store to the track to visit old friends was directly through the city.

I tried not to think about Rudi. The last thing she needed was to start over with someone like me with a boatload of trouble. If I could get in touch with her, I'm not sure what I'd say.

I didn't hurry to the house. Chances were good that it was a wild goose chase. If I was being watched, and I had to figure DiNatale would make it a priority, I should look like a guy who was lost with no place to go, instead of a horseplayer with a big-time hunch. Maybe Mabel's Fable had shined a light on Zany's safe house.

The best way to shake a tail would be a trip to the ER. Everyone knew that would take forever. I took a cab ten blocks over to Denver General and checked in at the desk. DiNatale's tail would think I required a patch job after last night's ass-kicking.

The receptionist smirked and handed me a clipboard of docs to fill out. I headed off to the men's room, flushed the docs, and headed out a side door. I ambled through a park, then a grocery store and caught a cab back downtown. Then I went to the parking garage and got the Crown.

The house sat back from the street in the sleepy workingman's suburb of Aurora, a few miles west of Aurora Downs Racetrack. I drove by several times. Like the other homes in the neighborhood, it was a two-story, four-bedroom house with a big front porch, but unlike others, the windows were shuttered. No cars in the driveway. Overgrown shrubs bordered the porch. The lawn dotted by dry spots.

I couldn't afford to take the extra time to wait around as I did that night at Zany's house. I'd have to use a different tact. I had some business cards in my wallet I kept for such occasions.

I parked at the end of the block and walked up to the front door. If someone answered, I'd say I worked for a roofer—need a free roof inspection? I pulled out the card. What was my fake name again? I read the card: Joe Bartolowski—Linsky Roofing Specialists. I prayed to God nobody was home.

I rang the bell. No answer. I glanced across the street and saw the curtains had been pulled tight against the sun. Like any hard-working suburbanites, both spouses worked and dropped the kids off at daycare. Still, I checked for nosy neighbors next door and took a look out back.

A high wooden fence surrounded the backyard and connected to the side of the garage. A Beware of Dog sign hung on a post. I rattled the locked gate. No dog. Trees and bushes ran along the fence line and beside the driveway providing cover. My old companion fear whispered caution. Tenorio awaited any wrong move. I took a long look down the driveway into the vacant suburban street and then scaled the fence.

The backyard was overgrown by weeds and bushes, without any domestic touches—no garden, swing set, or patio furniture. The sticker on the sliding door in back informed me of a security system. Thanks.

I did a perimeter check of windows and neighbors. The place appeared deserted. My heart beat faster.

I worked at the lock on the side door of the garage, hidden by the high fence. My pick didn't work and the tension wrench didn't do much better. I could break the window of the side door but it was probably wired with a security system.

Around the back of the house, I found a vent for the dryer and a laundry room door behind an overgrown vine. This time the pick worked.

I put on my gloves, raced inside, and found the controls to the security system inside the closed garage. I used the same code I had ready for Zany's residence. It worked. There were no vehicles, no bicycles, or toys. Best of all, no gas fumes.

I crept into the kitchen. The stale air hit me. I stood against the kitchen wall and listened. No sound of a TV or radio. No kids or dogs. No footsteps. My inner clock slowed, until I found myself back on the basement steps beneath the bar of O'Connell's Tavern, eavesdropping on the grownup world.

After an eternity, I went to the front window and looked out though a crack in the shutters. No one out front, no cars. I made the rounds through the house, checked on the backyard, and went upstairs. The place was furnished with shabby, outdated furniture but no signs of a recent newspaper or unopened mail. The heat wave had baked the rooms into ovens. I fought the impulse to open a window.

I went back downstairs to the basement door. I slipped in, shut the door behind me, and waited on the top step. The same precautions I'd taken at Zany's house were required here. If anyone hid down below, I'd be vulnerable on the open stairs. I pulled out my gun. I could out-wait anyone.

After the time it would take to smoke two cigarettes, I crouched down and took one slow step at a time. Fear crawled down my back. I glanced from one dark corner to the other. The basement was unfinished with concrete walls. It had a cool musty smell like a cave. Boxes of junk and old furniture were scattered everywhere. A million places to hide.

At the bottom of the stairs, I ducked behind a stack of boxes and listened to my own wheezing. My ribs cried out. All this bending and waiting—maybe I should've stayed at the ER.

I decided I was alone and began to search along the floor and walls. A moldy old rug covered one section near a wall that bordered the back of the house. I pulled the rug back and found a four-foot square drain. I pried up the grate and hoisted it to one side. The trap door fit snugly into the bottom of the one-foot indentation. My hand shook as I reached deep into my pocket and got the key—thank God DiNatale's muscle didn't find it last night when he searched my pockets.

I got down on my knees and slid the key into the lock. It fit like a charm. I pulled out my penlight and searched around the door for any sign of alarms or other devices to ward off intruders. I didn't see any, and I didn't have the time to get too technical. I pulled up on the door.

Concrete stairs led down. This was the bunker I'd been looking for. I thanked all the red-baiters and cold warmongers of the old days who scared people shitless and drove them to buy bomb shelters.

I wriggled down the narrow passageway into the dark enclosure. My penlight found the plastic wrapped packages of cash stacked up on shelves. I picked one up and stared through the plastic. Hundred-dollar bills, twenty-dollar bills. Stacks and stacks. I thought about the suckers who bet this money. How they could've used it to pay a mortgage, invest in their kids' college funds, or save for retirement. Guys like me. The sight of this cash hoard made me feel like a first-rate chump. Back in Chicago, I contributed to a stash like this one.

I'd found Zany's stash. What would Zany's Aunt Mabel say about this house and its lack of curb appeal? No doubt good-hearted Aunt Mabel had no idea. Maybe Zany's use of his trusted aunt had given him a reassurance of security and secrecy. She'd go to bat for him if there was trouble. She *had* taken his remains back to the Idaho ranch. Aunt Mabel probably had no idea of the maze of shell corporations she owned and forged paperwork that could've offered her pride of ownership. I'd tell her about the house when all this was over.

The discovery could put me back in good graces with Burrascano. Money meant everything to them and there was a lot of it here. Maybe a million, maybe more. There wasn't time to think about what this would mean for the mortgage on Uncle Mike's bar.

But would such a discovery be enough to get me back into the investigation?

The germ of an idea began to take shape.

41

I LEFT THE MONEY IN ZANY'S SAFE HOUSE. ON THE WAY BACK downtown, I drove down side streets and found another vacant home a few miles away. The bright red realtor sign out front and a quick check of the property records on the internet informed me the home had gone through foreclosure.

It was vacant. I took notice of the neighborhood and the sleepy street. The foreclosed house would be perfect.

When I returned to my car and headed downtown, I called Rudi.

This time she picked up. "Hello, Eddie?"

"Thank God. I've been trying to get a hold of you." Her voice sounded so great. I felt a rush of relief.

"Something wrong?"

I didn't want to appear overly needy and took a deep breath. "No, I'm fine." Except for my investigation, Uncle Mike's mortgaged bar, and a dozen other things.

"You are? You're sure?"

"Yeah." I didn't want to alarm her further, so I tried to keep a level voice. "No, no problem. Did you go back to Nebraska?"

"Hell, no. I spent time with Crystal. She's a wreck. I put my phone on airplane mode because of Warren. You heard about Zach?"

"I read it in the paper." Crystal must be devastated. Leave it to a woman like Rudi to give a friend's problems priority over her own welfare.

"Phyllis from the store called Crystal because she couldn't get in touch with me. That's why I checked my cell and saw you had called."

About a hundred times. "What did Phyllis have to say?"

"Things are terrible at the store. Lots of screaming and yelling. The employees are about to walk. What happened?"

Rudi had the store's interest in her bloodstream. True loyalty.

"That's a shame," I said.

"You don't mean that," she said.

I cleared my throat. "No, of course not. You know how Vic likes to take charge."

"Crystal said you were gambling yesterday."

I heard the note of concern in her voice. "Yeah, didn't do too bad." I thought of my nice exacta win.

"Can I help?"

This was unexpected but welcome. I did need her help. "Can you meet me?"

"Absolutely."

"Nixon's Diner in an hour? You know where it is?"

"Sure."

It was after rush hour by the time I parked the Crown Vic and took my zigzag route through alleys and side streets to meet Rudi. I had a plan but it called for plenty of risk. Each deep wheezing cough reminded me of my ass-kicking and got me pissed.

LoDo was almost vacant on a weeknight when the Rockies played out of town. I walked past a row of converted office buildings and felt the afternoon heat radiate from the old warehouse brick walls. My feet bounced with the thought that I'd see Rudi again soon.

A car sped past and instinctively I ducked. A shot rang out and something whizzed past. *Jeesus Christ, what the hell?* I dove onto the sidewalk. A bullet had ricocheted off the bricks. Tires squealed as the car swerved around a corner. A black Lexus sedan but I couldn't read the plate.

I stood up, one hand on the gun at the small of my back, and searched for the indentation in the wall. I should get out of there, but I couldn't resist the impulse. I found the fresh notch in the brick about where my head would've been.

I cursed myself for my lack of vigilance. Wake up for God's sake. It would only get more dangerous from now on.

Before I got to the booth at Nixon's, I called Uncle Mike from the back alley. I kept one hand on my gun and hoped the Lexus would try again, but this time I'd return the favor.

"Eddie, now what?" Uncle Mike got to the point.

"I found it."

"What?"

"I found Zany's stash."

"Goddamnit, that's great. Good work. Now we're out of the doghouse. Where is it?"

"That's the problem," I said.

"What? What problem?"

"I'm not going to tell them where it is."

Dead air and then the click of the lighter. "What the fuck are you talking about?"

"They let DiNatale stick his nose into this and now they're going to pay. All I want is some room to operate."

"Do you know what you're saying? For Christ sakes, Eddie."

Uncle Mike went on to explain the obvious. What if the cops found it or someone else? What if I was killed? I told Uncle Mike I'd mail the address to him as insurance. He'd have to try to sell my crazy plan to guys who were born suspicious. In their eyes, even Mister Rogers was out to screw them.

"Tell me one thing, Eddie. Be straight with me now or I swear—"

"Okay."

"Is this a bluff?"

"No, no way." I went on to explain what I'd found—the records, the bunker, the freeze-dried plastic packages of cash. But I didn't mention Aunt Mabel or anything that could give away the address.

Uncle Mike exhaled. His desk chair screeched. "It's your play. I'll do what I can. But I hope you know what you're doing.

I'm not sure how all this will help anyway. You still can't get into the Kelso Club."

"I'm working on it." I hung up.

I went into the diner and ordered a cup of coffee. My cell buzzed.

"Eddie? It's me."

"Hi, Rudi."

"On second thought, I think it's best if you come over here. I'm at a friend's house, and I don't want Warren to know where I'm at."

"Of course. What's the address?"

I assured Rudi I'd take the necessary precautions to be sure I wasn't followed. The address led me to a modest one-story home south of town near DU. There was a police car in the driveway.

I parked a block away and walked up the back alley. It had been a hot day but the dark clouds gathering teased us once again with rain and brought a cooling breeze. Rudi stood near the back gate of a wood privacy fence. She wore a pair of shorts and a sleeveless blouse.

We stepped into the yard and locked the gate from inside. I grabbed her in a bear hug being careful of the cast on her arm and lifted her up. "Rudi."

She giggled and tugged with her good arm around my neck. "What's wrong?" She kissed me. "What happened to your face?"

I set her back down and we kissed again.

"Fell out of bed."

Rudi shook her head. "That happened to me once too. Then I ran into a door. Before I kicked Warren out."

"How is the arm?"

"It's fine. Pain pills help."

I couldn't fool her. We walked into the house and sat down at the kitchen table. I couldn't keep my eyes off her. She was right here. She wasn't in Nebraska and she was okay.

"Coffee?"

"Sure."

She got up and grabbed the pot and poured two cups.

"How is Crystal? Zach didn't think the school would do it." I had lots of questions for Rudi. Should I get her involved again? She didn't need me and all my problems.

"She's taking Zach's suspension hard. You talked to Zach yesterday at the club? Then Preston kicked you out?" She sat back down.

I wondered what passed between Zach, Crystal, and Preston up in that penthouse suite. Maybe Zach went to bat for me. Preston must be at the boiling point—the poor, crazy fucker. "Crystal told you about that?"

"Yeah. She's ready to leave Preston. She's at the end of her rope. All she ever had was Zach—all she really thinks about. How did you get back into the club in the first place? I thought you and DiNatale were kicked out?"

"Arnold invited me. We played the horses, and Zach joined us." I liked how Rudi dug for information. It meant she was back in the investigation. But when I turned over all the cards, she might wish she'd headed off for Nebraska.

"You were gambling?" She tapped her nails on the Formica tabletop.

"Yeah?" Why did she care about my gambling?

"C'mon, Eddie. I'm not stupid. You've got a problem, don't you. You think I don't see how customers get turned on by the action. I saw the way you were fit to be tied on the Mulholland horse at Aurora Downs."

I felt exposed. How many others could see what she saw? "You're right. I saw the police car in the driveway."

"Changing the subject? Alright. My friend is a police officer. She's on duty but left her car here. Why are you fidgeting?" Rudi asked.

I'd tested out various positions on the chair, unable to get my back and ribs in perfect alignment without a shooting pain up my neck or down my leg. "Hurt some ribs when I fell. You packed up?"

"Maybe you should see a doctor," she leaned across the table and lowered her voice. "No, I'm not packed. I'm not going anywhere."

"You quit."

She smiled. "And you believed me? It's going to take a lot more than Warren's threats to make me run back to Nebraska for God's sake. But you were right about street smarts. Warren knew how to fool me all those years. He must be smart. How the hell did he get into the ER with a gun and get a lab coat? That's why I told you I quit. Warren was probably listening in on one of their intercoms."

"You're staying?"

She leaned toward me. "I'm all in."

"All in with the investigation?"

"The investigation—you bet," she said.

"That's great."

She sipped her coffee. "What's the next move?"

"I have to get back into the Kelso Club."

"Why?"

"I think the killer will kill again at the Allegro Martin Charity Tournament. The last two murders were both at Kelso Club events. It gives the killer freedom to move among the crowd and isolate his victim. People let their guard down believing there's safety in numbers. The Kelso Club is a mausoleum with rooms on every floor. The killer can lure his victim to one of those rooms. It's a way for him to make a statement. I'm not sure what. But I'm pretty sure the killer has snapped. The timing of the upcoming Allegro event couldn't be more perfect for him."

"Makes sense. But who is it? What can I do?"

"I'm not sure yet, but I need you to get in touch with Warren. Are you up for that?"

A sly smile lit on Rudi's face. "You think I've been hiding out, don't you? The employees keep calling. They think I've abandoned them. Well, all of you are wrong. The first thing I did when I left the ER and the drugs wore off was to get a new divorce attorney. Tomorrow I'm going back to Zany's store and straighten out that mess."

"A mess?"

"The employees are ready to walk. Grasso is running the store. You know him, right?"

"Sure, he works for Mags."

"Grasso thinks he deserves the store because he's worked for Mags all these years. Zany had told me how much he wanted to take over the store. That Grasso doesn't believe in outsiders. Instead of staffing up for football season, he wants to do layoffs due to the lack of ready cash. He doesn't know what he's doing."

Grasso and DiNatale must've bonded over their dislike for outsiders. "DiNatale was anxious to get me out, and now I know why. Grasso watched my every move. Last night the two of them kicked my ass. They used the excuse that I was gambling."

"Well, I could either let Grasso run it into the ground or save it for the employees who've been there forever for Zany. You want me to get in touch with Warren? That won't be hard. He still calls all the time."

"Want my gun?"

"I don't need it. I bought my own."

"You did? Can you use it?"

"My Dad had me out pheasant hunting when I was eight years old."

"The arm?" I nodded toward the cast on her left arm.

She raised a fist with her right hand. "I'm right-handed. What's the plan?"

"To get Warren out of your life and get me back into the good graces of the Kelso Club."

"You get your ass kicked and bounce right back."

She got up and I met her halfway. This time there weren't any demands of the store to get in the way. We kissed while she yanked at my shirt.

"Tell me your plan," she said.

I pulled at her blouse and undid her bra. She unbuckled my pants and slipped out of her shorts.

"We need to—"

We kissed again standing naked together in the kitchen.

"I have the back bedroom. The plan," she said. "Tell it to me slow."

42

Later that night, I drove back and waited inside the foreclosed house and resisted the urge to visit the money at Zany's safe house a couple of miles away. It was near midnight when Rudi called.

"Eddie, I talked to Warren."

"Did he buy it?" I wanted to kick myself for asking this stupid question, but I couldn't resist.

"Yes. I could hear him drooling over the phone. He acted all lovey-dovey. If he comes back here—"

"Don't worry. I'll give him a warm welcome."

Rudi had risked everything and if I failed, she'd face a husband bent on revenge. She wouldn't hesitate to defend herself, and I didn't want her to face that.

I hung up the cell and ran out front and grabbed the real estate sign. I'd given Rudi the address of the foreclosed property.

My upcoming ballet with Warren would be one performance only—at the foreclosed property.

I liked the plan. First, I had to think like Warren. It wasn't that hard. He'd been semi-successful at Zany's house so I figured he'd follow the same blueprint.

Warren's strange words in the ER had gotten me thinking. He'd said: "If you knew anything, you'd know." It was as if he knew something I didn't. He knew about Zany's cash as a rookie bagman for the store. In the ER he said Zany always had a wad of cash. Warren also said how he'd continue to stay a step ahead of me. The step on that river rock outside Zany's house. The explosion was rigged by an amateur—almost blew up the entire block. I could be wrong, but I'd wager big-time it was Warren.

He'd use the garage as his base of operations, hide his car there, and unload the tools and explosives. Then he'd rig the foreclosed house and search for the money. Once he found the money, he'd stuff it in the car and then hide the car down the block. If I got here early, he'd shoot me and then torch the place.

I'd wait for him in the garage.

My internal clock ticked on Uncle Mike time. My arms hung loose. In my head I smoked cigarettes. Scratched a match and held the flame to the end of the cigarette. Passed time with each imaginary smoke. Sat on those steps in O'Connell's Tavern. Used all the old tricks. Forty-five minutes went by.

Warren had gotten involved with a meth dealer back in his hometown. Drug money gets in your bloodstream and drives you batshit-crazy. Worse than a drug habit. I'd seen it happen plenty of times. All this jealous rage and harassment was just an act. When I told Rudi, she saw how it all fit. How Warren's demand that she quit was nothing more than a way for him to gain the upper hand. He used her good qualities against her, her loyalty, and her guilt over a busted marriage. But Warren's violence against me and the slashed tires told the real story.

The doorknob jiggled. Warren didn't have much imagination. No check of the perimeter, scaling of the fence, or search for an alarm. He might be an aspiring criminal, but he was a rank amateur.

I kept the door from the garage into the kitchen open a crack to allow some light and so I could listen. There wasn't much need. Each footstep seemed to crash through the empty house. No doubt his thoughts were consumed by greed and where he'd begin to smash walls and rip up floors in search of Zany's treasure.

A light flashed through the kitchen and into the garage. He must have a flashlight in one hand and probably his gun in the other. All the courage he needed.

I flattened against the wall beside the door. My sore ribs forgotten in the rush of adrenaline. Footsteps across the kitchen floor. He couldn't wait to trap *me*. I clenched my fists and held back.

The door into the garage eased open. The flashlight covered a short radius. A few seconds hesitation and he barged into the garage.

I caught the gun hand first. The weapon clattered to the floor. He swung the flashlight. It nipped my chin. My temper rose.

A quick left to the jaw made him lose his balance on the step.

"What the fuck? You?" Warren threw the flashlight.

I ducked. "Not such a big man without your gun."

"I'll kill that bitch."

"Not where you're going." I kicked the gun away and threw a right to the jaw.

Warren forgot or didn't know how to block punches. But he popped up again and swung wildly, first with the left and then with the right. I blocked them easily. Got him off balance and then struck back with a nice combination.

He wobbled on rubber legs but I wasn't finished. I connected again and he dropped to his knees. Then he tried to lock up my legs, but I stepped away from his lunge.

I could've finished him off as he rolled around the cement floor but maybe it was the boxer in me. I let him up to his knees.

"I don't have all night," I said.

Warren mumbled something that sounded like cuss words and held up a knife. He'd pay for that.

I shot a few jabs as he lumbered a few steps and slashed the air. Then I lit into him with a vicious combination. He flopped on his back unconscious. I had a flesh wound on the back of my hand as a souvenir.

I went to work with the rope I'd brought. Now I needed Tenorio to do his job.

43

I called the police operator from a payphone at a nearby strip mall and in my best 911 voice, disguised as a guy with a sore throat, told her of a burglary in process at the address of the foreclosed property. It was important she alert Detective Tenorio. This got her attention and she did her best to keep me on the line. I hung up.

Then I called Rudi to be certain she was okay.

"How did it go?" she asked.

"Warren needs a good cut man but otherwise he's okay."

"I mean you. How are you?"

At first, I thought she didn't have faith in my pugilistic talents then I realized her words had a deeper meaning. "I'm fine. I wish I could be there with you. You did good."

She sighed. "You could tuck me in."

"My luck. Goodnight."

Her comment wasn't what my imagination needed. Maybe if I could work my way out of this mess, we'd have a future. I drove the Crown Vic down a side street and watched for a tail then I did the same routine three blocks in the other direction. Finally, I felt I could head back to Zany's safe house. Except for one of those timer lights set inside and out on the porch, the house appeared empty. My heart beat fast when I slipped in again through the back. It was vacant and undiscovered.

Instead of seeing Rudi, I had to sleep with Zany's gold mine in a dark, dank basement. Just me and the spiders.

I woke up the next morning in a sweat despite the cave-like temperature. The money was safe for the moment but how many people were looking for me? In my bad dream, about a hundred people chased me down the street. But in the light of day, I could narrow it down to about fifty.

One of my disposable cell phones buzzed. I needed coffee.

"Yeah?"

"Eddie?" Uncle Mike asked.

"Did Burrascano give me a pass?"

"I haven't heard. But Joey L called. The cops found that woman's body. You know the woman Zany saw that night? Amity."

"What?" My breath came short. I didn't expect this. I'd hoped Warren's capture would get Tenorio off my back, now I had something new to worry about.

"It's not good. Makes them nervous."

"Where did they find the body?" I thought again of Amity, the contorted corpse on the bed of the seedy hotel room.

"I don't know."

"The last thing I needed."

"It's your call, Eddie. But there's one more thing."

Once again, I didn't like the tone of my uncle's voice.

"They found a slip of paper in her hand with your cell phone number."

"Damn it."

"Remember, Burrascano is the one who can pay the lawyers, not us," Uncle Mike said.

This was a body blow to my midsection. I tried to take a couple of deep breaths. "I'll think about it."

"By the way, Smiley called me. I guess you called him, and when he couldn't get in touch with you, he got concerned."

I didn't mind our old FBI contact talking with Uncle Mike. We'd been a team on more than one job. "Did he say anything?"

"No, the FBI isn't on your case—yet. He said he'd be around this morning if you want to give him a call." Uncle Mike coughed. "Let me know if you change your mind on anything."

I hung up then paced around the basement. Zany's killer poised to strike during the charity event and my status had not improved. I'd hoped that Warren was my ticket to get back inside the Kelso Club and now this.

I called Smiley. He answered the phone with all his southern charm, asked about Uncle Mike and things as a matter of courtesy, and I made certain to address him as Bertram.

Once the formalities were dispensed with, I got to the point. "I want to know what you guys might have concerning a Peter Leister in Denver. The guy is a bookie and owns a string of massage parlors dealing drugs and prostitution. I think you had an ongoing investigation."

"Well, it's not my district but I'll be happy to take a look into it," Smiley drawled. "But give me a few minutes, will you? I'll call you right back."

I paced around the basement some more, thought I heard something upstairs, and went up to investigate. It was nothing. Maybe my imagination or noise from the ice maker. I opened the fridge. A lot of Diet Coke and diet Dr. Pepper in the fridge and some frozen yogurt in the freezer. Damn jockeys in the habit of watching their weight. I popped open a can of Diet Coke, my caffeine substitute, and checked the backyard.

Why should I be paranoid? I had Mags and DiNatale, the black Lexus sedan with, I assumed, Leister's men, Zany's killer, and now the Denver police force after me. This wasn't good for my blood pressure.

I should've expected this problem with Amity. Mags and DiNatale had full access to the whereabouts of the corpse and provided it to the cops as payback for my ploy with Zany's money. The slip of paper placed in her hand was icing on the cake. I should've insisted it be found when I inspected the body but Mags probably had it in his pocket.

The cell buzzed. It was Smiley.

"You know, Eddie, this is a real funny thing you asked about. This Peter Leister? Our informant happened to be the manager of one of those massage parlors and ended up dead in a burglary. Our investigation is dead in the water."

I asked if he had anything else. Any open investigation on one Eddie O'Connell?

Smiley chuckled. "Nothing I can tell you about. Be careful, Eddie. You're in deep."

I sat down on a kitchen chair, rubbed my face with both hands, and tried to clear my mind of indictments and courtrooms. I was right. DiNatale's war with Leister was trumped-up. But why? I needed further proof.

The war started with Mancuso's delivery of the letter to Koransky. Was it a forgery? Did Leister actually "rat" to the school about Koransky? And then Leister's FBI rat ends up killed in DiNatale's raid. Too many coincidences to believe. Mancuso was no longer irrelevant—he was the key.

I'd been on my way to question Mancuso when someone ran me off the road. There was a reason someone didn't want me to talk with Mancuso, and I had to find out why.

I locked up Zany's safe house and got into the Crown Vic.

44

I TOOK I-70 TO BYPASS DOWNTOWN THEN HOPPED ON I-25 north toward campus to find Mancuso. I should've asked Rudi if she wanted to accompany me but then realized it would be bad karma. The last time we tried this together we ended up in a ditch.

As I left Zany's stash behind, I felt a pang of guilt and anxiety. The treasure had become my adopted child and its welfare my biggest worry. Would Zany's money be okay until I got back? Maybe a mysterious house fire would force me to find a remote south sea island to spend the rest of my days.

I got up to the school and asked some coeds for directions to the weight room. Lucky for me I'm in decent shape so they took my inquiry seriously. One of them even gave me an inviting smile.

The coach's office was located on the west end of the gym. The receptionist demanded to know if I had an appointment.

When I said no but it was urgent, she called some number, left a voice message, and told me to have a seat.

I asked for directions to the men's room then left to find the weight room. I'd spent time in a school weight room and it contained a unique smell, something between sweat socks and the inside of a jock. If I was a hound dog, I'd find it with my nose. Weight rooms cried out for ventilation.

I took a walk around the building, scaled a locked gate, and found an open door. Why spend money on more security—people don't break in to lift weights.

Inside, I scanned the room for a guy who was six-ten, Allegro's age, and all business. It was an impressive place. Lots of stainless steel and body-builder contraptions, enough to impress any high school recruit to sign on.

I spotted a guy who fit Mancuso's description near the free weights. His hair was white, but his stomach was flat, and his arms and shoulders stretched the fabric of the college athletic T-shirt to its limits. He stood with his feet apart as a young man bench pressed a couple hundred pounds. I waited.

When Mancuso came up to refill his water bottle at the drinking fountain, I walked over.

"Coach Mancuso?" He was even bigger when I got close. His arms stretched farther and were muscle-bound, even his chin jutted out like a rocky ledge.

He gave me the once-over. "What are you doing here? You're not authorized." His voice was deep and raspy as if he spent each day screaming and shouting.

Mancuso stepped into my space. His chest rose up around the level of my nose. The square footage of the man seemed super-human, a hulk, and caused me to shrivel up like a ninety-eight-pound weakling. But I didn't come here to get sand kicked in my face.

"My name is Eddie O'Connell. I took over for Zany."

"I heard of you. A goddamn bookie, get the hell out of here."

I wasn't about to leave. "You're old buddies with Allegro?"

Mancuso squinted. If he was a lion, I'd expect him to charge. "Didn't you hear me?"

"You were AM and PM in college, right? Could score day and night, anytime?" I'd researched it: Allegro Martin, AM, and Paul Mancuso, PM.

Mancuso's furry eyebrows rose. Maybe I'd made a few brownie points with the mention of the good old college days.

"Trying to piss me off? Do what I say." Mancuso hunched his shoulders and edged closer.

"You delivered a letter to a guy named Koransky?"

"You don't listen too well do you." He stared down a student ten feet away and the kid sprinted in the other direction.

I wanted more than anything to take a step back. One look at Mancuso's bulging biceps and one hand balled into a fist the size of a melon would make any reasonable human turn and run. I imagined him under the NBA boards fighting for a rebound.

"You got drafted thanks to Allegro. You owe everything you got to him."

"All I ever got was fucked over." Mancuso's voice rose. "By my school and by the NBA. Treated me like a piece of meat. Cut me from the team when I got hurt." His face turned red.

I expected Mancuso to throw a punch but his right hand still clutched the water bottle. "I talked to Allegro yesterday at the Kelso Club." Maybe I could make Mancuso curious, buy a few minutes.

His head turned to one side. "Why would he tell you anything?"

This told me that he and Allegro hid something. I had to string him along. "Because I'm on his side."

Mancuso placed the water bottle beside the drinking fountain as if annoyed by a gnat that he needed to swat. "You don't know shit."

I recalled Allegro's "tell." "Allegro is concerned about Zach, and so am I."

"He's suspended. End of story."

"It's bullshit. C'mon—grades?"

"I told Koransky what I'd do if he didn't clear out, now I'll show you. No more bookies on campus." Mancuso's mountain body quaked—a tremor in the thigh and muscle movement up the torso. He'd have every right to slug a bookie on campus.

At least I had a warning. Mancuso's muscular arm rose, the elbow swung around third base and twisted into a slingshot, aimed at my face. I danced away as his fist found nothing. He stumbled off balance from the momentum. It left him open for a right cross and I obliged with some extra pop—caught him flush on the chin and he tumbled.

Mancuso fell to one knee and then to both knees as he shook his massive head.

"Now tell me. I'm here to help. The killer will kill again at the Kelso Club charity event. You want that on your conscience?"

I allowed Mancuso to struggle to his feet. He groaned. Like most old pros his knees and joints held arthritic battle scars.

Somebody yelled out from the door to the locker room. "I called security, Coach Mancuso."

"Hear that?" Mancuso said. "You better get out of here. No way I'll tell you or anybody anything. Now get."

I left. No reason to wait around for security. But Mancuso had told me more than he intended. He told me someone other than the school was behind the letter to Koransky.

45

I called Rudi and we planned to meet at Nixon's. It was too risky at this stage to check on Zany's safe house—I might pick up a tail.

The important step would be to get back into the Kelso Club to find the killer. I was so close.

I breathed a heavy sigh of relief once more. If Mancuso had connected with one of those bombs, I'd be laid up for a week.

Back at the restaurant, I took my usual booth and ordered food. I'd skipped breakfast except for the Diet Coke.

It would be preferable to go to the Kelso Club this afternoon. Get a head start on things and question Preston and others. This was my original plan. But the discovery of Amity's body meant Tenorio would want me to answer questions. What did Warren tell the detective? Maybe if I waited until this evening, I could dodge the authorities.

But would I be allowed into the Kelso Club? I'd hoped the members would welcome me back with open arms upon Warren's arrest but now with the discovery of Amity's body—my best hope was that Detective Tenorio hadn't released this information to the media.

I spotted Rudi's rental car drive past.

I got up and went to the doorway of the restaurant and kept watch on the intersection. She parked across the street and walked up, a big smile on her face.

"We did it." She skipped over the sidewalk.

Inside, I pulled her into my arms and kissed her. So lucky Warren took the bait. Thank God she was okay.

She kissed me back. "I feel like a new person."

"Why is that?" We headed back to our customary booth. Some of the customers smiled up at us.

She fell into the red vinyl seat. "Haven't you seen it?"

"No, what?"

She pulled a rolled-up newspaper out of her purse and pushed it toward me. I pulled off the rubber band and unfurled the paper. The headline: "Killer of Attorney Found."

"Holy shit," I said.

I quickly scanned the front page and the continued article on page three for any report on the discovery of a young woman's body, found nothing on Amity, and then read the news on Warren.

The article described how he had been found mysteriously tied up at a vacant property in Aurora, his car parked nearby with gas tanks and explosives—the same materials, investigators believed, used to torch a home last Friday in the southwestern suburbs. A home titled to a company believed to be controlled by Zane E. Duran, a local bookmaker, recently murdered.

When asked how Warren Potts might be connected to two murders, Detective Tenorio replied that the investigation was still ongoing. But the newshound who wrote the article had lots of anonymous sources to fill in details.

The article dug up Warren's contentious divorce and that Michael Mulholland was the wife's attorney. Rudi's divorce filing described years of abuse and beatings and painted him as a madman. Track security monitors had picked up his presence the day of the Mulholland murder.

How this murder was linked to Zane E. Duran's murder was not clear but it appeared to be a romantic triangle. Mr. Pott's wife was seeing Zane E. Duran at the time.

Mr. Potts asserts the house contains stacks of cash squirreled away by the deceased bookmaker but to date, nothing has been found.

I stopped reading. A big smile played across my face and I realized such a gap-toothed smile might insult Rudi, whose marital trouble had been splashed across the front page for all Denverites to slosh through with breakfast.

I looked up.

"Enjoying yourself?" she asked.

"Sorry."

"It's okay. My new attorney got me right into therapy. I'm done feeling responsible for Warren."

"I'm going back to the Kelso Club tonight. If you're smart, you'll stay away."

"You don't think Warren killed Zany and Mulholland, do you?"

"No. He was just after Zany's money. And me."

"The killer will be roaming through the charity event to lure a victim. Who has the target on their back?"

"I'm going to find out."

She sipped her coffee and picked up the front page. A mug shot of Warren stared back at her. Maybe she didn't want to face people and their gossip. I failed sometimes to think through all the stuff she had to face.

"There's something else," I said. "I might be questioned about the murder of Amity. The cops might be waiting for me when I walk in."

"Why would you be involved?"

"I told the detective in Zany's murder that Zany had met with Amity at the ballpark the night of his murder. It bought me time with the detective, but now it's a problem."

"You do need somebody on your side tonight." She twirled a lock of her hair and glanced up at the lunch counter. Then she smiled at me. "The Kelso Club throws a great party. I wouldn't miss it."

46

THE ALLEGRO MARTIN FOURTH ANNUAL CHARITY Tournament kicked off officially on Friday. Rudi told me the night's itinerary included a buffet dinner in the ballroom on the third floor of the Kelso Club, an open bar, and a live band. On Saturday the old pros teed off at the exclusive Alpine Country Club at ten in the morning for what Rudi called the "hangover round." Then a formal charity dinner Saturday night back at the Kelso Club ballroom, complete with awards, speeches, and the presentation of a check to the local children's hospital.

Rudi met me outside the Kelso Club and knocked me out with her black cocktail dress. "You look great," I said.

"Everyone knows I'm available," she said.

I recalled the newspaper article that described her broken marriage. I felt a twinge of jealously. Lots of male hormones would be in attendance. "Keep a slot open on your dance card for me." I gave her a hug.

"Yes sir," she laughed.

"You better." Her kiss confirmed she teased me.

I expected one of Tenorio's men near the front entrance to the club but saw only the usual Kelso Club security. Then I expected a hassle from Raymond as we entered the lobby.

"Good to have you back, Eddie," Raymond said as he tipped his hat.

"Thank you, Raymond." I led Rudi toward the elevator and breathed a sigh of relief. Tenorio probably needed extra time to type out that novella of an indictment he'd serve on me for Amity. Fine, all I needed was time.

In the elevator, members who had stared daggers at me before said hello and shook my hand. They didn't come out and say they were wrong about me or apologize, but that was okay. I was back in the club thanks to Warren and those headlines.

I didn't celebrate. The killer would also feel free of suspicion.

On the second floor The Dave Brubeck Quartet's "Take Five" played on the club's sound system. The bar and dining room were jammed. Some were familiar member faces but many were unfamiliar. Lots of old ballplayers. Posters from their glory years in basketball, baseball, and football adorned the walls. No sign of Preston.

Rudi took a glass of chardonnay from a tray of various wines offered by one of the waiters in the hall. "It's your typical crowd." She almost shouted in my ear. "After a few drinks, the party will move up to the third floor and the Derby Bar. A few people will eat at the buffet before the dancing starts in the ballroom."

I felt uncomfortable in the wrinkled sports coat I'd retrieved from the pile of clothes in the backseat of the Crown Vic. I should look like the guy who took their money, not the guy who needed a handout.

More members came up and shook my hand. Rudi identified them by name. I rolled out some inane chatter.

Crystal, dressed in a sheer black cocktail dress, pushed through the crowd. "Hello, Rudi, Eddie. Welcome to my favorite party of the year. Rudi, you look stunning."

"So do you," Rudi said.

"Hi, Crystal. Yeah, nice dress." I tried not to stare but Crystal's dress didn't leave a whole lot to the imagination. Actually, it fired up my imagination. "Where is Preston? Isn't he the master of ceremonies?"

"He's in the office on the fourth floor doing his last-minute organizing." Crystal nodded toward someone in the crowd. "If you want something stronger than wine, you need to battle the crowd. Let me steal Rudi for a minute."

Rudi had warned me this would happen. Crystal wanted to catch up with some old boyfriends in attendance, and with Rudi as wingman, Crystal could mingle innocently.

I headed off into the throng that encircled the bar to order my iced tea, although my mind played tricks with a glass of scotch. The clink of ice cubes and alcohol-fueled laughter made me want to join in.

When I got to the bar, I looked back to check on Rudi and Crystal. Instead, I spotted a face I didn't want to see. DiNatale knifed through the crowd directly toward me. My blood froze.

Dressed in his finest black silk suit, white shirt, and gray striped tie, DiNatale oozed the image of cool. Not once did he look in my direction. It was as if he had a built-in homing device that allowed him to zigzag through the crowd toward me.

Grasso stood sentry at the bar entrance but appeared to focus on another part of the bar.

I wanted to punch out DiNatale as soon as he got in range. He came closer, his face fully exposed. I set my feet in a fighter's stance but kept my hands down by my sides.

If I slugged him, it would be my death warrant. This was what the mobster wanted. One punch and he'd be allowed to sweat me until I told him where Zany's money was hidden. Then he'd take me out. Burrascano would sign off and I'd be toast.

The ass-kicking in my hotel room came to mind. I'd been kicked around like a dog, my money taken. Then Amity's body turned over to the cops with my handwritten note. A frame job.

What more motivation did I need to clock this guy?

My fists clenched and unclenched. I needed payback. DiNatale came close. I grumbled hello or something.

DiNatale said nothing. Stood beside me and calmly ordered a Kettle One on the rocks as if I didn't exist. My feet shuffled slightly. Uncle Mike's talk about keeping my temper in check ran through my head.

The mobster picked up his drink and sipped. His hand betrayed a slight tremor and the glass tipped. A rivulet of the liquor ran down his chin and beneath his starched white collar.

I cracked up.

"What's so goddamn funny?" He slipped a hand inside his shirt where the vodka dribbled.

I choked back more laughter. "Nothing."

The crowd pressed in around us to get free booze. The loud conversation and music insulated us.

"You gave them Warren?" he asked.

"Why would I do that?" I wouldn't admit a thing. Let him read my memoirs.

"Who you working for?"

I shrugged. "I asked myself that the other night when I got my ass kicked."

"You know how these guys are," he said. "Mags and others. They're old school."

"Tell them the agreement with my uncle—no mob vengeance. We turn the killer over to the cops."

If DiNatale couldn't get me to take a swing and put my head in a noose, he'd try another strategy. He'd act like we were old friends. As if the ass-kicking I took had been a simple disagreement between buddies.

"I heard you took over the store," I said.

"Right. I know you're busy. All the employees can't wait for you to come back. Where's Rudi?"

He needed Rudi. The employees must be about to walk. No way I'd tell DiNatale that Rudi intended to go back.

"Preston let you into the club?" I asked.

DiNatale laughed. "We've got some deals going."

"That artwork?"

DiNatale slurped vodka. "Yeah, and franchises. Big money. You better be careful. Glad I found you."

DiNatale wanted to warn me about something else. "What?"

He drummed his fingers on the bar and looked around. "We found Moretti in the trunk."

Who the heck was Moretti? "Who?"

"One of Mags's boys. We found him in the trunk of his car. I could barely recognize the guy." DiNatale smiled, a smile coaxed by the warm emotion of violence.

"What happened?" Murder didn't give me a cozy feeling.

"Leister caught up with him."

"How do you know it was him?" Here was this trumped-up war in full bloom. Guys getting whacked for no reason. It made me sick.

"Grasso saw one of Leister's men."

Grasso was the witness. "Payback for your raid on Leister's massage parlor." I didn't turn it into a question. I waited for his reaction.

He chomped on an ice cube. "I don't know nothing about that."

Right. And I don't know nothing about the horses. "So, what's next—where will this thing with Leister end? The cops have their killer." When did DiNatale start this plan? He could've pulled strings from the beginning and had a deal with Leister to kill the informant for Leister and then take over Zany's store. Later, DiNatale and Leister could split up the territory. Maybe he killed Amity, a professional killing unlike Zany and Mulholland.

"It's Burrascano's call. All I know is Leister better not show his face." He set his empty glass on the bar. "We'll talk later."

He clapped me on the shoulder like a long-lost friend and zigzagged back through the crowd. He left with Grasso. A strange world. DiNatale could hide behind Burrascano when it served his purpose.

My cell buzzed. I checked for a name.

I had to take it, no question. "Hold on," I told the caller.

A path opened up at one end of the bar and I was able to squeeze my way through into the back of the simulcast area.

"Hello," I said.

47

"Hey, kid. It's me."

Joey L didn't identify himself over the airwaves. His aged voice, a bit frail, was unmistakable. I would avoid using his name. "How you doing?"

"When I heard, I had to call and apologize personally."

What the hell happened now?

"I told your uncle. It turned out to be bullshit," he said. "Something they used to scare you."

Now I was pissed. Nobody within earshot but I had to keep my words to a minimum. Maybe Joey L would get to the point. "Yeah?"

"The cops didn't find Amity's body or nothing. Like I said an embarrassment."

"What? You got to be kidding me."

He coughed. "No, I'm not."

I was numb. Tenorio wasn't about to throw the net over me. The big test had been DiNatale's exposed face—if I took the bait and slugged him, I'd sign my death warrant. I'd passed the big test.

Mags and DiNatale were clever. Of course, they could still turn over the body. They probably had that slip of paper locked up in a safe. The moral of the story? I better behave.

"Now look, kid," he said. "If you're playing a bluff on the money, don't count on me to help. I don't care how things turn out."

"I know. Yes."

"Good. Glad to know that. You know Zany was a good boy but he had a lot of Boy Scout in him. We couldn't tell Zany about Splendid Runner. I wish we had. Maybe he could've protected himself. We didn't tell your uncle either. But that kind of money needs insurance. Thank God the horse broke down *after* the wire. Too bad for Zany."

I got it. I'd heard rumors that Burrascano was my uncle's silent partner in horse ownership, but I'd never heard that Splendid Runner had been drugged. It masked the pain a horse might feel and allows it to run on—run until they break down. The amount bet by Burrascano required a guarantee.

Joey L had found Childress, my mother's rapist and murderer in Mexico. Uncle Mike had been with him. Joey L had Childress dragged behind a shrimp trawler, the sharks close behind. I lived with one foot in the mob's world, where a tradition of honor and bullshit ruled.

"I hope you find Zany's killer," Joey L said. "We owe it to him."

"We do." Zany's career ended when Splendid Runner broke down. Broke down due to drugs.

"I'll see you next time, kid. Keep your nose clean."

"Thanks."

I stumbled toward the handicapping carrels.

Arnold yelled to me. "Eddie, you're just in time."

The time was always right to gamble. I walked over to Arnold and Zach, two of the last remaining holdovers from the afternoon play. The other handicappers had congregated in the bar.

I was glad I didn't say anything to poor Joey L. The old man was simply the messenger.

What if he'd called a few minutes sooner? What if DiNatale's exposed face loomed up beside me at this very moment—I knew what I'd do.

Zach got up and moved to the next carrel over so I could sit between him and Arnold as I'd done before.

"Only one more race from Del Mar," Zach said. "You've got time. Here's my program."

I sat down and stared at the racing program. The horses were a game where trainers had to find an edge and played hide and seek with drug enforcers. A shadowy world where "things" happened. But I never thought it applied to Splendid Runner. The horse had ballooned into my own personal legend. I couldn't be more shocked if I'd learned Babe Ruth took steroids.

Arnold nudged me. "Take a look at that four horse, Eddie. What do you think?"

I didn't give a damn how it looked, but my fingers flipped the pages.

"Jim has been on a roll," Zach said.

"That's right," Arnold said. "I won the other night at cards, then won on those baseball games thanks to you. I'm back."

"Glad to hear it." It seemed like the last thing he needed. Some false hope until the next losing streak. How many cycles, winning streaks followed by losing streaks, had I been through?

I turned to Zach. "Sorry to hear about your suspension."

He hesitated as if he required a minute to concentrate in order to return to the real world. "I was so close." Zach stopped. His mouth worked as if he tasted something sour. Then his face lit up. "You watch—the team won't win ten games this year. Those hotshot guards from LA I told you about—my close buddies—they're transferring."

"You plan to transfer too?" I asked.

"I don't know. I'd have to sit out a year. I've got to think things through. I could declare for the NBA draft, but I'd get stuck in the second round. With the knee, the scouts want to see me work out. Plus, I need another year to show I should be a first-rounder. That's what Allegro said. Now don't let me talk too much and miss this race."

I checked the time. The post parade had just begun. "I won't."

"Preston has been looking for you," Zach said.

"I'll catch up with him." I couldn't force myself to look at the race. The old magic had drained out of me. "Sorry guys. I have a lot of customers to talk with. Let me know how you make out."

"Okay, Eddie," Zach said.

I clapped Arnold on the shoulder and glanced at all the flat screens, all the action.

Arnold didn't look up, too busy scribbling combinations.

As I walked out, I realized I hadn't even looked at the odds on the four horse.

I didn't look back.

48

I'D NEVER LEFT THE RACES ON SUCH A DOWN NOTE. AS IF ANY bet I made would lose, and if I did win, it wouldn't matter. I had to get all that out of my head. The bar played upbeat jazz, not a funeral dirge.

I went off in search of Preston. It seemed odd that he'd leave a message with Zach. I didn't think the two of them were on the best of terms after the suspension. Maybe Preston had apologized to stay in good graces with Crystal. Maybe he'd apologize to me too. I could hardly wait.

Preston was my key. He and Mulholland received those big payouts from Zany. With Mulholland dead, he was the lynchpin. Mr. Popularity Complex had become Mr. Loose End.

The second-floor bar and dining room had begun to thin out somewhat. Crystal and Rudi stood in a small group by the photograph of Kelso; Crystal locked in intense conversation with one of the old pros while Rudi appeared to make polite conversation with another man. She gave me a quick wave.

I walked over near the hostess station and flagged down a manager. I asked her if Preston was still in his fourth-floor office because he wanted to meet me. She called the office and told me that Preston had gone to the third floor.

I joined the attendees who crammed into the elevator with their drinks in hand. We got off en masse on the third floor.

I'd heard about the third-floor ballroom and Derby Bar but this was my first chance to check it out. Numerous gold chandeliers hung down from the high ceiling of the ballroom. The marble floor matched the floor of the lobby. A long buffet table had been set up along one wall, manned by chefs in big white hats at carving stations. The Thanksgiving smell of roast turkey pulled me toward the guest line, but I had to put business first.

The Derby Bar down the hall had an old-world Irish pub feel with its dark wood bar. I had the urge to find an open seat, order a Guinness, and study portraits of the past Kentucky Derby winners that lined the walls.

Tables had filled up fast. On the far side of the room, people played darts. I'd heard the card rooms were located behind this bar. Bartenders filled orders as waiters scurried about.

Preston walked into the Derby Bar from the direction of the card rooms with an assistant manager in tow, a tall thin man with the Kelso Club logo embroidered on his blue blazer. Preston shouted in his ear, turned red-faced, and gestured. The assistant manager nodded about a hundred times.

Drowned out by the noise of the crowd and Sinatra's "Luck Be a Lady" on the sound system, I couldn't hear Preston's rant.

He met me halfway, gave the assistant one final command, and stopped to address me. I felt like a combat soldier reporting to the general.

"Eddie, I'm glad you're here," Preston said.

That was a twist. "Zach said you wanted to see me."

He cleared his throat and appeared to be in pain. "Now, I know we have had our differences, and you have been quite patient during this difficult period. Recent news reports dictate a reconsideration of how the members' needs will be met this fall."

"You mean the fact I'm not a suspect in Mulholland's murder and you need Zany's store for football season?"

"Ah, yes." He cleared his throat. "As you can see this charity event is a strain on the club's resources. It's the biggest event of the year."

The biggest event of the year—how could the killer resist? But the killer was smart. I couldn't begin to guess his next move. "It's pretty awesome."

He glanced around the room as if to check on the quality of service. "But I hoped we could carve out some time later this evening."

"Yeah?" I liked how he talked circles around an actual apology. I should memorize his gibberish for future use.

"How about ten-thirty tonight in my office? Here's an appointment card—hand it to one of the fourth-floor staff people, and they'll show you in." He clicked his ballpoint, jotted something on a card, and handed it to me.

"Sure, I'll be there." I glanced at the card. He had written on his Kelso Club business card: "10:30; my office." He scrawled his signature at the bottom.

"We've had issues, but I think we can work to set things straight," he said.

Here were the magic words I'd waited to hear—"work to set things straight"—the exact same words Amity recited. The words Zany had told her. Was Preston the killer? Maybe this "crazy fucker" planned a trap.

I needed more information, so I rattled his cage. "Issues? I'll say we got issues. Like how you kicked my ass out of the club in front of everyone."

"What?" It was a high-pitched squeak. It took all my willpower not to laugh out loud.

"I'm treated like scum one minute and your buddy the next," I said.

"That was then and this is now, Eddie." He stroked his finely trimmed beard and lowered his voice. "We need to talk."

"I don't want to hear about another vote by the members. They've told me they'll stay with Zany's store. The headlines about the raid on Leister's massage parlors confirmed that they're a front for prostitution and drugs."

Preston stepped past me. "Mr. Leister is one of the issues I plan to discuss with you tonight."

"Arnold is down in the simulcast area. If you plan to apologize to me, you should apologize to Arnold, too."

He shook his head and pointed to his watch. "Ten-thirty. We'll discuss everything then." He strode away.

I had other stuff I wanted to use to get Preston peeved and talking, but I'd be able to do a better job sweating my witness when we were alone. At least I'd given him a taste and pushed him as far as I dared.

Then I thought of what might await me in Preston's office. The same magic words used to trap Zany. I'd never been to the fourth floor. Unfamiliar territory would give the killer an advantage.

49

Rudi and I slow danced to an old torch song, "Color My World" by the rock group, Chicago. More than twenty couples joined us on the dance floor. A quintet with a capable lead singer played from the stage. The buffet had been carried away and the dance floor set up with the precision usually reserved for a wedding reception. I was impressed.

The clink of glasses and loud laughter of the party crowd seated at tables in the back of the ballroom competed with the music. Couples clung to each other and swayed, unsteady on their feet. I could understand why they called tomorrow's round of golf the hangover round.

Rudi felt right in my arms. Her perfume reminded me of yesterday afternoon's lovemaking. The ballroom wasn't her friend's kitchen and lightning didn't flash outside, but the vacant corner of the dance floor close to the band would have to do.

She looked up at me. "Do you still think it's tonight?"

"What did Crystal tell you?"

"She said Preston was acting strange or stranger than usual. She didn't think tonight was a good time for another fight."

"She plans her fights?"

"I don't know. She wants to leave Preston, but can't afford it. She wants to stay with me tonight and needs to leave about ten."

I'd told Rudi about my scheduled meeting with Preston at ten-thirty. "That's okay. I'll find my own way back." Another night sleeping in the basement beside Zany's stash.

"She won't be staying with me and my friend. She's just using me as an excuse."

"I get it. That ballplayer she was talking to earlier? What's his name?"

"Yeah. Roger something. You'd think I'd remember his name. He used to be famous. Preston wants to iron things out with the store?"

"He should. Everyone I've talked to tonight plans to stick with Zany's store now that Warren is in jail," I said.

"Me, too. People are coming up to me. I think Leister has noticed."

"He's hanging out at the Derby Bar with a couple of his guys." Was Leister smart enough to kill his friend, Mulholland, to throw me off his track? These are the kind of last-minute second thoughts that can drive you nuts but save your ass.

"Grasso and DiNatale went downstairs. They tried to corner me about the store." Rudi laughed and gripped my hand hard. "They acted like we were best friends. But I wouldn't give them the pleasure. Let them suffer another night."

"Good work."

Allegro was working the Derby Bar the way he'd worked the crowd at the racetrack. His old celebrity charm hadn't faded for a night like tonight.

"Do you think it's Preston?" Rudi asked.

All I had were Preston's chosen words: "we need to work to straighten things out." Was it enough? I told Rudi about what Amity had told me. That Zany was headed to the Kelso Club to "straighten things out." The band played another slow song: "One For My Baby (And One More For The Road)."

"If it isn't, I think he knows something. I tried to get him to talk earlier, but he refused. Wants to wait until tonight."

"I'm worried. What if something happens to you?"

"Tell you what," I said to her, pulling her closer. "If I run into trouble, I'll text you with the letter 'P' to call the police." It was the same signal Uncle Mike and I had arranged to use tonight, but it wouldn't hurt to have Rudi as backup.

"Good. My friend the cop is at home tonight. She'll get someone there in no time. I'll tell her to have them focus on the fourth-floor office."

She edged closer and snuggled against my chest. With Warren locked up, she probably felt safe.

I watched the crowd, the killer among them.

50

I TOOK THE ELEVATOR TO THE FOURTH FLOOR AT 10:20. IF you're to be trapped by a killer, you should be on time.

It looked as if the administrative offices were locked. Most of the crowd downstairs had wobbled home or back to hotels. The band stopped playing at 9. Like Rudi had said—Denver was not a late-night town.

When I knocked, I was surprised that someone answered.

"Yes?" A man with unkempt hair and a loosened tie opened the door.

I handed him Preston's card and offered an explanation.

"What is this?" the man asked. "He knows I've got to leave at ten-thirty."

"It's okay," I said. "I can wait in his office."

The man inspected me closely. "This is against policy."

"Don't worry," I said. "I'm an old friend. I won't steal anything."

The man smiled and then studied the card again. "Nothing to steal. Okay. His office is in back. I have to go but if you need anything, pick up the phone and dial zero."

"Thanks."

He led me through the rows of vacant cubicles and small offices. Remnants of lives strewn about—family photos, coffee cups, employee of the month awards. These people with real jobs made me nervous, even when they were absent.

"It's crazy this time of year," the man said.

"When does the cleaning crew come by?" I asked.

"Not tonight. They're busy downstairs. But we'll survive."

He unlocked the door with Preston's nameplate then left. It was a large office and boardroom combined. A long shiny mahogany table ran the length of one wall. Another elaborate photo of Kelso hung above the table, this time the champion racehorse stood in the winner's circle. If there was a board, this is where they met.

At one end of the room sat a big executive desk. A truckload of paperwork had been dumped over it. I hoped the pile consisted of a million past due invoices. Behind the desk hung a wall-sized wood carving of a jockey on a horse in midstride near the finish line. I studied it. I liked to stand by the finish line when I attended the races; the last seconds were the best.

Those days at the track could not be over for me. I cast this worry about my gambling aside and turned to inspect the rest of the room.

Along the wall opposite the boardroom table, an artificial putting green and a pinball machine offered relaxation. I chuckled. I couldn't begin to guess at the pressure Preston endured to spend that trust fund allowance.

The disorganized mess on the desk matched my image of Preston as a "crazy fucker." The trap had been set. The administrative office was empty. The last man scheduled to leave at 10:30. The night's guests filing out.

What was next? Would Preston jump out from behind this wood carving or enter through a secret passageway from behind the bookshelves?

Surely the killer would strike tonight. Wasn't it obvious or was it obvious only to me?

If it wasn't tonight then I might not find Zany's killer. Warren would take the rap. I'd be gone. Because I couldn't go another day worrying about the welfare of Zany's stash. No way. And since I no longer ran the store, the need for my services would end. Perhaps abruptly.

I took a deep breath and touched the butt of my gun for reassurance. Would Preston commit murder here in his own office? But Zany was killed in a public place. So was Mulholland. Murder came easy.

I heard footsteps. Someone at the outer door. I crouched and turned, one hand on my gun.

"Hello?" A voice called.

"Yeah?" I didn't recognize the voice.

The tall, thin assistant manager with the blue blazer walked in. "Are you Eddie O'Connell?"

"Yes."

"I was told to let you know Mr. Williston has taken ill and can't make your appointment. He sends his apologies."

What happened? Maybe Preston got cold feet.

"I'm here to lock up." He held up some keys.

"What else did he say?" I walked through the door of Preston's office and the assistant manager closed and locked it behind me.

"He didn't say anything. He sent me an email."

"Thanks." Preston hadn't appeared ill and he seemed committed to our talk. A lot of trouble to go through just to cancel.

An email sent to Preston's assistant. Anyone with access to Preston's email could send it. Just because I stepped into Zany's shoes didn't mean I would become the target. Preston was the loose end.

I ran through the offices into the hall.

51

I took the elevator to Preston's penthouse on the fifth floor.

Was I too late? I might stumble onto a murder scene with the cops on the way. Tenorio would be smiling and bouncing that eraser if I ended up in the wrong place at the wrong time.

From the elevator, I walked up to the double doors. Preston's nameplate with the words "Private Residence" etched in gold. No detail had been overlooked at the club. The doors were locked. I listened for a minute. Nothing. I got down on one knee and went to work with my pick.

My hand shook. I had to be quiet and this was the only way in from what I could tell. I'd had trouble with the lock at Zany's house. I took it slow and easy and held my breath. The lock clicked, and I opened one of the heavy wooden double doors.

The room inside was dark but some light seeped through the curtains from the terrace. I shut the door behind me and crept inside.

The penthouse oozed all the cold comfort of a museum with faceless statues, the endless gurgle of a fountain in the entryway, and ornate antique furniture. Fancy throw rugs slipped beneath me as I scrambled to a spot behind a couch. The sound of traffic told me a door or window must be open.

The terrace would be the perfect place. Sweat dripped beneath my arms. I crawled through the room toward the sound of traffic.

I thought of the two hotshot guards from LA planning to transfer. Why? That was the key. They tore up the league two years in a row. One more year and they'd cash their ticket to the NBA. Why disrupt their careers simply because Zach was kicked off the team?

Arnold had refused to explain the payouts to me when Zach appeared.

Did it start as a dare two years ago? Something Zach and the two guards did because they could. Shaving points might be impossible to resist for those players in control of the game.

A fixed sporting event was the biggest scandal a school could face.

The cover-up boggled my mind. The school had so much to lose. A point-shaving scandal could set a college program back to the dark ages and alumni contributions would dry up. The school went after Zach for poor grades but that was the cover story. Mulholland followed through on the cover-up and kept the point-shaving allegations secret to protect his alma mater even taking the extreme precaution of maintaining an office file that referred only to the issue of grades. The attorney's conflict between his alma mater and his client would be motivation for murder.

No way Zach or the two guards could place a bet without a strawman. That's where Preston came in, the founder of the Kelso Club. He'd dreamed of being on the inside. He'd given those two guards part-time jobs to keep the money flowing.

The payouts to Preston and Mulholland by Zany must have been proceeds from winning bets on the fixed games. Zany must've informed the school. Like Joey L said, he had too much Boy Scout in him.

Zach's behavior had escalated. The dream was dying. He and his mother were trapped in the penthouse with Moneybags. Arnold would notice Zach's erratic behavior and drugged state.

Zany had been thrown off the roof of the baseball stadium. "Get gambling out of sports," the murderer proclaimed.

Preston, the last loose end in the scheme. He could provide hard evidence, eyewitness testimony. Wrap up Preston at his own charity event and then, in the middle of the night, throw him from the roof of the Kelso Club. What a statement that would be.

I made my way, half-crawling, through a dining room and into the kitchen. Some faint voices could be heard. I found a sliding door that led from the kitchen onto the terrace. It was left open a crack. The wind caused the closed blinds to bounce back and forth. I made my way closer.

I pulled out my gun. Got down close to the sliding door, careful not to cast a shadow, and listened. The voices were a jumble at first. The street noise made it difficult to distinguish words. I had to concentrate and block out the background noise.

A voice outside said, "So, Preston, old buddy. Are you comfortable?"

I couldn't quite tell who uttered the words. It sounded like Zach. At least Preston was still alive.

"I've wanted to have this conversation for a long—"

A truck rolled down the street followed by a brigade of motorcycles and the voices outside were drowned out. What if this was a simple conversation? Maybe Preston had actually become ill.

I peeked through the blinds. I saw part of an elbow but then the figure stepped back out of sight. Must be in an alcove off to the left, behind a wall.

"Sorry things didn't work out between you and mom." The man laughed.

The voice was off, but I was ninety-nine percent sure it was Zach. The laughter gave him away. I waited for Preston's response.

"You did such a good job," Zach continued. "You did so much to help, you and Mulholland. I hope I can repay you—"

A police siren wailed down the block. No response from Preston. The arrogant bastard couldn't stand to be quiet this long—he must be bound and gagged.

"Should've done better with that attorney. He sure deserved it. Don't worry, I'll make up for it with you. You can—" Zach's words again were lost in the street noise.

I placed one finger behind the blinds and into the crack of the sliding door. What kind of noise would it make? Did Zach have a gun? Where exactly were they positioned on the terrace?

"You're not the last either. Those people from the school—"

I thought through the police report on the torture of Zany. What did they speculate came first—the cigarette burns, the chipped tooth? The castration rites came last.

"I wish Zany and I could've talked. I was a beginner."

How would Zach react when I jumped out? I'd get the drop on him and then text Rudi for the police.

"You suspected me, didn't you, Moneybags? I could tell."

I heard the clink of metal on glass. What did he have—knives, pliers, what else? The police report faded from my memory as I planned my move.

"Maybe they'll have a charity tournament in your honor next year. Here, I've got a pack of Mom's cigarettes."

I smelled cigarette smoke. Then I heard some muffled whimpering and rustling. The stench of burned flesh. Zach's hands would be busy. If I caught him by surprise—

I flung back the blinds and threw open the sliding door and jumped out.

"Stop." I took several steps and pointed the gun. Zach stood over Preston lying horizontal on a chaise lounge. The terrace extended the length of the building bordered by a short, brick wall and dotted by numerous potted plants and bushes.

Zach threw something then the basketball star dodged and weaved and ran toward me.

I got hit on the shoulder. Pliers clattered on the wood deck.

Zach lunged at me. I fired.

Zach grabbed my arm then hooked the other arm, forcing my gun straight up. Did my shot miss? We wrestled upright.

Zach's hot breath and stupid grin. I felt the wetness against his chest. We slid back and forth like mud wrestlers and his lanky frame made it tough to gain any leverage.

Blood over everything. I tasted it. Sticky. Where did Zach get the strength? No knee trouble.

Preston sat up straight, his arms and legs bound with rope, mouth wrapped in duct tape, and a black mark on his forehead. His eyes bugged out.

The gun slipped from my hand. Hips and chest shoved as I tried to gain position. One step back to free myself and Zach was on me, pushing. His cat-like moves anticipated my every move. As if we fought for a mythical rebound.

The smell of alcohol on Zach's breath. He gasped for air. The weird smile never left his face.

Then I felt the brick wall at my butt. Zach had pushed me toward it. I pushed back. If I went over, I'd be in Zany's shoes—parts of my brain found across the street.

I tore and kicked and fought. The kid could fight and had leverage. One hand got free and I smacked him across the jaw but he kept pushing. My foot slipped. I sensed Zach would make one last push with both feet to hurl his body at me and drive us over the wall.

His feet and legs failed him. We slumped against the wall. I heard him gag and his muscles tighten. I'd never had someone die in my arms.

At the end of the terrace, a figure emerged and walked toward me. A gun in his hand.

52

Allegro walked toward me in the shadow of the Denver skyline behind him. I was about to explain but his smile told me everything I needed to know.

"Hey, the twenty-nine to one shot. I thought you two would go over."

He pointed the gun at me. My arms still interlocked with Zach's arms. Dead weight but he became my shield. Allegro came closer.

If Preston was involved in the scheme, Allegro must've been part of it as well. I recalled the way the two of them stood in line at the racetrack's betting windows. Joined at the hip when it came to wagering. Allegro's gambling itch had caught my attention. Preston made the perfect strawman for Zach and Allegro.

Now I knew why Allegro was so concerned about what Zach may've told me when we were gambling in the Kelso Club.

"Sorry to disappoint you," I said. Blood ran out of Zach's chest and mouth. Trickled down my shirt. Gurgling sounds like the fountain inside.

Allegro glanced at Preston. "Hate to lose my biggest fan too. All that fucking money."

"You've got that broadcast job," I said.

"That's right. Too bad you'll miss it. I'm pretty good."

"This won't be good publicity."

"Won't be nothing to connect me. Zach killed his old buddy, Moneybags, and then you and Zach killed each other. Preston gave Zach this gun for his birthday." Allegro inspected the weapon in his hand. "You can't hold him up forever."

I didn't like the easy way Allegro handled the pistol. No way to free my hands to text Rudi.

Preston twisted on the lounge chair and emitted muffled sounds through the gag and duct tape.

I had to keep Allegro talking. "People know." I looked across at the dark commercial buildings around the Kelso Club, all of them closed up tight on a Friday night. It was the perfect murder scene. Shots mistaken for a car backfiring. Everything drowned out by city traffic noise and a string of bars a block away. Crystal on a sleepover. No one would find anything until morning.

Allegro took a step closer. "I give you credit, Eddie. You were one cool dude. I knew that from the first day at the track."

My muscles ached. I couldn't hold Zach much longer. I spied my gun a few feet away on the deck. "That was one neat trick you pulled with Koransky."

"You like that?" Allegro chuckled. "My old friend Mancuso. He'll do anything for me. He hates gambling. Thinks it's a disease. It got you and Leister fighting each other." He stared at me. "You didn't tell anyone."

He was right. Too bad I didn't tell DiNatale. He could be the one here to hold up Zach.

Preston slid around on the lounge chair. Allegro stood between Preston and the wall at the foot of the chaise lounge.

I inched closer to my gun. "Gambling runs in your blood."

"You got that right." Allegro raised the gun toward my head. "If you knew how much I've won. I got guys like Zach in lots of good places."

I could imagine how young players flocked to the NBA great to learn every tidbit he might be willing to share with no idea the advice came with a price tag. Allegro's pride in the scheme made it clear I'd take what he said to my grave.

Allegro waved the gun and smiled. "You're letting him slip."

I tightened my hold beneath Zach's arms and dragged my shield upward, slowly losing all feeling in my arms.

A siren blared down the street.

"Somebody called the cops," I said.

Allegro took his eyes off me, turned, and looked down. Preston rolled sideways like a log down the chaise lounge.

I threw Zach's body off to the side and dove for my gun. Preston's body walloped Allegro's knee—twisted as Allegro turned to look down.

"Fuck," Allegro yelled.

I reached out and grabbed my gun as Allegro pushed up off the ground with one arm and tried to aim with his other hand.

I fired first. Hit Allegro in the shoulder. His gun flew out as he fell back.

I scrambled to my feet and held the gun on Allegro. Preston, a duct-taped worm, squirmed beside Allegro.

"Go ahead, Eddie," Allegro said. "Finish the job."

My finger slick on the trigger with Zach's blood. I gathered my senses. "It won't be that easy."

53

I tied up Allegro's hands and feet then wrapped his mouth in duct tape. Since his shoulder wound seeped blood, I wrapped duct tape around that too.

I could've done a lot of things next. I could've unwrapped Preston—a cigarette burn on his forehead. I could've called Tenorio. Instead, I went into the kitchen and closed the sliding door, called Uncle Mike, and I told him what I had.

"Jeesus Christ."

"And I'll only turn Zany's cash over to Burrascano."

"What? Are you nuts, Eddie?"

"That's the only way. I can't trust anybody out here. DiNatale and Mags would take the money and kill me."

"Damn. I hope you know what you're doing. Shit. When did you get to be such a hard ass? I like it. I'll call Joey L."

It never ceased to amaze me how quick Burrascano could get the cavalry on site. I'd seen it time and time again. My only condition: that it not be Mags or DiNatale's guys.

Two guys showed up and told me that Burrascano would fly out sometime that morning. I kept in constant touch with my uncle throughout the night. I texted Rudi with an "all clear."

"I hope you know what you're doing, Eddie." My uncle repeated this line about a hundred times.

"Why don't you get some sleep," I said. "You sound beat."

"Shit, I can't sleep. Tell me again what happened."

As I led Uncle Mike through the maze of clues, Burrascano's men brought in a cleanup crew. They didn't flinch at the sight of the deck. Their experience with corpses, blood, and gunshot wounds became clear. Preston's penthouse transformed into part M.A.S.H. unit, part environmental cleanup site, and restaurant. These guys worked up an appetite.

Preston was overjoyed to provide his residence. Especially now that he'd escaped certain death. When we unwrapped him, I thought he might do cartwheels across the terrace.

"Eddie, allow me to say I never thought I'd see the sun again," Preston said. "When you jumped out from the kitchen— what else can we do for this crew? How are you, are you okay?"

This was a side of Preston I'd never seen before and probably hadn't existed until now. It wouldn't last.

Allegro requested my presence. "Eddie, why are they doing this?"

"You'll find out. I don't make the call." I had the guard replace the gag in his mouth.

One of Burrascano's lieutenants dug through Zach's bedroom and found a diary. From what I was able to learn, they'd use the last page, a page that didn't mention point shaving but did describe in detail his depression and despair over his lost career. I guessed they'd use this page as a cover story for Zach's disappearance. They couldn't allow the cops to reconstruct the murder scene or find Zach's body. They had other plans.

Zach's death would haunt me. He didn't deserve this, but I couldn't change the past. At least I'd prevented more murders.

Why did Zach go this far and get those LA guards involved? The only explanation I could come up with was what he told me about that damn dream that takes on a life of its own.

Burrascano showed up around 8:30 that morning and summoned me for a private chat. The mob's gambling czar sat behind Preston's antique desk. His steel-gray hair slicked-back, fashionable eyeglasses low on his nose, and not a wrinkle in his thousand-dollar bespoke suit. He could out-dress DiNatale.

I expected trouble. I hoped I didn't look half as nervous as Uncle Mike had sounded over the phone. He pointed to one of the desk chairs. I sat down and waited.

He rubbed his chin. He had bags under his eyes but for being in his early seventies, he was fully alert. Maybe he'd slept on the plane. "Okay, Eddie. First of all, good job. Congratulations. But why the hell am I here?"

I took a deep breath. "Because this war you've got with Leister is bullshit." I talked fast. "You got a rat in your organization. That massage parlor manager killed in the raid—he was a rat for the Feds. Leister knew it. Whoever organized your raid, works for Leister."

"What?" He slammed the flat palm of his hand on the desk. A war costs money not to mention lives and publicity.

I didn't mention DiNatale by name. I didn't have enough proof. It could be Mags, but my bet was Charlie Grasso.

Burrascano's jaw worked as if he might spit but he restrained himself. "What else?"

I continued. "With a rat around I have to be careful about turning over the money. It's a shitload of cash."

He nodded. "Zany's stash? Sure, I understand. I'll send two of my best men with you."

"Good." I thought about bringing up the bullshit interference I got on this job from DiNatale but decided to let it pass.

My mood had changed. I'd done what I'd come out here to do: I found Zany's killer. That meant more to me than anything. And I'd bet good money that when Burrascano smoked out the rat, he'd have his hands on the throat of Amity's killer.

"Anything else you need?" he asked.

I shrugged. "We're good on this mortgage on O'Connell's Tavern?"

He didn't appear surprised that I knew. It told me that he, Joey L, and Uncle Mike had been talking. "The fee on the job and your finder's fee on the money should cover it. What about this Allegro Martin?"

"My uncle says with Zach's death, we don't have enough evidence to turn Allegro over to the authorities." Uncle Mike and I had discussed it thoroughly. Since Zach had done the murders and was no longer around to testify against Allegro as a Svengali or mastermind, a smart lawyer would exonerate the NBA great.

"Fine." Burrascano nodded as if he'd analyzed the legal situation already.

"But Allegro has contacts with players who fix games. He's got a job with the sports network as a sports commentator." I knew what this meant for Burrascano, a man whose business involved taking action across the country and setting the lines. Not only could he influence games through Allegro's contact with players, he'd use Allegro to provide commentator opinions favorable to Burrascano's strategy on the betting lines.

Burrascano didn't need "admissible" evidence but he'd gather affidavits from Preston and those other players just in case. He'd have his hooks in Allegro.

Did it make me sick? Yeah. But if not Allegro, it would be somebody else. A crooked ref, a penny-ante criminal who bought players—so many ways to influence a game's outcome. At least Burrascano would do it in style.

His eyebrows shot up. "I'll talk to Allegro. Very good."

The government had declared sports gambling illegal and pretended it didn't exist. Somebody had to maintain order.

Burrascano's fingertips came together. "I'm impressed, Eddie. Maybe you'd like to stay and handle the store?"

It was an attractive offer and it said that the mob's gambling czar trusted me to run a major cog of his empire and that he trusted my gambling problem was under control. But I graciously declined. I didn't have the expertise to run the shop and my luck was running low. I'd fuck up the store somehow.

"It's not for me. But I know someone who can."

The ride out to Zany's safe house with Burrascano's two top lieutenants pushed my shattered nerves to the breaking point. If the money wasn't there, then what? I stared at the two pros. What were their orders? If the money was gone, would they drive another twenty-five minutes to the empty sagebrush fields surrounding Aurora Downs and find a quiet resting place for me?

"This Zany was one smart guy," one of the lieutenants said.

"Eddie, we'll let you go in first," the other man said as we drove up.

It was nice of them to let me do the honors. If the cops lay in wait, I'd be able to greet them.

It was my most unprofessional daylight break-in on record. My heart almost burst out of my chest. I kicked open the front door. Then I ran downstairs and didn't bother with a perimeter check. My hands shook as I brought out the key and unlocked the trap door. Then I almost fell down the narrow concrete steps into the bunker. The plastic-wrapped packages remained on the shelves.

I walked back outside to the limo. "Okay."

"You got a set of balls, buddy," one of the men said as he followed me into the house. "Demanding Burrascano fly out here and holding out on the stash."

"I'll need a count." I didn't want to leave anything to chance when it came time to settle the mortgage on Uncle Mike's bar.

54

That night I met Rudi inside the Kelso Club for the evening's festivities. We sat at a table beneath the portrait of Kelso. She wore a formal dress and I'd rented a tux. If you sandblast the blood and grit off me, I clean up pretty good.

"Did you hear about Allegro?" Rudi asked. "I guess he had to get emergency surgery this morning due to an old shoulder injury—a blood clot or something."

I nodded. I didn't smile. I didn't laugh. The blood clot was a good story.

"Of course, everybody says Allegro had the surgery now so he wouldn't be embarrassed out on the golf course," Rudi said.

I laughed on cue. "Good one."

The waiter came by and she ordered white wine while I ordered iced tea.

"Still on the iced tea?" she asked. "You look relaxed for once."

I'd spent the afternoon with professionals counting cash. Tenorio had set an appointment for me to come in for questioning. I was the opposite of relaxed. Must have put on a good show, though.

"That crowd stopped me when I came in." She nodded toward the members at the end of the bar. "They asked me about Warren."

"It will get worse." Warren's case brought a new batch of headlines every day.

"The court will decide if he did it," Rudi said. "I'm still not convinced he did it, but then I ask: what the hell's wrong with me?"

With luck, he might get a deal for life in prison. I didn't shed any tears. "Right. He'll have his day in court." Where did I come up with that bullshit? I wish I could've told her everything that had happened with Zach and Allegro, but for her own protection, it was best to let things lie.

"I wonder if Zany had a safe house?" She lowered her voice and leaned in close. "I know the police deny it but a lot of cash passed through his hands."

I shrugged. "The more Warren talks about it in the papers, the more people will search every corner of every neighborhood." And find nothing. At least Zany's old store would have the resources to take Denver's action this fall.

She clasped my hand. "Eddie, I've been thinking—about the store."

"What?"

"I don't think you should go back."

"Why?"

"Because. You know." She glanced up at the photo of Kelso then over toward the doors leading into the simulcast area. "It won't be good for you. It's too easy to get sucked in by all the action."

I couldn't believe it. She continued to think about my welfare and my gambling. I laughed out loud. "You're right. I can't go back to the store."

She laughed with me.

"What about you?"

Rudi pulled her hand back and stuck out her chin. "Well, I'm not about to head back to Nebraska. The employees called . . ."

"You need to think of yourself."

"They need me," she said. "I have to tell you something." She reached out and took my hand again. "I've been offered the job to run Zany's store. I've accepted."

I wouldn't tell her about my talk with Burrascano. Those discussions had taken place behind closed doors. I'd heard that Mags was more than happy to have Rudi in charge. Especially when the rumors came out about Charlie Grasso. They concluded he was the one behind the trumped-up war with Leister. It was also my bet Grasso had killed Amity.

I wanted to ask Rudi to come with me to Chicago. I needed the love of a good woman. But I'd seen the mountain of money. Rudi and the employees had been a big part of that success.

"Zany would've wanted you to run the place," I said. I raised my water glass in a toast. "Here's to the store."

Rudi smiled and raised her glass. "And Splendid Runner."

I hesitated. "You bet. Here's to Splendid Runner." Our glasses touched. "As close to a sure thing as I ever got."

ACKNOWLEDGMENTS

I really appreciate the support I've received from so many. I'd like to thank my critique partners who see the pages before the second or third draft. These brave readers include the Tuesday Night Mystery Critique Group: Suzanne Prouix, Chris Jorgensen, Don Beckwith, Mike McClanahan, Jedeane MacDonald, Laurie Walcott, Kay Bergstrom, Val Moses and Scott Brendel. In addition, my Thursday night critique group: Bill Brinn, Steve Reinsma, Luke Dutka, Judy Green Matheny and Jim Morris. Special thanks to my beta readers: Scott Brendel, Chris Jorgensen, Jedeane Macdonald and Sue Thomas. Many thanks to my mentors in the publishing world: Karla Jay, Wendy Terrien and Barbara Nickless. I would also like to thank my fellow writers at Rocky Mountain Fiction Writers, Pikes Peak Writers, Thrillerfest and Rocky Mountain Mystery Writers of America for the meetings and conferences they've presented over the years that have provided me with insights into the craft of writing.

To my fellow handicappers, best of luck. Stay in control and seek help, if needed.

To my editors, developmental editor Steve Parolini and copy editor Susan Brooks, thank you. To my design team, book cover by Steven Novak and Interior by Ali Cross. Thanks for your hard work.

Lastly, to my family. My wife, Kathi, and sons, Greg and Mark. You make it all worthwhile.

ABOUT THE AUTHOR

Tom Farrell has worked as a golf course starter, a chemist, and clerked at City Hall in Chicago while attending law school. He has served as Vice President of Rocky Mountain Fiction Writers, a nonprofit corporation, and was a past finalist in the Pikes Peak Writer's Contest in the Mystery, Suspense and Thriller category. Now retired from practicing law, when he's not handicapping, he can be found on the golf course or at a local jazz club.

www.tomfarrellbooks.com

Made in the USA
Columbia, SC
03 August 2021